'I — I think there has been some misunderstanding, Mr Brogan. The filly is not for sale and I would like you to go.' She tried to push past him but he refused to move. She could smell horses and tobacco, mixed with a faint tang of sweat. What could he smell — soap and cabbage probably, she couldn't remember when she had last used perfume. He took hold of her shoulders and stroked her gently with his thumbs.

'I mean it, you know. I want you, the children and even that God-awful dog. Come and live with me, Mary. I want you.'

His voice was very soft, his hands caressing. She lifted her gaze from a detailed study of his jumper — machine knitted she noticed — and met his eyes. They were half closed and his breath came through parted lips. She realised with a shock that he passionately wanted to make love to her.

'So you think you can have us all for your money, do you?' She sounded shrill but could do nothing about it. 'We may be desperate but we haven't sunk that low. Get out of my way you — you —' she searched for something bad enough to suit him and found it ' — you bloody Irish mick, you!'

Also by Elizabeth Walker

Conquest
The Court
Rowan's Mill
Voyage
Dark Sunrise
Wild Honey

A Summer Frost

Elizabeth Walker

KNIGHT

First published in 1985
by Judy Piatkus (Publishers) Limited

First published in paperback in 1986
by Grafton Books

Reprinted in this edition in 1991
by HEADLINE BOOK PUBLISHING PLC

This edition published 2000 by
Knight an imprint of Caxton Publishing Group

10 9 8 7 6 5 4 3 2

ISBN 1 84067 189 0

Typeset by Medcalf Type Ltd, Bicester, Oxon

Printed and bound in Great Britain by
Mackays of Chatham PLC, Chatham, Kent

Caxton Publishing Group
20 Bloomsbury Street
London
WC1B 3QA

A Summer Frost

Chapter 1

The wind nagged at her as she struggled with the gate, it pulled at her clothes and tangled her hair across her face. The buckets were heavy and even carrying them one at a time she still slopped water down her boot. This cannot go on, she thought, looking wearily down at the big-eyed milky faces of the calves in their pens. It was cold in the barn, too cold and the heat lamps cost too much to run. Everything cost too much; and she was so very, very tired.

Screams met her as she opened the back door. Ben, strapped in his high chair, was hurling wordless insults at Anna, who had stolen his toast. Too depressed for involved parenthood Mary returned the mangled offering to Ben and placated Anna with a chocolate biscuit. It was the last in the packet and with a spurt of rage she screwed the paper into a ball and hurled it into the sink. It bobbed reproachfully on top of the washing up water but there it stayed, keeping company with the unwashed dishes.

She was sorting the washing when the dog's roars galvanised her into action. Once more and he would refuse to deliver the letters George had said and here she was again, breaking all records in an attempt to get to the gate before Jet did. She made it with barely inches to spare, and grabbed the dog's collar, bawling at him to shut up. He subsided into muted grumbles, fixing the postman with a baleful stare as George climbed painfully from his perch halfway up the dead elm.

'You said you'd tie him up, Mrs Squires,' he sighed, brushing moss and twigs from his dingy trousers. 'I'm getting too old for this lark. You don't know what it does to me system.'

'I'm sorry, George, really I am. I meant to but – anyway, I'm sure he wouldn't bite you. He's all noise.'

George looked sceptical. 'It's just Tom he likes the taste of, is it? He won't deliver here no more, I can tell you.' He handed her three letters and pulled his bike out of the hedge. The front mudguard was bent, but it might have been like that when he came.

'You will still deliver, George, won't you? Please?'

He sniffed and then looked at her anxious face. 'Just you make sure you keep him tied up. Them Alsatians is dangerous.' He settled his chubby bottom on the tartan cover of his bicycle seat and creaked off down the lane.

God bless George! She glanced at the letters. A circular, her mother's elegant hand and – it was from the bank. Suddenly she felt very, very sick and she turned to go inside, but slowly, to put off the moment when it had to be opened. Then she was fumbling with it, to get it over and at last to know. And this time there was no escaping the message. She must sell the farm.

Stephen had died at harvest. The big Ferguson tractor had broken down, something to do with

2

the drive. It was an irritating delay and he had set to work furiously, surrounding himself with oily bits and pieces, all the while cursing that it should happen now, at harvest. It was there that she had found him, so unmistakably dead, his face empty of all but surprise. And her only thought, the one that she could not stop thinking, was that now she would never get the tractor back together again. The guilt was with her still.

How many times had she begged him to take things more easily? Just half an hour after lunch would have been something, but no, there were fields to plough and fences to mend and after all, they had years ahead of them. There would be time, one day. 'Give it five years and we can relax, love. When the loan's paid off. Things are tight until then, but afterwards – just think Mary, our own farm! It'll be worth it, I promise.' And he had died three years too soon.

The neighbours helped of course, in a haphazard way, leaning corn and baling straw, but their labour was casual and uninterested, lacking Stephen's enthusiastic energy. Mary was grateful, of course she was, but she was glad to see them go. To have the farm to herself again, without people. There was balm in being alone.

She took the children for a walk that afternoon, wanting in some vague way to imprint the scene on their young minds. They would not remember the cold air, the bare trees leaning against the wind, the huddle of cattle in a muddy field. Anna skipped beside the pram, splashing in all the puddles, while Ben gazed from the confines of his cherry red balaclava with a benign solemnity.

Thoughts chased each other through her head;

memories of spring days when they would go and watch Daddy ploughing; happy summer afternoons picking daisies in the pasture. Gone like petals in the wind.

'He might have known. He should have foreseen. He should never have left me in this mess,' she thought miserably, kicking at stones on the path. It was unjust and she knew it but she felt no remorse. Only anger at being left to cope alone, when she hadn't the strength – and God knows it needn't have been like this. That last loan wasn't necessary but Stephen had insisted, brushing aside her counsels of caution. 'We can't grub along with a handful of cows and some broken down machinery. Yes, it'll be hard but we can't do the thing by halves. It's no good owning land if you can't make it pay. Trust me, Mary. Please.'

And she had. Bitterness rose in her throat to choke her and she swung the pram round and headed for home. Perhaps a cup of tea would help.

The stock sale was almost upon her. It was strange that although the days themselves dragged the past weeks had rushed by, bringing her here before she knew. Things which take so long in their beginnings take no time at all about their ends. She was finding it hard to believe what was happening to her and wandered about in a fog of indecision, sure that if only she could clear her thoughts she would see a way out. This disaster could not be going to happen.

Mr Booth, the agent, patted her shoulder, a solid pat, intended to console.

'I'm sorry – did you say something?' The man

must think her an idiot, gazing vacantly into space when they were meant to be discussing the stock.

'The bull, Mrs Squires. We were going to look at the bull.' He was a kindly man, red-faced and corpulent, but he did not think women capable of farming. Perhaps he's right thought Mary, despondently plodding to the barn. The big Charolais was snoozing in his pen, his vast creamy rump looming over the concrete divider.

'You'll be glad to be rid of this fellow,' said Mr Booth cheerily, giving the bull a hearty slap. There was a snort and a massive head, restrained by ring and chain, swung irritably into view. Mary leaned over and scratched between the bull's ears.

'It's all right, Bill old lad,' she soothed and at the sound of her voice the bull subsided into his habitual doze. 'It doesn't do to take liberties with him, Mr Booth,' she said crisply, wondering if she should explain that Billy had nearly flattened Stephen once when he had been taking hay up to the suckler herd. If the fence had been three feet further on, Stephen had gasped, he'd have been mincemeat. They had never forgotten it and however calm the animal appeared made sure he could never use his great strength against them. She hoped he would fetch a good price. He was pure Charolais and had taken a second at the Great Yorkshire Show. That had been a lovely day.

Again she was lost in thought. Billy was such a good bull, even if he was a bit heavy nowadays. Her mind began to juggle with figures. If he made a lot – well, as much as she could hope for and heaven knows she was due for some luck – it might clear that last loan and then with the money from the cows and the machines she might be able to buy a house. Oh, it would be such a relief.

'How much do you think he'll make?' she asked abruptly.

The little man shook his head, hitching his trousers and shuffling. He poked at the bull with his stick, almost a reflex action when he came near stock, and Billy grumbled at him.

'How much?' repeated Mary, her voice tight.

'Well − it's hard to say rightly, but − a fair bit. Oh, a fair bit.' Mary beamed at him, forgiving him everything.

'Would you like a cup of tea, Mr Booth?' she asked sweetly, heading towards the house. She might even give him a piece of cherry cake.

She was almost at the back door when she realised she had lost him. He was standing before the loose boxes. He'd better not wave his stick about there, she thought aggressively, and hurried over.

'Selling these are you, Mrs Squires? Some quality horseflesh there.'

Mary sighed and leaned on one of the doors. Soft lips nuzzled her hair and she breathed the sweet smell of hay. Her horses. Her beautiful, expensive babies. They should have gone months ago, but she could not bring herself to do it, just the old brood mare now, in foal again, and the filly. After all, it was only sense to keep them. The mare threw super foals that always fetched a good price, and as for the filly − Mary was sure she had a winner. How sickening to sell for a song and find out two years later that she was heading for the top.

'I thought − I thought I might keep them,' she said quickly, aware that her voice trembled. Mr

6

Booth was looking at her, rubbing at his plump red neck beneath a too short haircut. He knew the mess she was in, all right.

'Nice to have horses around,' he said noncommittally. 'But – Mrs Squires, excuse me asking, but you've nowhere to go yet have you? No house or anything?'

She shook her head wordlessly, tears pricking her eyes. She would not cry in front of this horrid little man, she would not. 'It depends on the sale, you see. What's left. I – I'm sure I shall manage, Mr Booth.'

'Well then. Yes. But managing's a bit harder than we'd like sometimes. Look Mrs Squires, I can find good places for these, in fact the filly might suit my daughter. Bring a fair bit, they would. Help you out.'

'I don't need helping out!' Her voice was cold and she gazed at his podgy red face with real dislike, amazed that a moment ago she had been going to give him cake. The man was an obvious shark, out for what he could get. 'Come along, Mr Booth. I think we should go and have that tea.' She stalked to the house, as cross as two sticks.

Watching television that evening she thought it over. A little house and a little paddock, that was all she wanted, and surely the sale would bring enough for that? She would have to get a job of course, though heaven alone knew what with the children so young. Then of course it would be time that was at a premium, time to spend with the children, to look after house, garden and livestock. She might just be able to keep the mare, but the filly – oh, Mr Booth was right. The filly

7

would have to go. It didn't bear thinking of. She sighed and turned the television up, problems in Cambodia or somewhere. There didn't seem to be much fun anywhere in life these days.

The stock sale was on a Friday, and Mary was sick with apprehension. Anna was at playgroup but Ben remained with her, toddling about merrily, totally unaware of his mother's tortured state of mind. Who was the halfwit who said children are sensitive to mood, she thought, as she went to the toilet for the fifth time, nearly deafened by Ben's toy drum. At least he could provide an excuse for her to hide in the house if she really couldn't face it. Cars were already arriving and the sale didn't start till ten.

A rap on the door made her jump. Jet was shut up and it was odd to hear the knocker. She peered timidly round the door, despising herself for her cowardice, but it was only Mr Booth and relief made her effusive.

'Do come in,' she gushed, flinging wide the door and realising too late that she was ushering in two burly farmers as well as the agent. Favoured customers, surely. Perhaps they would buy the bull. She gave them all coffee and fruit cake – this was no time to be churlish – and chatted about the weather.

Mary wondered idly why such individualists as farmers should all wear exactly the same uniform at sales. Tweed suit, dark tie, flat cap and cane. She had often walked past men she knew quite well at the market because they merged so completely into the tweedy backcloth. She could only tell these two apart because one had hardly any teeth, and those that were left looked like a

8

dentist's nightmare, and the other exuded a faint aroma of pig. At last Mary could bear the suspense no longer. 'Are you interested in the bull?' she asked, toying casually with a spoon. Her fingers were stiff and it fell to the table with a clatter.

'Er – the bull?' They all looked shocked. She should have let them stall.

'Yes. The bull.' It might be a game to them but it was life and death to her.

'Good bull, said one farmer.

'Bit heavy,' said the other.

'In the prime of life,' insisted Mr Booth, taking up the cudgels on Mary's behalf. 'Bull like that's hard to find, strong, upstanding–'

'Thing is,' said one farmer, 'I heared his temperament's bad.'

Mary gulped. 'Temperament?'

The man nodded. 'Not to be trusted.'

Mr Booth let forth a gale of laughter, sending Ben scurrying for cover under the table. 'Only another bidder would say that, Harry. No, he's gentle as a lamb that bull. Why Mrs Squires handles him don't you, ma'am?'

'Yes – yes,' agreed Mary distractedly, visualising the trail of blood the bull would leave if anyone tried to treat him like a lamb. To hell with it, let the buyer beware.

'You are so right Mr Booth, he's quite a family pet really, we shall all be sorry to see dear Billy go.' She opened her eyes wide. 'I do so hope he goes to a good home – we don't want anyone being nasty to him, you know. More coffee gentlemen?'

Ben wriggled and jiggled in her arms as the bidding

began. Cow after cow was peered at, prodded and finally sold. The prices were not good and she felt cold with fear. What if there wasn't enough money in the end? What would she do then? Stephen's mother had telephoned last night.

'You know you're always welcome to come to us, Mary dear. We'd love to have you and the children.'

The children, possibly, but not me she thought viciously. Let the old besom take over my family? Never.

She knew she was being unjust, that the offer was kindly meant, but the thought of them all cooped up in that tiny bungalow in that twee street, condemned to live with the net curtain brigade for ever and ever, filled her with horror. That left her parents, and they hadn't offered. The house was big enough, heaven knows. They just didn't want any disruption of their ordered life, collecting antique silver and entertaining like-minded friends to cocktails. Two lively children and an independent daughter just wouldn't fit in. She supposed they'd have her if she was desperate. Please God it never came to that.

They were selling Billy. She wondered if anyone else could feel the sudden tension. Which of these brown, weathered faces was actually going to bid? Mr Booth's farmers were both there, leaning on their sticks with studied unconcern.

'What am I bid?'

Mr Booth rapped the concrete with his cane. The bull, unsettled by the crowd and the change in routine, spun round in his pen, dragging the chain to its full extent and pawing the floor and bellowing, murder in his eyes. Mary felt accusing stares and busied herself with Ben. If she'd had any sense she'd have tranquillised the brute, heaven knows what this performance would do to the price.

She felt a sudden shock. What was happening to her? Six months ago she had believed in honesty, integrity and a good name, and here she was now, money-grubbing, lying, and seriously considering doping. She could end up in gaol! At least it would be a roof over my head, she thought dismally.

She couldn't see who was bidding. It was going up fast and it took a trained eye to see the lifted finger and slight nod. All at once it slowed. Mr Booth took a deep breath and looked round in amazement. 'Come now, gentlemen, please. We're talking about a prize bull here. Pedigree Charolais, show winner. Always gets good calves. I need hardly remind you, gentlemen, of the tragic circumstances that bring about this sale – a rare opportunity for someone I should say. Now, shall we be serious? Do I hear . . .' and off they went again.

Suddenly the tempo changed, the bidding must have passed a magic figure because the agent became quite frenzied. 'Selling all the time now gentlemen, selling all the time. Chance of a lifetime and we're selling, thank you Mr Vane, what about you Harry, you're not going to miss it for a few hundred are you?'

He punctuated his words with raps of his cane. The bull swung his massive head from side to side, his roar bouncing against the stone, filling the barn with sound, but Mr Booth talked on, apparently understood although no one could hear him. Then he stopped.

'All done?' The dramatic pause. 'SOLD to Mr Vane.'

He thwacked the stone with a force sufficient to break the cane, and it was done. Too little by half.

Chapter 2

That evening, when the children were in bed, she walked round the empty yard and listened to the silence. The night was clear and very cold, frost already twinkling on the roofs and cobbles. Soon, very soon, she would have to leave here, abandoning not only a place but a whole way of life. She needed courage and she had none.

Small sounds caught her attention: the far off whines and snuffles of Jet rabbiting in the long field; the low champing of the horses at their hay. She moved to look in at them and they were quiet and trustful in the dark. Large, warm, familiar shapes. She leaned her head on the door and let Bella blow into her hair. It soothed her.

'Excuse me.'

She spun round, heart pounding. A man, a stranger, and she was alone here with just two small children in the house and the dog away across the fields. He was walking towards her across the dark yard; he looked very tall and there was nowhere to run.

'What do you want?' Her voice sounded thick. Oh God, if only the dog would come back.

'I was looking for Mrs Squires. I didn't mean to frighten you.' He sounded faintly Irish. Her brain started to function again. If he'd been going to murder her then surely he wouldn't waste time with pleasantries, but then again, perhaps he would, she didn't know many murderers. Either way there was very little she could do about it. Her mother's training asserted itself – always be polite.

'I am Mrs Squires. What can I do for you?'

She sounded ridiculously social and at once regretted that she had told him who she was. He would know she was alone. She should have said he was at the wrong farm, that her husband was in the house, anything. He took the few remaining strides towards her, his step sounding measured, menacing. She couldn't stand it. She pushed past him and raced for the house, slipping and sliding on the frosty stone. The kitchen door banged behind her. She shot the bolt home and scuttled into the hall. He couldn't see her there. She sat on the stairs, holding her knees and shivering.

A knock came on the back door.

'Mrs Squires? Mrs Squires? It's quite all right really. I only want to talk to you for a moment.'

He kept on knocking.

The stupidity of her position annoyed her, she felt like a rabbit with a ferret at the hole. She walked into the kitchen, turning on the outside light as she did so. She could see him now.

'What the hell do you want, sneaking up on me in the dark?'

He was trying to look through the frosted glass panel of the door. 'For God's sake, I called at the house, there was no one there. I walked over to have a look at the horses. Look, do you always hold conversations like this? I feel as if you're about to shoot me or something.'

Now there was a thought. She would have to get a shotgun.

14

Suddenly the night erupted in a frenzy of growling and snarling. Jet was back from his sortie and was making up for lost time. Muffled cries drifted into the kitchen. Quite at ease with this familiar situation Mary flung open the door, collared the dog and helped the man up.

'Won't you come in?' she asked sweetly.

Ten minutes later they were sitting opposite one another at the kitchen table, drinking coffee.

'I really am extremely sorry about your coat,' Mary said again. He glared back at her. His eyes were very blue, his hair fair, but he had had an accident at some time it seemed. His cheekbone was out of line and it was irritating to look at. It was as if a picture was crooked or a tablecloth rumpled; you automatically wanted to straighten it.

'That dog is really dangerous. You should get rid of him.'

She had heard that once too often. She drew herself to her feet. 'I would rather get rid of you. Creeping round houses in the middle of the night, you deserve everything you get. You're some horse dealer I suppose, hoping to pull some nice big con on a silly little woman. Give her some tale about splints and curbs, knock hundreds off the price and waltz off with a champion. I should have let the dog eat you.' She was fighting angry tears.

He looked up at her, without emotion. 'It is only half past eight, you know.'

'What's that got to do with it?'

'Well, it's not the middle of the night. Anyway, how was I to know you were on your own? Has your husband run off with the milkman?'

She sat down again. 'My husband is dead.' She

spoke with conscious dignity, expecting the usual embarrassed mutter.

'Don't tell me the dog ate him by mistake.'

Mary stared at him, in outrage, and then started to laugh. It went on and on, and she knew that if she didn't stop soon she never would. The man leaned over and caught her wrist, she choked on a giggle and was silent. 'It's been one hell of a day,' she said wearily. The man still held her arm, loosely, his fingers brown against the white inside of her wrist. Her skin prickled and she pulled away, embarrassed.

'It's cold in here,' she said, apropos of nothing.

'You're tired. Look, I wanted to talk about the horses but I can come back tomorrow if you like.'

She shook her head and dragged herself to her feet. Oh, he was right, she was so tired she thought her bones might fall though her skin and on to the floor.

'You might as well come now. But don't think you can con me because you can't.'

He grinned and pushed his coffee cup aside. His cheek twisted when he smiled, which was a pity. 'I never con pretty ladies,' he said lightly, and she thought 'smoothie'.

She led the way to the loose boxes. 'This is Bella, my brood mare,' she said, switching on the light.

He grunted. 'It's the filly I'm interested in.'

'Now, how did you hear about her?' It was flattering to know people thought the horse worth discussion. There, that proved she was good.

'Bloke called Fred Swallow mentioned her. Know him?'

She was impressed. A rich industrialist who had taken to the country, Swallow was fast becoming

16

a name in the horse world. His house had kept two firms of builders occupied for the best part of five years. Mercifully he had planted a tree screen which would one day hide it from the public gaze but in the meantime it was a local tourist attraction.

'We do not move in the same circles.' She hoped he thought she was socially superior to *nouveau riche* Mr Swallow, when of course she was just too poor. 'How did he find out? She's only just broken, no one's seen her.'

'The vet told him. Chatty fellow, Swallow said.'

She should have known. Ted was better than a telephone exchange.

'Well, you'd better come and see. As it happens I've sold the mare anyway.'

They stood and looked over the door at the big, sleepy three-year-old, straw in her tail, blinking in the light. The man pulled out a cigarette and started to smoke. Mary coughed ostentatiously but he took no notice, and just stood there, smoking, saying nothing. The silence began to grate on Mary's nerves.

'What do you think?' she asked shrilly.

'What? What about?' He was peering down at her, a little perplexed.

'The filly of course. But if you were studying the stars or something you can give me your opinion of them too.'

He was laughing at her. 'You don't sell many horses. Take your time, lady, it pays.'

'But what do you think?' she asked again, softly, her eyes large and worried.

'I think – I think I'd like to try her. Tomorrow. Ten o'clock. All right?'

She nodded and turned to go into the house. The day had been so awful and this man was too much. Let him come back tomorrow, she would talk to him tomorrow. Without a word to him, the dog at her heels, she trailed into the house and off to bed. The man stood in the dark yard, looking after her, and then walked to his car.

She overslept. Normally the children would have been racing round the house by half past seven, but not today. When ten o'clock came they had only just finished breakfast and the house was a shambles. She was desperately washing dishes when he drove up, and the dog was loose. She had to catch Jet before he raked his claws down the car door, the blasted man would probably run him over after last night's little incident.

Anna joined in the chase, yelling, 'I win, I win!' and obstructing her mother's every step with the result that Jet was only apprehended seconds before the dreadful deed was done. Red-faced and panting, she looked up to see an expression of mild interest on the face behind the glass. He extended a languid hand and pressed a button. The window descended noiselessly.

'Can I get out now?' he enquired sweetly.

'By all means,' replied Mary with as much ice as she could manage while hanging on to an exuberant dog.

They proceeded towards the stables in silence. She showed him the tack and returned, with Anna, to the house, there to undertake frenzied tidying. She suddenly remembered the sack of flaked maize in the corner of the sitting room. She gazed at it in surprise. What on earth was it doing there? Of course it was safe from the mice, but really . . . perhaps things had been getting a little out of hand lately. She hadn't time to move it so she'd just have to get the kitchen presentable.

At the last moment she noticed a pile of soggy nappies underneath the kitchen table. She swooped on them and stuffed them into the cleaning cupboard, jamming the door shut with a chair. Not a moment too soon – in he walked.

'Do sit down,' said Mary with her most charming smile, and too late saw which chair he was going to choose. She watched resignedly as nappies, shoe cleaning gear, a half full packet of washing powder and a dandy brush spewed on to the floor. Never apologise, never explain she thought, kicking a path to the table. She plonked two cups of coffee on it and sat down. The silence became oppressive. He cleared his throat.

'Well,' he said. 'Just you and the two children, is it?'

'And a horse I think you want to buy.'

'Not to mention a dog that – ' he caught her eye and grinned. 'I suppose he grows on you in time.'

'About the horse.'

'Yes.'

Anna wandered into the kitchen, accompanied by her Jack-in-the-box, a toy renowned for its eldritch scream. The man leaned down and plucked it from her grasp, his features contorted with pain. 'Little girl,' he said patiently, 'why don't you go outside? Your mother and I are talking.'

'That's mine,' said Anna.

'Yes. You can have it later.'

'Now.'

19

'Later.'

Anna gave him a measuring look and decided to give in. She leaned against his knee, sucking her thumb and staring at him. 'What's your name.'

'Patrick Brogan. What's yours?'

'Anna. And I've got a little brother called Ben. Daddy's in heaven. Mummy doesn't like it, and –'

'Time to play outside,' interrupted Mary scooping her up and plonking her unceremoniously outside the back door. Anna thought about wailing then changed her mind, content instead to chase the straw that blew around the yard. Mary watched through the window for a moment and then came back to the table.

The man, Brogan, was watching her. 'I like your little girl,' he said. 'She's pretty. Like you.'

Mary brushed this aside with an irritable shake of her head. 'Mr Brogan, you must understand something. I'm selling the filly because I have to. The mare, Bella, the farm agent's going to take her and she didn't – there wasn't – well, I didn't get very much. She's old you see, and – but the filly's different. I've got to get a decent price for her. I thought you should understand.'

'How bad are things with you?' He was smoking again, without asking. She did not offer him an ashtray.

'I don't want charity. She's a good filly and I want a fair price. That's all.'

'I don't buy horses out of charity.'

'Well then.'

They stared at each other. Mary's heart bumped against her ribs and a pulse in her throat fluttered. His eyes were very blue and very steady. All at once he seemed to decide something. He reached into his inside pocket and pulled out cheque book and pen, the one leather covered, the other engraved gold.

'There you are.' He tossed the cheque towards her. Mary looked at the figure and gasped.

'You're not serious?'

'She's worth it. She's a great horse. All right, I know I could get her for less, but you need the money. I'd feel a heel if I didn't pay.'

'But – what will you do with her? I thought she might make a hunter or something and then one-day events, that sort of thing. This is race horse money.'

'Or show jumping.'

'Oh. That's what you do, is it?'

He grinned ruefully. 'You sure know how to hurt a guy. It's what I do and I'm even supposed to be quite good at it. You don't watch?'

'Not really. It always seems to be very boring when it's going all right and then dreadful when it goes wrong – you know, horses falling and people squashed and so on.'

'Thank God the rest of the world doesn't think like you.'

'And you think my filly could jump?'

He nodded. 'She's got all the makings. Of course she's too young yet but she's the right shape, and she's got a nice nature. She showed really well over the poles.'

Mary beamed at him, delighted with his approval of her treasure. Plans began to form for what she might do with the money and she stood lost in thought, the cheque in her hands. Was it enough for a deposit on a house? But she wouldn't get a mortgage, you needed a job for that and how could you get a job when you had nowhere to live? Brogan coughed, and Mary started back to life.

'Oh, I'm so sorry. More coffee? A biscuit?'

'Yes, please.'

She bustled about fetching things but her mind was still wrestling with bills and bank balances.

'Where are you going to go?'

She jumped, turned, and gave him a strained smile. 'I don't know yet. You see, even with this it's going to be — we have debts, you see. But you must understand that Stephen never meant to leave me in this mess, neither of us ever thought this could happen. In a few years it would have been fine.' A deep sigh racked her, but again she forced a smile. 'I'll sort something out. And it's so wonderful of you to take the filly.'

'I think I'd like to take something else as well.' It was almost a whisper. She blinked at him, without understanding, and turned away. Did he want the old plough?

'What is it? What do you want?'

He was standing behind her. His finger traced the curve of her cheek.

'I want you,' he said softly.

'What on earth do you mean?' She was sure she must have misunderstood him.

She really must not jump to conclusions, he surely couldn't mean . . . she looked up into his face and looked away quickly, feeling herself go scarlet all over. Oh yes he could.

'I — I think there has been some misunderstanding, Mr Brogan. The filly is not for sale and I would like you to go.' She tried to push past him but he refused to move. She could smell horses and tobacco, mixed with a faint tang of sweat. What could he smell – soap and cabbage probably, she couldn't remember when she had last used perfume. He took hold of her shoulders and stroked her gently with his thumbs.

'I mean it, you know. I want you, the children and even that God-awful dog. Come and live with me, Mary. I want you.'

His voice was very soft, his hands caressing. She lifted her gaze from a detailed study of his jumper – machine knitted she noticed – and met his eyes. They were half closed and his breath came through parted lips. She realised with a shock that he passionately wanted to make love to her.

'So you think you can have us all for your money, do you?' She sounded shrill but could do nothing about it. 'We may be desperate but we haven't sunk that low. Get out of my way you – you –' she searched for something bad enough to suit him and found it ' – you bloody Irish mick, you!'

To her fury he was laughing and the grip on her shoulders was no longer gentle. Suddenly he let her go and she rushed to the other side of the kitchen. She stood for a moment trying to decide what to do, there was no way she could throw him out if he didn't want to go.

He was still smiling. In a spurt of anger she marched up to him, kicked him hard on the shin and stormed over to the sink. She started to peel potatoes, her fingers flying. At least she had wiped the smile off his face she thought viciously, listening to his extensive range of swear words. If he came over here she'd stab him with the potato peeler.

Ben was awake, shouting to be rescued from his cot and she went to get him. He was pink and rumpled, very warm. She spent some minutes holding him close but he wriggled. To her surprise Brogan was still there when she came down. He was smoking.

'I want you to think about it.' He was blowing smoke rings.

'Go away.'

'I'll come and see you tomorrow. You've nothing to lose, you know.'

'If you discount reputation and self-respect, I suppose you're right.'

'They won't keep you warm at night.' He walked to the door. 'See you tomorrow, love. You think about it.'

She waited until the sound of his engine had faded to a distant purr and then sank limply into a chair. He was right of course, she had absolutely nothing to lose. If she stayed on her own she would be well and truly in the poverty trap, the children would be farmed out heaven knows where while she struggled to find a job, and anyway, what could she do? Nothing that would pay very much, that was certain. Suppose she moved in with her parents? For a moment she toyed with the idea, imagining herself welcome, loved and indulged, but she knew it was a lie. The reality would be rows and complaints, hurt silences and scratched rosewood. And she knew she could not live with her mother-in-law.

She wondered what Stephen would say if he could see her now, seriously considering becoming a kept woman. She wouldn't of course. It would be the terraced house in Leeds, child minders and a job in a factory. She sighed and went to start the lunch.

She lay in the bath for ages that evening, letting her thoughts drift. Finally she had to get out, there was no more hot water. She dried herself slowly, thinking about Patrick Brogan. What kind of man was he? He seemed very rich, but then one never knew; expensive cars can always be hired and promises are easy to make. Was there money in show jumping? There must be or Fred Swallow wouldn't be interested. The man was certainly Irish and really that settled it, she wasn't going to live in Ireland.

She wiped the steam from the mirror with a corner of the towel and studied herself. A pretty face – dark hair, huge green eyes and soft, curving features – but lately she had looked white and strained and new lines had been drawn on her forehead. Giving the mirror another rub, she stood on a chair to look at her body. No stretch marks thank goodness and the worry of the past few months had put paid to any flab left after Benjie's birth. Yes, she looked slim and fit and small breasts were fashionable these days after all. She thought of Brogan's hands and her nipples suddenly hardened. Climbing down, she hurried into her dressing gown. It was very thick and unbecoming but practical in the draughty farmhouse. Central heating had been one of their dreams for the future, when they would banish damp walls, peeling plaster and smoking chimneys. Now it would be someone else's dream. She went to bed.

Chapter 3

She was awake early. The stupid man hadn't said what time he would come. Perhaps he wouldn't come at all – but anyway, it was best to be prepared. Suppose he came for lunch? She could hardly give him beans on toast but on no account must she appear to have made an effort. Steak and kidney pie would be ideal – she could casually offer to stretch it to accommodate him and if he didn't come the left-overs would keep them going for at least two days.

Then there was the question of clothes. In fact, this did not present too great a problem as her wardrobe seemed to have conspired recently in a campaign of mass disintegration, so she quickly settled on her least awful pair of jeans and a tight red sweater. She knew red suited her, it made her skin look very white. A little, a very little make-up and she was ready.

The morning crawled by. The children seemed determined to get their matching denim dungarees and pale blue sweaters absolutely filthy and Jet, shut in the sitting room, was scratching the remaining paint from the door. All this effort just to tell him to get lost, she thought dismally, and her stomach turned over as she heard a car.

It was only Jim Pearce in his battered Morris Minor. He had the farm to the north of her and had been very kind in recent months. He reached over the front seats – the rear ones had been removed decades ago and the space was used for an assorted cargo, sometimes including the odd pig – and produced a chicken. It was still warm, and he advised Mary to pluck it at once. Not today I won't thought Mary, even if I have to take the eyebrow tweezers to it tomorrow. She put it to one side and invited Jim in for coffee, it would pass the time.

The man was glad to sit down out of the wind. Fifty years of scratching a living on too small a farm with too little money had taken their toll and he was permanently tired. Each winter was just a little harder to bear than the last. Mary wondered how long it would be before he too had to leave. The little farmers would all have to go in the end.

They talked companionably of crops and weather, stock and prices. Suddenly Jim thought of an interesting snippet of news.

'Heard about High Wold House, have you?'

'You mean that place about ten miles away? I heard it was for sale.'

'So it was, though who'd want it I don't know. Way up in the hills, gets all the worst weather and the house is in a real state. Take a mint to fettle that I can tell you.'

'How much land?'

'About forty, mostly grass. Anyway, it's been bought. Now who d'you think it was?'

Mary laughed. 'I can't guess. The Queen? Lord Halifax? Go on, tell me.'

He took a deep breath. 'Patrick Brogan. Now what do you think of that? There, I can see I've surprised you. And there's more. He's done some sort of deal with Fred Swallow – buying horses, bringing them on, that kind of thing. That's why he wants to live here.'

Mary found her voice. 'He's in show jumping, isn't he?' She sounded anything but normal but fortunately the farmer didn't seem to notice.

'Yes, and very good he is too. Me and Betsy always watch him on the telly. He's moving from Ireland I heard, it should do wonders for the horse trade hereabouts and I said to the missus, Betsy, I said, what about Mary's filly?' He looked at her triumphantly.

She got to her feet. Her legs felt most peculiar and she leaned on the table. 'I'll think about it, Jim. I don't know if I want to sell just yet. Anyway, I must pluck that chicken – '

Pearce took the hint and picked up his hat, bracing himself before opening the kitchen door. It was a raw day and the wind raced across the flat fields and hurled itself against the house. Mary waited until he had started the car and then went back into the kitchen. Ben had crawled right over Anna's bricks, ruining what she assured her mother had been an airport, and the resultant war took five noisy minutes to settle. She heard the door open just as she finished rebuilding the runway, diverting Ben with some pegs.

'Forget something Jim?' she called without looking up.

'Sorry to disappoint you but it isn't Jim.' The voice was unmistakable.

Mary stood up. She couldn't remember when she had felt so embarrassed, but she was pleased to see that he too had dressed with care – smart grey trousers, sports jacket and tie.

'Really Mr Brogan, it is usual to knock you know.'

'Do we have to be so formal? My name's Patrick.'

'So I gather. I've found out quite a bit about you since yesterday as it happens.'

'I thought you might. This place has a grapevine that makes telephones look ridiculous.' He sat on the old pine table, swinging his legs and fiddling with his watch strap. Mary realised that he too was nervous.

'Are you living there now?'

'High Wold House you mean? No, I move in at the end of the month. I'd like it very much if you came too.'

There was a silence, tense and unpleasant. She turned to face him.

'I wanted to ask you something.'

He looked at her expectantly.

'Are you married – or anything? I mean, it seems strange, asking some woman you don't know to live with you. I wondered if you had a wife somewhere.'

The question plainly bothered him. 'I'm divorced. It's been over a long time and it's nothing you need think about. I haven't seen her in years.' His manner shut her out. She wanted to ask more but his face warned her away.

She gulped and said, 'But why us? We're nothing very special you know. Just a rather pathetic little family that's hit a bad patch. What's in it for you?'

He smiled and rubbed his cheek in a gesture that Mary was beginning to recognise. 'It's quite simple really. I don't like living alone and I don't intend to. The house is very isolated and I'm away quite a bit, especially in summer. I think you could cope with it. And anyway –' he slid easily off the table and stood in front of her, studying her face intently

' – you're so very lovely, Mary.'

Again there seemed nothing to say. The air was thick with meaning. She moved away, saying loudly, 'We need to settle a few things. You'll keep us all, will you? Pay all bills and so on, clothes, food, the lot?'

'That's right.'

'And I get the money for the horse?'

'You've got the cheque. It won't bounce.'

'It had better not. When would you like us to move in?'

'At the end of the month. Do you want to take your furniture?'

This was starting to sound like an interview with the bank manager. Mary looked round the kitchen. The old, battered table, the rush matting on the tiled floor. She thought of the shabby sofa in the sitting room where she and Stephen had sat together in the firelight talking and planning, looking forward eagerly to the morning. The nights in their big double bed under the patchwork quilt made by his grandmother in her youth.

She sighed. 'No,' she said softly. 'I don't think it will quite suit this arrangement.'

He stayed to lunch and they drank champagne. He had brought a bottle and she wasn't surprised. He left soon after, saying he'd be back in a week or so to show her round the house, but she could organise everything herself couldn't she? She could. He kissed the top of her head and was gone.

Mary told no one of the arrangement. Living with someone you loved was one thing but this smacked horribly of prostitution. She did telephone her parents but said she had taken a job as a housekeeper. She dreaded the neighbours finding out, as they surely must. They would be so shocked. Still, he had said the place was isolated, perhaps she need not meet many people.

They drove to see the house on the last day of February. Occasional flurries of snow hit the car windows as they threaded their way through lanes that became narrower and steeper by the minute. The house could be seen from some distance away, standing tall and square amidst a jumble of outbuildings, its only shelter a small clump of leafless trees. No other dwelling could be seen, just the dark brown and greens of the rolling hills with here and there the wavy grey line of a road.

The drive was potholed and muddied, leading not to the front door, but as in all Yorkshire farmsteads, to the courtyard at the back. Mary got out of the car slowly, unaware of the bitter cold. This farm had been young hundreds of years ago. The barn roofs, of red pantiles, sagged and leaned. Doors hung askew in walls that bulged alarmingly and the raised walkway that led to them had crumbled completely in places, with the result that the central sunken area, originally intended for manure, was now half filled with assorted rubble, weeds and litter. She turned to look at the house. Dead creepers clung to the walls, surrounding windows that were dirty and cracked. The grass growing in the gutters could be seen even from here, and the house was three storeys high. She would look round later, first she must see the garden.

All around was rubbish only dignified by age. Old cans, bottles and bricks lurked in every grassy clump to trip her. Then she saw a brick archway where once must have stood a wrought-iron gate. She climbed through and stood staring; it was a walled garden, knee high in weeds and half filled with scrap. But here, where the wind always blew and spring came in June it was everything, a haven of shelter and sunlight. She might even keep bees she thought excitedly as she made her way back to the car, suddenly aware that for the very first time since Stephen's death she had something to build. Only now did she realise how hard it had been to pull everything apart, piece by piece, and to be left with nothing. She needed this place and most assuredly it needed her.

He was smoking a cigarette, his coat collar turned up, listening to the radio. Mary climbed into the passenger seat, sat for a moment and then looked at him.

'If you've got the money,' she said slowly, 'I can make this place . . . beautiful!' She sighed happily and then was galvanised into action. 'Come on, I haven't seen the house and I have to pick the children up at five. Have you got the key?' She was already halfway across the yard. Brogan laughed softly and opened his door. This was a strange one and no mistake.

The house was as Mary expected, dark, cold and damp. The kitchen was a nightmare of peeling plaster and cracked tiles. As they opened the door a flash of movement confirmed Mary's worst fears. They had mice. An ancient coke boiler lurked in one corner, daring anyone to touch it. Apparently it heated the water, although where it dispensed its bounty was a mystery as the sink sported only one wobbly cold tap.

Eventually they discovered a bathroom of

mammoth proportions, the actual fittings hiding embarrassedly in the farthest corner. Mary felt no desire ever to get into this bath, brown stained and flaking as it was, even if the taps worked, which seemed doubtful. She looked accusingly at Brogan.

'We'll have a new one,' he said apologetically, and led the way next door.

'The master bedroom,' he announced grandly. Mary refused to meet his eye. The room was lovely, with windows on two sides giving marvellous views of the hills, and a curly plaster cornice. It was light even on this wintry afternoon. Stephen would have loved it, thought Mary, and her mood became shadowed.

'We must go,' she said gravely, and they returned to the car in silence.

The old van wheezed up the last incline in bottom gear, shuddering with the effort. Mary turned thankfully into the drive. The removal wagon was hard behind her and for one dreadful moment she had thought it was going to crush her faithful little car beneath its gleaming wheels. An even more enormous pantechnicon already stood in the yard and the humble van crouched next to it like a mouse at the feet of an elephant.

In the end she had brought some of her own furniture, the children's beds, her wedding presents and so on. Try as one might to abandon the past it just was not possible. Besides, she needed the security of familiar things around her; she could not help but realise how perilous her position was likely to be. At least she would have the money if he did abandon her. She had put it in the building society, it seemed the safest thing to do.

34

'Mummy, Mummy, Benjie pinched me,' wailed Anna and Mary hurried to let them out before blood was shed. Jet jumped out unbidden and began a tour of inspection, his mere presence driving the removal men back into the safety of their cabs.

' 'Ere missus, the dog's loose,' one called nervously and Mary sighed. Her first task would be to find an outhouse for the dog.

'Is Mr Brogan around?' she asked, trying to sound casual.

'Said he'd be back around ten tonight,' replied one of the men, apparently uninterested in her novel domestic arrangements. Thank you very much Mr Brogan thought Mary. I am obviously expected to work for my keep.

The next few hours were chaotic. Confronted with furniture she had never seen before and a house in which she repeatedly lost her way, she evolved a simple system. Tables, chairs and china were all deposited in the vast front room and everything else went upstairs. They just went along corridors and if they found a room with nothing in it, put something down. Things came to a halt when Mary discovered them trying to shove a piano upstairs. She diverted them to the dining room and declared a tea break.

The cooker wasn't connected and the electric kettle had the wrong plug, but one of the men attended to that. They drank out of a wondrous assortment of vessels, sitting on packing cases in the darkening kitchen. The children were cold and a little frightened. Anna asked continually to go home while Benjie just sucked his thumb and trailed around clutching his blanket. If she did nothing else, thought Mary, she must make their room habitable. The problem was, which room was it to be? She finally settled on a small bedroom above the kitchen. The wallpaper was peeling but it faced east and would catch the morning sun. Best of all, Anna's bed was already there and she only had to locate the cot. By the time she had found it and some bedding the men had almost finished. She said goodbye to them as if they were friends of a lifetime for after all, they had been through much together.

'I should let that dog out, missus,' they advised sagely. 'Bit lonely up here. You want to be careful.'

She thanked them but did not do as they said, Brogan would not appreciate the welcome.

They had ham sandwiches and milk for tea and the children cried and complained throughout. Mary knew how they felt. She too wanted a fire, familiar things and her own bed. She too wanted to go home. The children slept eventually but they were restless, muttering and occasionally crying out. Mary felt very gloomy which she knew was only to be expected after such a day. Somehow, knowing that didn't make it any better. She wished for company, but at the same time dreaded Brogan's imminent arrival. The men had unpacked a huge, brass-knobbed double bed which they placed unerringly in the master bedroom. She made it up, pointedly with only one pillow. She would sleep in the room next to the children tonight, surely he couldn't demand a night of passion on the day they moved in. Apart from anything else, she was exhausted. It would be best if she was in bed when he came back.

She was scuttling off to her solitary couch when

lights dazzled the windows as he turned into the drive. With a sigh she started back downstairs. This was one scene that couldn't be postponed. He came in like a whirlwind, clutching a brown carrier bag and a bottle of wine.

'Here, I brought a Chinese meal, I had to drive like the clappers to get it back hot so don't hang about.' There was no room for embarrassment in the rush for plates, forks and – impossibly – a corkscrew. In the end he impressed Mary enormously by knocking off the neck of the bottle against the fireplace. They drank out of teacups.

'Where were you today?' she asked gently as they finished the bottle.

'Arranging for the horses to come over. I thought you'd do better on your own.'

'I bet you did,' said Mary, with heavy sarcasm. He ignored her.

'What have you done with my filly?'

'You really are the soul of tact.' She put her feet up on a packing case. '*Your* filly is with my neighbour, Jim Pearce. He thinks I've gone to my mother.'

'Hiding your guilty secret? He's going to get a bit of a shock, isn't he, when we roll up together to get her?'

Mary said nothing. He leaned over and took her hand.

'Come on, it's time for bed.'

She looked up at him, her eyes wide and luminous in the dim light. 'I thought – tonight – that possibly – '

'Stop behaving like a frightened virgin. We are going to bed. Together.' He really was the most boorish man.

'I can behave any way I like,' she declared, flouncing to the door.

'Not when you're under contract to me you can't.' His voice was very hard.

Mary felt as if he had hit her. Her shoulders drooped and her step was heavy on the stairs. She flung another pillow on to the bed then undressed quickly and got in naked. A nightdress, even if she could find one, would surely be superfluous. She sat up to begin with but her head was aching so dreadfully that within minutes she had laid it down. He was locking doors, the sounds echoing in the old house, but she did not hear him come up for she was asleep.

She awoke quite early, with cold feet. She turned over and instinctively snuggled up to the large warm body beside her. She was drifting back to sleep when she realised he was gently stroking her thigh. A vague feeling that something was wrong stirred in her consciousness but it was soon dispelled by warmth, sleepiness and the delicious sensations produced by that stroking hand. A little moan escaped her as the hand moved to cup her breast, sending sharp darts of feeling through her. Suddenly she was no longer passive; she had been too long without a man and she wanted him. She rolled towards him, putting her arms around his neck in the darkness, feeling him hard against her. Her lips moved on his throat.

'Please, please . . .' she whispered. He heard and rolled on top of her, letting a great draught of cold air into the bed. Neither of them noticed. He sank into her and she groaned with the familiar pleasure of it. She was as urgent as he, but her climax took her by surprise, leaving her dizzy and gasping beneath him. His breath rasped in his throat as he gave a last desperate thrust before subsiding on top of her. She could hardly breathe, and she pushed feebly at his shoulders. He rolled off and lay on his back, panting. Mary lay beside him, refusing to think. They had made love without a single kiss.

When she woke again it was daylight and a thin rain was spattering the windows. She could hear the children bouncing around and was about to get up when she remembered she was not alone. She shut her eyes again quickly.

'You're going to have to wake up sometime, you know.' He sounded amused, he had been watching her. She turned to look at him. He looked very strong, his shoulder muscles bulging into a thick, tanned neck. The hair on his chest was a fine gold and she would have liked to touch it. Instead, she swung her legs out of bed and started to dress. She tried to hide her acute embarrassment by refusing to hurry, but the cold beat her and she pulled her sweater on with shivering hands.

'This house is freezing! What do we do about washing? It may be strange to you but it's an old Yorkshire custom, even in winter.' She felt much braver with her clothes on. He too started to dress and Mary watched him covertly, pretending to look for a comb.

'Don't worry,' he said cheerfully, wearing nothing but his socks. 'Six months and we'll have it sorted out. Central heating and all.'

'If we live that long,' said Mary dolefully, venturing into the icy corridor. At least it sounded as if he still expected her to be here in six months' time. Once Ben was three he could go to nursery school. She needed Brogan for those two years.

By the end of the day she was really wondering if she could take it. Brogan left the house entirely to her, informing her as an afterthought that the builders would be starting next week. He had more important things to take care of – namely the stables. There, the builders started today. Fond as she was of horses Mary was amazed at Brogan's complete obsession with them. To him, they were simply the most important things on earth. His abstraction when discussing damp courses and boilers for the house contrasted completely with his long and enthusiastic discourses on hay racks, feed stores and exercise yards. They were to have a jumping course in the bottom paddock, an all weather area in the long meadow and cross-country fences built into all the field boundaries. When Mary asked if they could please have two bathrooms, he said, 'Bathrooms? Yes, of course you can have bathrooms. Look, you see to all that, I'm busy.'

So she decided to have three. She was sure he wouldn't notice.

In the meantime she had to cope with conditions that would have brought tears to the eyes of pioneer women on the Oregon trail. She liked to think that she understood fires but it took her most of the day to fathom the mysteries of the boiler. Eventually she established that it had to be brought to a white heat by feeding it half a tree twig by twig before you dared ask it to accept anything from the pile of anthracite outside the back door. Once lit, however, it heated the water with creditable enthusiasm.

Cooking was another matter entirely. They were to have an Aga, Brogan informed her. Mary was

thrilled and demanded to know whether it would
be installed this week or next. He lifted his head
from the plans of the stable block for long enough
to take another cheese and pickle sandwich and to
say that no, that would come when all the other
work was finished. She could manage with the old
electric one he'd brought, couldn't she? It had been
his mother's until she bought a new one.

That afternoon Mary confronted the monster.
One of the builders had jury-rigged the connections
and she felt sure that she was well on the way to
an early grave if she so much as touched it.
Nonetheless, the children must be fed. They all sat
down at six o'clock to a meal which Mary felt to be
a triumph of ingenuity; she had found just the right
size book on which to stand one of the front legs,
had jammed the oven door shut with a piece of
wire and knew which ring she must on no account
use unless she wanted to fuse the lights. She had
in fact done this and since no one was the least
interested in her plight had taken the fuse out and
substituted a rusty nail. She almost wished it would
set the house on fire.

The children were in bed by seven and since the
kitchen was the only warm room in the house,
Brogan worked at the table while Mary washed up
and searched for more and yet more mouseproof
containers. They were in bed by ten.

This set the pattern of their days. Brogan worked
outside, transforming the ancient buildings into
lines of loose boxes worthy of a racing stable. To
Mary's unspoken fury, a large modern flat was
being constructed with all speed in the granary.
This, Brogan informed her casually, was for his girl
grooms. The man is a brute, thought Mary viciously

41

as she lowered herself into three inches of rusty water in the bath; she had let the boiler go out. That very day a shining white bathroom suite had been delivered post haste to the granary. And it was not as if the grooms even needed a bath – they weren't even here!

She, on the other hand, was daily fighting a losing battle against the piles of brick dust the builders were producing. No sooner had they knocked holes in all the walls for central heating pipes than they bashed all the plaster off for the new wiring and when they finished that they dug the floors up for the damp course. The final indignity was when the plumbers got to work; within hours the toilet no longer flushed and buckets of water had to be carried to it up two flights of stairs.

'I thought being a kept woman was supposed to be a life of luxury,' she complained to Brogan that night, filing her blackened nails. He just laughed, poured her a drink and went back to reading *Horse and Hound*. Conversation between them was polite but limited. Mary never used his name but he never mentioned the fact. They behaved almost like strangers.

During the day, that is. The nights were a very different matter. From the moment they got into bed there was a warmth and intimacy between them that took them both by surprise. They made love often, sometimes tenderly, sometimes with violence and passion, whispering their need for each other in the dark. Come the morning they rose and went their separate ways as if the night had never happened.

Chapter 4

The horses were to arrive at the end of March, half
to High Wold House, to fill the hastily completed
boxes, half to Fred Swallow, who was to put them
up until the work was finished. Brogan was
anxious to start working them; the season was
getting under way and he had been idle too long.

'How many do you have?' asked Mary one day,
at breakfast. Ben threw his feeder cup over his
shoulder, the top came off and milk swilled round
the floor.

'Fifteen at the moment,' he replied, deftly
moving his feet out of range of the flowing tide.
Such incidents never seemed to annoy him, he just
did not get involved. Quite a sensible policy really,
thought Mary as she mopped up. Many breakfasts
with Stephen had been marred by remarks like
'Can't you make those children eat properly?' and
'Are we never to have a civilised meal?'.

The children's attitude to him was very
different. He made no attempt to win them over
yet they adored him. Anna was his shadow and
wherever he went on the farm there followed a
little figure in a blue anorak, red wellingtons
flashing in her efforts to keep up. Mary had tried
to discourage her by keeping her in the house as
much as possible but as soon as her back was
turned Anna was off. She was surprised that

43

Brogan never complained and often worried in case his policy of non-involvement extended to letting Anna fall into the cement mixer, or at least wet her knickers. One day Anna had been gone so long that she left Ben asleep in his cot and went in search of her. Brogan was mending a gate in the long meadow and a familiar little figure was with him. They did not see her approach and she was able to watch as they worked in obvious harmony, Anna handing nails and even the hammer on request.

Brogan looked up in surprise as Mary hurried to them.

'Is she being a nuisance?' she gasped apologetically.

He was off-hand. 'Not too bad. Do you want her? Go on, Anna, back to the house.'

The little girl started to protest but was silenced by a stern glance. Mary tried not to feel resentful. He had no right to hold such sway over her child. At least Ben still loved her best, she told herself, but even he would cling to Brogan's trousered leg, yelling, 'Da, Da, Da.'

She went for a walk on the day the horses were to arrive. She felt very shy of the unknown grooms and dreaded their knowing stares. They would almost certainly know more of Brogan than she did and it was likely to prove humiliating. He never spoke of his family or his wife, he seemed to have no past.

The day was cold, but bright and sunny. The promise of spring was in the air, in the tiny buds on the hawthorn and the new greenness of the winter wheat. Jet ran wildly through the fields, chasing rabbits both real and imagined. He needed more exercise. When Stephen had been alive Mary had taken the dog with her when she went riding, leaving her husband with the children. The dog was starting to look quite portly, she thought sadly.

When she returned the yard was filled with noise and bustle. She stood unnoticed by the gate, a child holding either hand. Horses were being led from an enormous green and yellow horse wagon with the words 'Patrick Brogan' emblazoned on the front and sides. Each animal wore a matching green and yellow rug, a travelling hood and bandages on legs and tail. Mary paid them scant attention and concentrated on the grooms. There were three, all girls, all young. They wore what was almost a uniform in the horse world, jeans, jumper and green quilted jacket, and they were working with smooth efficiency. Mary dreaded them noticing her, but she had to walk through the yard to the house. She was halfway across when one of the girls caught sight of her, stopped what she was doing and marched confidently over.

'I say,' she called out in somewhat mannish tones, 'you can't just walk through here you know. What do you want?'

To her horror Mary felt herself blushing. Surely at her age she should have grown out of that. 'I live here,' she said weakly and began to walk on, but the girl pushed herself in front of her.

'Oh no you don't,' she said crisply, taking her by the shoulder with one firm, brown hand. 'Paddy!' she bellowed, and Brogan appeared from within the barn.

He strolled over. 'What's up, Edna?' he

enquired lazily. The girl looked like an adoring spaniel presenting a dead bird to its master. 'Why are you clutching Mary like that? Let her go, girl, do.'

'She says she lives here,' explained Edna in incredulous tones.

Brogan took out a cigarette. 'So she does. She's what you might call the mistress of the house.' He bent his head to a match, drew on his cigarette and blew a long cloud of smoke. 'Come on, love.' He threw an arm casually round Mary's shoulders and together they walked to the house. Edna was left to stare furiously after them.

'What a terrifying girl,' exclaimed Mary as they reached the safety of the kitchen.

'She is a bit,' he agreed. 'But she's a damned good groom. You should try to make friends with her.'

'I didn't know you were called Paddy,' she said softly. He met her eyes.

'You don't speak to me at all.' His voice was thick and she knew he was thinking of last night. She had taken the lead, her hands and lips stroking him into readiness before she sat astride him, pushing him deep within her. Afterwards he had held her very close and had called her his darling girl, kissing her hair. She had pulled away from him, turning her face into the pillow, as so often taking refuge in silence. He had stroked her back, whispering her name, but she had still not replied. Eventually he slept, but it was a long time before Mary did so.

He sighed, sounding tired, and walked to the back door. His hand was on the knob when Mary spoke.

46

'Patrick! Would you like a cup of tea?'

'So we are going to communicate, are we? Thank God for that. Yes, tea would be lovely.'

'I don't think I'm going to like that girl,' said Mary, filling the kettle.

'Edna? Why ever not, she's a bit bossy but that's all. She's a cracking rider too, so don't think I'm getting rid of her on your account.'

'I don't think she's going to like me much either.'

'She'll just have to put up with it then. She does what I tell her anyway.'

Mary searched in a packing case for some cups. Would this kitchen never be finished? 'Has she got a crush on you?' she asked cautiously.

'Don't know. Yes, probably. Me and Knight Errant.'

'Who's he?'

'My best horse. Look, hurry up with that tea and I'll introduce you to him.'

Edna was grooming the horse when they walked up.

'Leave that now please, I want to show him to Mary,' said Brogan, going into the box.

'He's had quite enough upset for one day,' replied the girl, not even pausing.

'Don't push your luck, Edna.' His voice was quiet but menacing. She flung her brushes violently into the box and stormed out, giving Mary a look of such venom that she recoiled.

'I don't think you're helping things,' she said ruefully as she joined him in the stable.

He was uninterested. 'What? Oh, never mind that, what do you think of this fellow?'

Mary looked at the horse properly for the first

time. He was tall, about 16.3 she thought, but so well made that he looked smaller. His head had the unmistakable quality of the thoroughbred but the legs were so powerful that Mary suspected something more plebeian somewhere in his ancestry. He was in beautiful condition, the deep browns of his coat gleaming in the fading afternoon light. Brogan threw a rug over the big gelding, pulling his ears affectionately.

'Seen enough? What do you think?'

Mary laughed. 'Now I know you paid far too much for my filly. With something like this you don't need her.'

'No, no, your filly's good.' He caught her eye and grinned. 'Not that good, but then I had my reasons. That reminds me, we must go and get her this week. Out you come now, Edna will want to get on.'

They moved round the rest of the boxes and Mary was hard put to it not to show how impressed she was; she wasn't prepared to let him have things too much his own way. She was introduced to the other two girls. One, Susan, was quite pretty in a plump way but she was very shy and obviously terrified of Brogan. The other, Mandy, had been well primed by Edna. She gave Mary a cold stare, running a grubby hand through fair hair darkened by grease and too little washing. Mary felt a pang; the bath would be wasted on that one. Feeling an outsider, she trailed back to the house, alone.

Jim was washing out his little milking parlour when they drove the horse box into his yard. His dozen or so dairy cows were his pride and joy and he never begrudged the hours of labour that went into squeezing a tiny profit from them. His equipment was old-fashioned and unreliable, but there was no hope of replacing it, or of enlarging his herd to economic proportions. It was only a matter of time, thought Mary sadly, drawn back into the insecure world she had known for so long. To a farmer, too little money meant that nothing could ever be done properly. You could never buy the best in stock or machines, which meant that illness or breakdown were everyday occurrences, eating into precious time and even more precious energy. So often Mary had heard a big, prosperous farmer pouring scorn on the squalor and filth of a neighbour's yard, knowing nothing of the treadmill on which the man laboured, day after day.

Mary jumped down, calling, 'Jim, Jim, it's me!'

She was ridiculously pleased to see him. She hadn't realised how isolated and friendless her life had been of late. He hurried out, wiping his gnarled hands on the sides of his trousers.

'Well, Mary lass, I've been wondering where you disappeared to. It's right good to see you, I'll say. And pretty as a picture. Come on, come see that blasted filly of yours, you'll have been worrying about her I dare say.'

'We thought we'd take her today Mr Pearce, if that's convenient.'

Brogan's words as he climbed from the cab brought the farmer up short.

'Aren't you – I mean – well, bless me, Mary, I never thought you'd sell that quick, I didn't really!' He gave her a sly wink, intended to convey that he thought she'd done really well in hooking such a prestigious buyer.

Brogan strolled to Mary's side and placed a casually possessive arm round her waist. 'Come along, darling, let's see the filly. We must get home before dark you know.'

Jim Pearce looked from one to the other in obvious bewilderment. 'Well . . . Mary, you're not . . . I mean you're working away, aren't you?' He looked at her hopefully. She was stiff with embarrassment, her cheeks flaming.

'I'm living at High Wold House, Jim,' she said flatly.

The little farmer looked at her for a long moment. He sighed. 'Well, I'm sorry to hear that, lass. Still, you know what's best I suppose.' He turned and led the way to the filly.

They hardly spoke on the way home. At last, Mary said, 'Why did you do it?'

'People have to find out sometime. You can't hide for ever. And anyway, what are you ashamed of?'

'Stephen has only been dead six months.'

'But he is dead. And look at the mess he left you in, damned irresponsible if you ask me.'

'You know nothing about it. You don't know what it's like to be poor. Look at you now, throwing money about as if there was no tomorrow. I only hope you can afford it, I should hate to be destitute twice in as many months.'

'Oh, but you've always got your escape fund, haven't you?'

'What do you mean?'

'What I gave you, plus what was left from the sale. You're sitting on that like a damned broody hen. You buy food, things for the house, clothes for the kids, all with my money, but nothing for yourself. And you won't touch your little nest egg. Not if your life depends on it.'

'I don't need anything,' said Mary defensively.

He snorted in derision.

'All right, well I can't spend that money. It makes me feel safe.'

'Then why don't you spend mine? For Christ's sake woman you don't even possess a decent pair of jeans.'

'I don't know. It would feel so – immoral, somehow.'

He laughed so hard that the horse box swerved dangerously and Mary squawked in alarm.

'Do be careful! I really don't know what's so amusing. It's not as if I need many clothes, we never go anywhere.'

'We're going out on Friday week, as it happens. Dinner at Fred Swallow's. So, leave the kids with Susan and go and buy some clothes. That's an order.'

'I don't think I want to meet Mr Swallow.'

'Pity. His house is incredible.'

She was silent for a while. 'What sort of thing do I wear?'

'God, I don't know. Something glamorous.'

'Kept women are supposed to have wardrobes full of black suspender belts and see-through nighties. Shall I stock up with those as well?'

'That's the most sensible thing you've said so far,' he grinned, turning into the yard.

'I was joking,' she said coldly, opening the door. He caught her free hand and raised it to his lips, placing a long, sensuous kiss on her palm.

'I wasn't,' he whispered.

Mary pulled her hand away and ran to the house, ignoring the giggles of the watching grooms.

Chapter 5

Once she had made up her mind to spend money Mary found it an odd and invigorating experience. Setting out that morning in her least dreadful underclothes, much-washed jeans and a sweater, she resolved that Brogan should be taken at his word however much it cost him. She resolutely ignored the whisperings of her thrifty conscience, flitting from shop to shop with an ever increasing load of parcels. When Stephen had been alive she had limited her purchases only to the barest essentials, making as many of her clothes as possible. Not that she had needed many, there had been no money to spend on outings and besides, they had found a rare pleasure in just being together. The comfortable closeness of their life was a world away from the tension of living with Brogan, swinging from rage to indifference, passion to humour in a moment.

The memories threatened to cloud her day and she walked quickly into yet another boutique and began rifling through the dresses with firm, decisive fingers. A pale blue silk cocktail dress caught her eye and she whisked into the changing room without even a glance at the price tag, something she had never done in her life before. It fitted perfectly and she gave her reflection a grin which she quickly replaced with a bored stare when the assistant appeared.

'That is absolutely wonderful!' gushed the woman, and for once it might have been true. The bodice was tight, with shoestring straps, but the skirt was full, to mid-calf, with the folds studded with tiny rhinestones. The silk hung softly, clinging as she walked emphasising the leanness brought about by hard work and worry. It was a very sexy dress, and just the thing for Fred Swallow. She wrote the cheque with a flourish and swept into the street to stand trembling against a pillar box. You could buy two calves for the price of that dress.

Feeling chastened she arrived at the hair salon for her appointment with Henry and sat in dumb humility as he lifted a lock of her hair, letting it fall from limp, exhausted fingers.

'This hair has been totally neglected!' he shouted and everyone turned to gaze in accusation at the sinner. 'What can I possibly do with this? It's had nothing done to it, nothing at all!'

Mary looked wildly around, realising that unless she made a stand she would shortly emerge with an Afro perm at the very least.

'I just want a decent cut,' she declared in ringing tones. 'I know it's difficult, but that's what I want.' Henry glared at her in the mirror and she cringed.

But, a mere forty-five minutes later, she had her new style, sleek, shining and beautiful.

'I knew you could do it if you tried,' she said kindly to Henry as she left.

Brogan was in the yard when the van made its usual noisy entrance but he was talking to Edna and did not turn round.

'I've spent a small fortune,' said Mary hopefully,

longing to show off her purchases even to an unresponsive audience. 'And I've had my hair done,' she added.

Brogan turned his head. 'Oh? Very nice. Look, I need Susan, run along and get her there's a good girl. The kids have been driving her mad and she's got better things to do than baby sit for those horrors. I thought you'd be back hours ago.'

He resumed his conversation leaving Mary deflated and near to tears. The man gave with one hand and then took away with the other, she thought furiously as she flounced into the house. She should have foreseen this, of course. To him she was just another employee, much the same as the grooms but with responsibilities on a more personal level and a more flexible wage structure. As such, he expected her to be a credit to him and her lovely dress was simply part of her pay. Clenching her fists into tight balls, her stomach churning with suppressed rage, she forced herself to speak calmly to Susan and the children, then began to prepare the tea. The children were hanging round her legs, showing their drawings and telling her of the little happenings of their day and gradually she was soothed. In the future she would remember that the relationship was strictly business.

Brogan and the grooms were reaching a fever pitch of activity and Mary felt very much out of it. They began working horses at seven-thirty in the morning, walking and trotting endless circles, changing horses constantly. They all ate breakfast in the house at eight-thirty and the conversation was always of horses, exercise programmes and forthcoming competitions. Mary felt like a waitress, producing full plates, removing empty ones, pouring cups of tea and toasting bread, all without a word spoken to her. At nine o'clock she was left amidst the wreckage and they started serious jumping. Brogan returned to the house for lunch but he rarely spoke, he was too preoccupied with entry forms and timetables. He continued with this until three while the girls had a well-earned rest, then he went out again to ride yet more horses, leaving Edna to supervise grooming and strapping in the stables. They were leaving to start the round of shows in two weeks' time, only Susan remaining to care for the horses to be brought out later in the year.

'How long will you be away?' asked Mary over lunch one day.

He was distracted. 'Oh, I'll ring you.'

Mary sighed. 'You can't. The phone's not connected.'

'What? Oh, of course it isn't, I forgot. Well, chase them up while I'm away. I'll write or something.'

She tried another tack. 'Can I take the filly out this afternoon? Susan said she'd look after the children.'

'Your filly you mean? No, that's not on, I'm afraid. Edna's been working her and has just about got her going, we can't risk having her spoiled.'

'But she was my horse! I've been riding her for ages!' She was very offended.

'Yes, and it showed. You've been letting her get away with murder, good thing we caught her when we did.'

'Well, isn't there anything I can ride then? I never get out of this damned house and the

56

builders are driving me mad! Jet needs the exercise too.'

He looked at her thoughtfully. 'I suppose you could have Merlin for an hour. He wouldn't take too much harm. Talk to Edna.' He returned to his paperwork.

She found Edna in the tack room, sorting bits.

'Patrick say I can ride Merlin.' She felt like a schoolgirl reporting to the games mistress. Edna looked at her with unconcealed scorn, her tall, thin figure radiating confident superiority.

'Well, if you must you must, I suppose. But don't blame me if he carts you all over the countryside.' She took a saddle and bridle from the loaded racks. 'Go and tack him up. I'll come and check him over before you set off.'

Mary scuttled out, wishing she had never started this. Edna was on her own ground and would not hesitate to make the most of it.

Merlin was a twelve-year-old, and on the way down in the world of show jumping. He had never been one of its brightest stars but he had been consistent and would no doubt soon be sold on to some up and coming youngster who could learn from the old horse. He opened his mouth obligingly when Mary offered him the bit and ambled into the yard with as much enthusiasm as a seaside donkey. Edna bustled up and tightened girths and buckled straps officiously.

'Just make sure you don't bring him back in a lather,' she ordered as Mary swung herself into the saddle. She could feel Edna's eyes upon her as she started up the lane, Jet following close on the horse's heels.

The countryside calmed her, as it always did.

From Merlin's back she could see over the hedges
to the gentle roll of the hills, dipping smoothly
down to the valley. Tractors worked in the
distance, ploughing and harrowing, each followed
by its flock of gulls, feeding on the worms in the
newly turned earth. She sniffed the tang in the
air, made up of rain and grass and living things,
and wondered how it was that she could live in
this paradise and see so little of it, engrossed as
she always seemed to be in the house and its
occupants.

There was a bridlepath some halfmile along the
road and she turned down it. She had no idea
where it led but had often longed to explore. She
set off at a trot, making the transition with an
uncomfortable bounce. She was out of practice.
Jet sauntered along in her wake, as delighted as
she with their temporary freedom. The path was
narrow and overgrown and as they rounded a
bend Mary could see that it was blocked by a fallen
tree. She slowed to a walk and took a good look
at the obstacle, which turned out to be only about
three feet high although surrounding branches
made it rather wide. She turned to take a run at
it, wondering anxiously if she and Merlin would
still be together in a few moments' time. She need
not have worried, the old horse ballooned over the
log, Mary hanging on for dear life, one hand
prudently lodged in his mane. They cantered on
for a few yards, delighted with themselves, before
Mary decided it was time they returned to a trot,
and tightened the reins.

Merlin's ears pricked, he leaned on the bit and
started steadily to increase his pace. Not as yet
alarmed, she tried again and once more felt that

determined resistance and gentle acceleration. They were now flying along the track and Mary began to worry. She sat down hard in the saddle and leaned on the reins, turning his head to her knee as she did so. He merely dropped his nose almost to the ground and continued his headlong gallop, apparently quite happy not to see where he was going. She released him quickly, thinking that he must tire soon, but the horse seemed set for miles. She could hear Jet's frantic barking far to the rear as he struggled to keep up, realising in some vague way that she was in trouble. If only she knew where the path led, she thought, visualising Merlin careering out on to a main road.

She could see a gap in the hedge some way up the track and resolved to try and turn the horse into it, hauling on his head as if trying to raise a sail. She succeeded and they skidded round the corner and into a ploughed field, still at breakneck speed. He started to slow as his feet clung to the heavy earth and she aimed him straight at the hedge. For a terrible moment she thought he was going to try and jump it but he must have had second thoughts because he finally ground to a halt within inches of the hawthorn, hanging his head and drawing gasping breaths. Mary climbed down, ashamed to find that she was shaking. The horse was in a dreadful mess, plastered with mud, the sweat and foam on his neck cut into great slices by the reins. She looked round for Jet but he was nowhere to be seen. Perhaps he had decided to go home.

She spent some minutes trying to smarten the horse up, using her handkerchief supplemented by wisps of grass, but the final effect was not

much better than when she started. She
remounted and set off at a walk – the exhausted
horse was incapable of anything faster – wondering how they were to get home. They were neither
of them in any state to negotiate the log. She
decided to cut across the fields, hoping the gates
would be in the right places, which of course they
were not. At last and after endless circles she
came out on to the road above High Wold House
and turned towards home, dreading her reception.
Edna and Brogan were standing in the lane waiting for her, bursting with righteous indignation.

'Where the hell have you been?' roared Brogan
as she rode up. He had been worried to death
about her. 'Do you realise you've been gone three
hours? Susan's got better things to do than look
after your brats and I've had to send Mandy out
looking for you. And what on earth have you done
to this horse?'

'He bolted,' said Mary weakly.

Edna smirked. 'Just what I expected. I told you
she couldn't ride, Paddy, and now we've got all
this work cleaning the old boy up. I wouldn't be
surprised if he's broken down.'

'I'm sorry.' Mary was near to tears. 'I just
couldn't hold him. I did try, I did really.'

'Of course you couldn't hold him,' snarled
Brogan. 'What's he doing in a snaffle? He's got a
mouth like a bucket, we always use a gag.'

Mary turned and stared at Edna, who had the
grace to flush.

'Merlin will be getting chilled,' she said
defiantly.

Mary got off and handed the reins to the girl.
'Thank you, Edna,' she said gently. 'I do hope I

60

can return the compliment some time.' She turned and walked into the house.

'I've spoken to Edna,' said Brogan when he came in later that evening.

Mary looked up from her ironing. 'Jet's not back,' she said, failing to keep the wobble from her voice.

'He'll be rabbiting. He'll be back in the morning.'

She was not comforted but turned her attention back to the pile of shirts just the same, wincing as she picked up the iron. There was nothing she could do until the morning anyway. Brogan caught her hand, turning the palm upwards, trying to look at it, but she pulled away.

'Let me see.'

'No.'

'Don't be stupid, let me see.' He held her wrist in an iron grip.

'You're hurting me.'

'Open your hands.'

She did so reluctantly, standing in front of him, palms outstretched.

The raw flesh oozed.

'Edna should see this.' His voice was grim.

'I wouldn't give her the satisfaction.'

'Why can't you two get on? She's not a bad girl, you know.'

Mary turned back to the ironing. 'She's jealous. And I can see why, she's missing out on a lot.'

'What on earth do you mean? Head girl here, all the riding, all the travel, lots of girls would give their right arms to be in her shoes.'

'How old is she though? Twenty-eight? Thirty? And no boyfriend, or any hope of one I should think. What will her future be? Horses don't keep

you warm at night and Edna can see the day
coming when the travel palls and she'd like to
settle down and have some babies. Grooming isn't
a job for one's middle age.'

'That's true. But she's not that bad looking. Bit
masculine, perhaps.'

'Yes, and can you imagine Edna in a romantic
situation? If someone told her she looked
gorgeous she'd tell the poor fellow not to be
soppy, slap him on the back and go and get two
more pints. She's just not the stuff that dreams
are made of.'

'You're right there,' laughed Brogan. 'And you
I take it, have all that she wants and you're not
very grateful for it either.'

'What she wants is you, as well you know. You
trade on it, you know you do. I think you should
find Edna a husband, you owe it to her.'

'It would get her off your back, you mean. No,
she's too good to lose. You'll just have to learn to
love her I'm afraid. Or is that too much for your
superior soul?'

Mary sighed. 'I'm going to bed,' she said wearily,
in no mood for verbal sparring this evening.

Brogan sat looking after her. God, that woman
was prickly. Every now and then they would talk
and it was real, and honest, and relaxing. Then
down came the shutters, either she snapped and
snarled like a cornered vixen or she froze; and
walked out and left him feeling stupid, because
he had no idea what he had said. 'I should finish
it now,' he muttered to himself, knowing that he
would not. In the night, when he reached for her,
the fire and ice of her fused into thrilling, wanton
need. It was as if everything she held from him

in the day was his for the taking at night and he took it, rousing her to frenzy and then leaving her spent and weary. It gave him a power over her, and at the same time put him in thrall. The woman was a witch.

When morning came Jet had still not returned. The atmosphere at breakfast was dreadful, Edna and Mary not speaking to anyone, Mandy and Susan conversing in nervous undertones. Even the children for once noticed something and reacted predictably; Anna complained of tummy ache and Ben wailed. Only Brogan seemed unaffected, reading the paper much as usual, but as they all rose at the end of the meal he said, 'Mandy I want you to help Mary look for her dog. Susan, you see to the children.'

For a moment Edna hesitated, and seemed about to say something, but she thought better of it and went out into the yard.

Mandy took one of the horses and rode down the bridlepath Mary had visited yesterday. Mary walked the lanes, calling. Suddenly she saw something large and black in the hedge. She walked slowly towards it, knowing what she would find. He was quite cold and must have been dead for a long time, lying where he had fallen. The dog had run and run, trying desperately to stay with her but too old and too fat to do so. His heart had just given up.

She walked back to the farm, cold and desolate as never before. Jet had been Stephen's dog and his passing seemed to place the final seal on her dead marriage. She cried, she did not know if it was for Stephen, for Jet or for herself. Brogan caught her arm as she stumbled across the yard, and she turned on him in a fury.

'You got rid of him in the end, didn't you, you always hated him. You let her do it, you know you did. Oh God, I wish I could get away from here, I wish I had somewhere to go. I wish, I wish . . . oh, I wish I was dead!' She collapsed against him, shaking with sobs. Faintly she heard a voice, Edna's voice, rather high and tense, say, 'What a fuss to make about a dog. Anyway it was vicious.'

The words seemed to echo in her head, going round and round and suddenly she was screaming and crying uncontrollably. She was dimly aware of hands holding her, soothing her, of the frightened faces of Ben and Anna, of being coaxed between cool sheets. She lay there exhausted, an endless river of tears still streaming from eyes closed against an uncaring world.

They called Doctor Bateson, who had delivered both Anna and Ben. He held her hand and talked softly to her, asking about her life since Stephen had died. She replied in strangled whispers, still unable to stop crying. She didn't think she would ever stop crying. After half an hour he patted her hand and stood up.

'You stay there for a day or two, my girl. You can't expect to lose your husband and go on as if nothing had happened. The day of reckoning has to come and yours has arrived.'

The Yorkshire accent was very strong and Mary found it comforting. He was a nice man if you were really ill. Malingerers never called twice.

'I seem to have got myself in rather a mess,' she said apologetically.

'You'll get out of it,' laughed the doctor, putting

on his coat. 'You're a fighter if ever I saw one. Now, I'll just have a word with these people downstairs and I'll be on my way.'

'What are you going to say?'

'Only what I've told you. Now, you have a little sleep, you need it.'

He shut the door and marched downstairs, his feet very loud on the uncarpeted treads.

Brogan met him in the hall, closely followed by Edna.

'Is she going to be all right?' It was Edna, made miserable by guilt.

The doctor glared at her, but replied with distant civility. 'I think she will. She never really let go when she lost her husband and now she's making up for it. A day or two in bed should do the trick.'

He moved towards the door, but Brogan caught his arm.

'She'll be alone here for a bit, just her and the children. Do you think . . .?'

He sounded strangely uncertain.

Doctor Bateson drew himself up stiffly. 'I should think, sir,' he rapped, 'that she would have been very much better if you had left her alone in the first place. A little time to herself is just what she needs. Good day to you.'

Brogan was left looking at the peeling paint of the closed door. By Christ, anyone would think he had kidnapped her or something. He was supporting her, wasn't he? And not only her but the children, although somehow he didn't like to put them into the scale to be weighed against things. No, those two gave as much as they took, the noisy, sticky horrors. It was Mary that was the problem. He had known some women, but not one like her. Leave her alone the man said, as if she was ever anything else, away from them all, away from him. He knew her not at all.

There was nothing for it but the lumpy, too short spare bed, and Susan would have to do the housework which was a damned nuisance. He directed a venomous stare at Edna, who recoiled as if from a snake, and stumped off into the yard.

Susan fumbled messily around the house for the next two days. She was an indifferent cook but Mary did not notice, hardly touching the food set in front of her. Brogan did not come near her, she did not know where he was sleeping. Very early on the third morning she decided to go in search of him. She washed her face, looking ruefully at her white cheeks and red eyes, and walked along the corridor, peering into rooms, moving quietly to avoid waking the children. He was lying on his back staring at the ceiling when she softly opened the door. She was embarrassed, she had expected him to be asleep.

'I couldn't find you,' she said feebly. He did not reply and she stood uncertain in the doorway, wondering if she should go away. She half turned, but changed her mind, shutting the door and walking over to the bed. Their eyes met and she rushed into what she had to say.

'Look, I feel I've rather let you down. You wanted someone to look after the house and . . . everything, and here I am, just a neurotic nuisance. I just wanted to say that if you want us to go, we will. To my mother, probably. Or something. I just wanted to say that.'

He sat up slowly and Mary noticed how drawn

he looked, the crumpled cheek very much in evidence.

'Do you want to go?'

She looked out of the window at the misty spring morning. 'No.'

'But you've not been happy.'

'I don't think I would have been happy anywhere.'

'Then stay.' He was almost offhand.

'Do you want me to?'

He busied himself hunting for a cigarette and would not meet her eyes.

'Yes, I want you to,' he muttered, and Mary almost laughed at his embarrassment.

She leaned over and gently kissed his cheek. He pulled her to him and they kissed again, softly, thoughtfully.

'We're leaving today.'

She looked at him in surprise. 'I didn't realise. And I never did get to wear my blue dress.'

He smiled. 'No. When we get back, perhaps. Anyway, I've asked Fred to pop in and see how you are.'

She wrinkled her nose. 'Keep an eye on me, you mean. Still, I've got Susan. And I'll try and get everything sorted out by the time you get back.'

'For God's sake get the phone connected if nothing else. Spend what you have to, carpets, curtains, the lot, just get it finished. I'll be back as soon as I can.'

'Can I get in touch with you?'

'Not very easily, we'll be on the move all the time. I'll leave you an address to write to, I should get the letters eventually.' He stroked her hair.

'We'd better get a move on, there's a lot to do today.'

'Yes.' She sighed and stood up. 'I'll go and get dressed. And Patrick – ' he was looking at her expectantly ' – thank you.'

'I've used you, Mary.'

'Well, I've used you too. But that's business for you. Let's talk about it sometime.'

She walked slowly from the room, leaving a faint scent behind her, soon dissipated in the draught from the door.

The morning passed in a rush of packing, for people and animals, culminating in the deafening clatter of horses being loaded. Edna and Mandy were pink with excitement while poor Susan became more depressed with every passing moment. At last she and Mary were standing in the yard, saying goodbye. Brogan was full of last minute instructions.

'Now remember, don't hesitate to call the vet if there's the least problem. And there's always Fred Swallow to call on. And get that tap fixed before I come back. Any questions?' They shook their heads obediently. 'Right. We'll be off.'

'Good luck,' they chorused, and he nodded, already thinking of other things.

'Look, about the barn roof . . .' he began, and caught Mary's eye. He grinned ruefully. 'All right, you can cope. We'll go and leave you to it.' He caught her to him in a quick hug and climbed into the horse box.

Mary and Susan waved as they drew out of the yard, both feeling rather dismal, left in a dull, everyday world whilst others embarked on adventure.

Chapter 6

Left alone at High Wold House Mary began to
relish her independence. The builders had reached
the plastering stage and it was not long before a
beautiful pale yellow bathroom suite made its
appearance. It was the first of the three Mary had
promised herself, although now that it came to it
she wondered if she had gone too far. A house this
size needs three bathrooms, she reasoned, one for
the master bedroom, one for the children and one
for the guests. She had grave doubts about Brogan
seeing it that way, so she assuaged her guilt by
undercoating woodwork in readiness for the
decorators. Unfortunately her amateur efforts
were treated with great scorn by the professionals
and she was relegated to painting the wooden
flower tubs with which she intended to decorate
the yard.

She was engaged in this one day, fighting the
combined attentions of Anna and Ben who were
helping, when a large limousine drew into the
yard. She stood up, wiping her painty hands on
the oversize boiler suit she used for such tasks and
feeling less than presentable. It was the legendary
Mr Swallow.

'Mrs Squires?' he boomed, hand outstretched,
bouncing towards her with a short, energetic
stride. 'Swallow's the name.' The small, round

figure radiated confidence. Mary waved her sticky fingers apologetically and he withdrew his arm with slight distaste.

'How do you do?' she said with an attempt at dignity spoiled by the need to grab Ben before he wiped his hands on Swallow's pearl grey trousers.

'We'd better get cleaned up,' she murmured.

'Yes indeed,' said her visitor with emphasis.

She left him in the kitchen amongst the decorators' paint pots while she found them all some respectable clothes. For herself she selected a new pair of jeans and a cream silk shirt, brushing her hair to a shine and putting on some make-up. She wanted Mr Swallow to think well of her and his first impression had not been favourable, she felt.

His beam when she reappeared told her that she had succeeded.

'Tea, Mr Swallow?' she asked, and then as he looked somewhat disappointed, 'or something stronger?'

'Scotch would do nicely, thank you, love,' he smiled and Mary went in search of the bottle she felt sure must be here somewhere. She wasn't used to drinking at three in the afternoon.

He insisted that she join him and as they sat there, chatting and drinking whisky, Mary began to enjoy herself. He was passionately interested in what she was doing to the house and was full of ideas. Remembering his own edifice she was a little doubtful when he offered to bring wallpaper samples for her to see but it seemed churlish to refuse. They were on safer ground when it came to show jumping.

'I can truly say that it's changed my life, Mary

70

lass,' he reflected, his words tinged with religious awe. They had been on first name terms since their second drink. 'The excitement of seeing your own horses out there – there's nothing like it. And now Paddy's come in with me we can really go places.'

'Is Patrick very good?' she asked casually.

'My good girl, he's the best! It took some brass to tempt him here, I can tell you. But he's worth it, I don't need to tell you that.'

So, you are paying for this lot are you, thought Mary to herself, looking round the half-finished kitchen. She had wondered about the bottomless purse.

'Of course he had a bit of a setback when his wife left him, but he's got over that now. Going really well. He's a man for the ladies though, I don't need to tell you that. Had one really fast piece, Sylvia I think she was called, but I suppose that's all over now.'

'Yes, I suppose so,' said Mary doubtfully, and rose to her feet.

'Do you mind if I start getting the children's tea?' It was a tactful hint to go but he merely moved his legs out of the way and poured himself another drink.

'No, no, you get on, love. And what about you, then? Paddy told me you'd been ill.'

'Are you being discreet, Fred?' His heavy-handed tact amused her.

'Well, I suppose I am. We all know what you've been through lately. Set the place by the ears when you moved in here, I can tell you. But I don't suppose you care about that.'

'Why should you think that?'

'Oh, so you do care? Well it's not worth it, love, take my word for it. The old biddies'll gossip about anyone.'

'It's the children I worry about. I wanted them to have a respectable mother.'

'You look respectable enough to me. Which is more than can be said for Paddy. Gets about a bit, he does,' he said again.

'I don't think I like the sound of this,' said Mary, running a hand through her hair.

'Well, that's the way he is, love.' He heaved himself up. 'I'll be off now. Look, I'll pop in again towards the end of the week, bring those samples, see how you are.' He belched loudly and lurched to the door.

'Do you think you ought to drive, Fred?' He looked very much the worse for wear.

He ignored her, muttering, 'Sound like the bloody wife, you do,' and made his way to his car, staggering slightly as the fresh air hit him. Mary watched him go, churning the gravel under his wheels. She hoped he made it home, in an odd way she was looking forward to seeing him again.

Susan came in for breakfast next morning looking rather glum.

'The milkman says he won't deliver any more. He's sold the round and the new man won't come this far out. It's the end of the world, this place.'

Mary grinned. She liked Sue and they got on well together.

'You should learn to drive. Get a licence and I'll teach you on the van, if it'll stand the strain, then you can go out a bit. It's rather awkward about the milk though, we can't trail into town every other day.'

'We'll have to get a cow,' laughed Susan, delighted with the thought of driving lessons.

'Yes,' said Mary thoughtfully, 'we will.'

They bought Violet from a farm about ten miles away. Mary assured herself that they were only going to look but she and Susan were no match for the charm of the Jersey's little black feet and luminous eyes.

'Calved last week, so you won't have no bother. She bulls well, too,' said the farmer.

Mary had bought many cows but never a dairy breed. 'How much will she give?' she asked.

'Oh, about four gallons. She's a good cow.' He noticed the stunned expressions on their faces and misinterpreted them. 'More if you feed her right,' he urged. 'Better than a Friesian any day. Think of the cream!'

'We'll be able to make butter!' Susan was really entering into the spirit of the thing.

'I like this "we",' said Mary caustically, bending to take a hopeful prod at the cow's udder. She wondered how long it would take to extract four gallons from that odd-looking set of bagpipes.

'We'll rear calves,' she said decisively. 'That at least is something I know about.'

Susan looked dubious. 'What about Mr Brogan?' she asked anxiously. 'All his boxes . . .'

'We can use the end ones, they're empty. And anyway, this is profitable, Susan. We're not being frivolous, after all.' She met Violet's brown gaze and looked away. That cow knew the truth; Mary longed to have a cow and here was the cow and Brogan was nowhere to be seen. If there was to

73

be a row it was some time in the future and she would worry about it when it happened.

She wrote the cheque quickly. It was Brogan's money but it was an investment after all. The farmer promised to deliver Violet the following day.

'There's just one thing,' Mary said casually, as they prepared to leave.

'I don't know . . . well I've never actually . . . *milked* a cow, if you know what I mean.'

The farmer leaned against the barn door, his eyes watering with mirth.

'I hope the cow can't hear you,' he gasped, 'she'll refuse to leave home!' He took pity on her worried face. 'It's only practice, lass. Just keep trying, it comes.'

Mary was not reassured, but what others managed so would she. It was a knack she would acquire.

Violet duly arrived the following morning, walking daintily down the ramp of the trailer and into the box as if she had lived there all her life. Mary and Susan spent most of the afternoon hanging over the door looking at her.

'They say Jerseys are very docile and she seems to be,' said Mary happily, watching in fascination as Violet blinked her long eyelashes and chewed the cud, her jaw moving lazily from side to side.

'When do you milk her?' asked Susan.

Mary noted that the magic 'we' was no more. 'Now,' she said dolefully.

Sadly, milking cows is not easy. Mary heaved and prodded, poked and tugged, and was rewarded with a swingeing kick.

'I'm not sure that you're as nice as you look,'

she complained, and Violet's sour expression made
it clear that she returned the compliment.

'Be firmer,' advised Susan, from the safety of
the door.

'Firmer! My hands are like jelly already. I should
have realised when I saw that farmer, his were
like spades.'

'So will yours be soon,' comforted Susan.

Mary's face became pained. 'That will be nice.'

After an hour's sweated labour there was a
bucket of milk.

'It's bound to get easier,' said Susan cheerfully,
but Mary only sighed. The thought of tackling that
cow night and morning for the foreseeable future
depressed her utterly. Nonetheless, within a week
she could do it. Twenty minutes flat, night and
morning, to achieve a pail of creamy yellow milk
topped by a froth whipped up as she sent the jets
whizzing into the bucket. It was fun! They had
custard, and blancmange, and cocoa, and rice
pudding and still the milk flowed. In desperation,
using Brogan's money, Mary bought three calves
from a dealer and installed them in the box next
to the cow, and at last some sort of order started
to emerge.

'I thought we were going to drown in it,' said
Susan thankfully, as they presented each new
arrival with its bucket of milk.

'We almost did,' agreed Mary. 'You don't realise
how much four gallons is until it's washing around
the kitchen.'

The weather was warmer now, and Violet went
out to graze during the day. As Mary walked her
in from the field one day she reflected that this
was as she had imagined. A quiet spring evening,

a slight chill in the air, the snipe calling far away and the sound of soft cow feet on the muddy path. They strolled along, enjoying the idyll, until suddenly Violet thought of her tea, waiting for her in the yard. She took off at a run, hotly pursued by Mary who was handicapped by giggles. Trust a cow to bring you down to earth with a bump she thought, watching the pink udder swing obscenely from side to side as Violet careered down the path. She gave up the chase, the old girl would wait for her, and sauntered along on her own, quietly content.

Fred Swallow was in the yard when she wandered in.

'I was nearly run down by a cow,' he spluttered, 'it went in there! I've never seen anything like it.'

'Don't worry Fred, it's only Violet,' soothed Mary. 'She only kills on command. Come and be introduced.'

Swallow peered at the cow from a safe distance, keeping his light tan brogues well out of reach of anything nasty.

'Does Paddy know?' he asked as the milk swished into the bucket.

'Er . . . not exactly.'

'I thought not. Well, it's your funeral, I suppose. What you want with a cow beats me. Nasty, smelly things.'

'It's an investment, Fred. And we had a milk problem, they wouldn't deliver.'

'You've gone too far the other way, I should think. What do you do with it all?'

Mary wordlessly led the way next door. Fred was silent as she fed the calves and said nothing until they were seated in the kitchen, drinking scotch. He took a deep breath.

'Mary, love. Far be it from me to interfere. You know best, I'm sure you do. But Paddy is running a jumping stable here, not a bloody farm! Next it'll be hens and ducks and things. It's just not on, you know. He'll be livid and he'll have reason.'

She was very much on the defensive. 'He said I could do as I liked and I have. We are going to have a few geese as it happens, they arrive tomorrow, but it's nothing very terrible. It's not as if I'm neglecting the house or anything.'

He took a sip of his drink. 'Well, I've warned you. Just don't ask me to house the brute if he throws it out, we have enough trouble with the Pekinese.' He leaned back and gazed round the room. 'House is coming on, isn't it?'

Mary grinned at him fondly. 'Yes, we've got hot water at last. Did you bring the wallpaper?'

He had and they spent half an hour wrangling over it. Swallow felt that the dining room, tall and gracious with deep windows, would be best presented in red flock, of the type often seen in Indian restaurants. Mary held out for green and gold and at last he gave way.

'It's your house I suppose,' he muttered and then realised his error.

'Well, what I mean . . .'

'Don't be coy, Fred. It's not my house as we both well know. What about this for the sitting room?' She indicated a delicate cream stripe.

'Bloody washed out if you ask me,' he declared and chose orange squirls instead.

By the end of the evening they had sorted out most of the decorations. Swallow's influence had pushed Mary into being rather more adventurous than she was at first inclined but she was well pleased with the end result.

'I think it will have flair,' she declared, making some much needed coffee.

'Still think the lounge needs more zip,' he mused, looking regretfully at his rejected choice.

Mary patted his greying head. 'It'll be lovely, you'll see.'

Fred was silent for a moment and then burst out with a suddenness that made Mary start. 'You know, Mary, I hope Paddy appreciates what he's got in you. You don't want to let him take advantage. He can use women you know, and I'd hate to see you hurt. I would that.' His ears were rather pink and Mary was touched.

'It's all right, Fred. I'm not pinning my hopes on him. But with the children so young . . .'

'Yes. Well. He'll be on the telly tomorrow night you know.'

'Who, Patrick? Good heavens. I shall have to watch.'

'I shall be there too, as it happens. Driving down tomorrow.'

'Then I shall definitely watch, Fred. You won't tell him about Violet, will you?' she added anxiously.

He grinned, looking suddenly boyish. 'Nay, lass, I'll keep me trap shut. Take care of yourself.' He gave her a quick peck on the cheek and left.

She was stationed in front of the television well before the show jumping was due to come on. She felt strangely excited although she could not say why, and relieved her feelings by eating her way

78

through a box of chocolates. There were only three to go when the programme at last came on, and almost immediately she saw Fred Swallow, talking to someone in the collecting ring as the initial announcements were made. It was the first time she had ever seen anyone she knew on television and it was an odd sensation, almost as if they weren't quite real. Fred was overacting for the camera, laughing and talking with far too much animation and Mary felt rather embarrassed.

To her relief the camera soon switched to the jumping. Horse after horse appeared and each time her heart gave a bump as she realised the rider was not Brogan. She was beginning to wonder if Fred had been mistaken when there he was, calm and confident on the striking bay, Knight Errant. The crowd gave a roar – he was popular it seemed – and then he was jumping. It was a faultless round, gracefully executed, he was every bit as good as Swallow had said. Mary was fascinated, this calm stranger seemed to have nothing to do with the man she knew. The camera followed him out of the ring but he seemed oblivious of its presence, handing the horse over to a waiting Edna and strolling off to talk to a small, pretty girl in riding clothes. She sparkled up at him and Mary felt her stomach contract. Swallow was right, this was not a man to trust.

The jump-off was very close, all clear rounds with split seconds between them. Brogan showed little sign of strain, perhaps just a slight hardness about the jaw. He was pushed into second place by the smallest margin, and it was only then that Mary felt she knew him. His fingers strayed briefly to the broken cheek in a gesture which she recognised as one of tiredness or indecision. But the smile was still there, again for the small dark girl. Mary switched off the television quickly, busying herself tidying the room and preparing for bed. She did not own him, she did not seek to do so, but if he must be unfaithful – and that word alone meant a commitment which he probably did not feel – then she would rather not know. As so often recently she missed her dog, his presence now would have been a small but comforting thing. She went to bed thinking of him, it was safer than thinking of Brogan.

Chapter 7

Her life became very full over the next weeks. Violet and the calves took up several hours a day and the dozen newborn goslings keeping warm in the airing cupboard kept her busy for a week. But, as the house took shape she was able to concentrate on the garden, at first just removing scrap and slashing nettles. She constantly hoped to find an ancient and beautiful sundial or statue embedded in the undergrowth, but had to content herself with old pram wheels and bottomless buckets. As she worked one day, energetically heaving and scything, she realised that she was almost happy. Insecurity and loneliness had no meaning on this sunny day, the walled garden echoing to the wild shrieks of the children playing on what had once been a lawn. They would have a bonfire for the rubbish, the children could help. Ben was enthralled and had to be stopped from putting his hands into the licking flames, almost transparent in the thin spring air. Mary and Anna fed their creation with sticks, finding a primitive satisfaction in watching leaves shrivel and branches turn black, then red, before crumbling to dust.

'Hello, everyone.' It was Brogan, looking tired and dishevelled in jeans and sweater. Mary felt her face flame, she could think of no way to greet him. The children had no such problems, they ran forward, Anna crying, 'Daddy, Daddy,' Ben thankfully wordless. They hung on to his knees, skipping with excitement, and he bent to talk to them.

'What have you been doing? Have you been good?'

'Oh yes, and we got a bonfire, look! And we got Violet and that man came.'

He looked up at Mary. 'What man?' he snapped accusingly.

Mary spread her hands. 'She means Fred Swallow,' she said softly. She felt a spurt of anger as she thought of the small, dark girl. There were rules and rules, it seemed.

'I didn't expect you,' she added coldly.

'I'm only back for two nights. Thought I'd see how things are coming on.'

There was an awkward silence, broken by Anna tugging at Brogan's hand and saying, 'Come see our bonfire, Daddy.'

'He's not Daddy, darling, he's Uncle Pat,' said Mary firmly.

'It's all right, I don't mind if you don't,' said Brogan easily, and Mary opened her mouth to say she *did* mind, but then closed it again. The best policy was intensive indoctrination of Anna in private.

They stood round the fire, Brogan watching for a time as Mary worked, hampered by Ben clutching her hand. Finally he took the rake off her and did it himself, transforming her higgledy piggledy pile of sticks into a neat heap from which smoke and discreet little flames issued decorously. She had much preferred her own inferno but of course this was more efficient. Brogan caught her eye and grinned.

'Not so pretty, but works better,' he said and Mary suddenly felt in sympathy with him. She reached up and kissed his cheek affectionately, saying, 'Come on, it's time for tea,' and starting to gather up the tools.

'Mary.' His voice was almost a whisper but it sent a warm tide through her. He caught her arm, fingers digging into the flesh and dragged her to him, kissing her so hard that their teeth met before their tongues did. His hands were tearing at her clothes, he had her breast, and then his teeth were there, biting hard. She gasped and pulled away violently.

'The children,' she croaked, remembering them rather too late. For a moment she thought he would hit her but then his face cleared and resumed its usual calm. He touched his cheek.

'Yes. Tea, you said.' He strode to the house.

Susan joined them in the kitchen and the tension relaxed. Mary buttered bread on her brand new work surface and heated soup on her bright red Aga and waited for a compliment that never came. At last she could stand it no longer.

'Haven't you noticed anything?' she said plaintively. Susan sniggered.

Brogan looked blank.

'The kitchen,' wailed Mary, waving her arms dramatically.

'Oh,' said Brogan and she threw a tea towel at him, wishing it could be the teapot. He laughed knowingly and she knew he had been getting his own back for the scene in the garden.

'I did notice, actually. Very nice. Very nice indeed.'

'You didn't want tiles with gold flecks in? Or onions on the wallpaper?'

He looked mystified. 'There isn't any wallpaper.'

Indeed there was not. The walls were rough plastered and painted white, against which glowed old pine cupboards, some with glass fronts, holding the chunky blue pots they used for every day. The floor was quarry tiled in dusky red, with plain rush mats here and there. The Aga warmed the room and the kitchen clock filled it with its loud tick.

'It's just that Fred had all these ideas,' explained Mary, sitting down.

'You haven't put any into practice, have you?' squawked Brogan, looking apprehensively towards the hall door.

'Only some,' said Mary with a sweet, revengeful smile.

She took him on a tour as soon as the children were in bed. He liked the dining room – green and gold – and the hall – white with red carpet – but stood silent at the sitting room door just staring. Mary's heart sank.

'Don't you like it?' she quavered.

He turned a fierce, blue gaze on her. 'How much did that carpet cost?' he demanded and Mary almost giggled.

'Nothing,' she said lightly. He seized her arm.

'Now, look here madam . . .' he began but she stopped him.

'All right, I'll explain. Yes, it is Persian, it is valuable and it's on loan. My parents lent it to

Stephen and me when we got married but we
never had anywhere to put it. And when I saw
this wood floor, and thought of it polished, it
seemed – perfect. That's all.'

'Oh. I see.' He let her go and studied the room.
The walls were pale cream, making the colours in
the carpet sing. More furniture was needed – the
few pieces were dwarfed and the chairs huddled
round the ornate Victorian fireplace. The curtains
were natural, heavy linen, braided round the
edges in red and gold. The effect was warm, rich
and slightly exotic.

'We need a sofa,' he declared. 'If not two.'

'Mmmm,' said Mary noncommittally, thinking
of the expense of the unseen three bathrooms.
Spending money still came hard, she had taken
to asking everyone to send accounts and then
paying by cheque. The time lapse made her feel
less spendthrift, though she still had nightmares
in which she stood barefoot in the wind, the
children crying for food. She would have liked
to tell Brogan about it, but of course she would
not.

Fortunately most of the bedrooms were still
being decorated and Brogan curtailed his
inspection after a quick glance.

'What colour do you want for our room?' asked
Mary as they went downstairs. 'I haven't decided
on anything yet.'

He put his arm round her as they reached the
bottom of the stairs, and nuzzled her neck.

'Anything you like,' he whispered, pulling her
on to the carpet.

He was urgent, refusing to wait. He wanted her
now, right now, while she was warm and smiling

and open, before she had time to close and turn away, like a flower in the night. When it was over she sighed and licked a droplet of sweat from his shoulder.

'Oh Mary,' he murmured, but she did not reply.

Later that night they sat in the kitchen – the sitting room seemed far too grand to use – and chatted with unusual warmth.

'How did it go?' asked Mary, sipping red wine. He was in the rocking chair in front of the fire.

'Pretty well. Horses could have been fitter, but Fred's pleased. You warm enough? Come and sit here.' He tossed a cushion on to the floor by his feet and Mary sat on it, leaning back against his legs.

'Has Susan taken good care of the horses?' she enquired, really meaning had he seen Violet yet.

'Haven't looked. Tomorrow's soon enough. I must be getting old or something.' He yawned and reached for the bottle of wine.

'Well, there's something I should mention . . .' began Mary and fell flat on her back as the legs she was leaning against removed themselves at speed.

'What's happened? They're not dead surely? She hasn't sent them all lame, has she, what can you expect, stupid girl like that, I should never have left her in charge . . .' His words drifted back to Mary as he raced across the yard, she trailing in the rear.

'But it's nothing to do with the horses!' she shrieked.

86

There was a silence. 'What do you mean?' Brogan had returned to face her.

'It's this.' She turned and led the way to Violet's box.

The little cow was lying down but struggled to her feet as they switched on the light. She mooed plaintively, and was answered by a small chorus of moos from the neighbouring boxes. Brogan closed his eyes for a moment and then went to inspect, finally returning to Violet.

Mary started to gabble. 'It was because of the milk, you see, they wouldn't deliver, and there was Violet and she didn't cost much, mind you when you get to know her you can see why, but she was an investment you see, and I've made some money on the calves already, so it's not as if I squandered it . . .'

His shoulders had started to shake and she realised with relief that he was laughing. 'When I said you could spend money I meant on the house, not on a blasted herd of cows,' he gasped. 'I should be furious, but I'm so glad it's not the horses. But you can't have these boxes, I need them.'

'Well, where can I put them?' complained Mary. 'There's only the old barn and the roof leaks.'

'I told you to get it fixed.'

There was a small silence. 'I forgot.'

'So it seems. Well then, get it fixed and put them in there. Otherwise they're out.'

'Yes, Patrick.' She was very meek.

He sighed and ran a hand through his hair. 'Oh God, I never knew a woman like you. Like a lamb one minute, yes Patrick, no Patrick, and then off doing things like this. I hardly dare turn my back.'

'Don't worry,' comforted Mary, 'I'm not going to buy any more cows.'

He laughed. 'That doesn't reassure me at all. Let's go and finish that wine, it's freezing out here.'

The next morning he told her that they were to spend the evening at Fred Swallow's.

'Can I wear my blue dress?' she asked. 'Or would it be overdoing it?'

'You can never overdo it with Fred,' he said feelingly, and Mary grinned.

They were happy together that day, confident enough to treat each other to little kindnesses. He fetched her jacket when she was cold, she made his favourite cake. Mary made excuses to touch him, trailing her hand casually across his shoulder as she walked past his chair, only to have it caught and gently kissed.

They were in sparkling mood when they arrived at the Swallows and were laughing as they walked up to the heavy, iron-studded front door. Fred flung it open, bent on his role as the genial host, but he kissed Mary with real affection.

'You look cracking, lass, you do that. Let me introduce you to Jean.'

Mary turned and met a cold stare from a short, plump woman with small eyes and too-blonde hair. She was also dressed in blue, but blue satin a size too small, her bosom bulging painfully from the sequined bodice.

'Pleased to meet you,' rapped Mrs Swallow, turning immediately to Brogan.

'How do you do,' faltered Mary to the hostile back and looked questioningly at Fred. He was

pink with embarrassment and quickly introduced
her to the other couple in the room, a banker and
his wife. Mary drank two large sherries too
quickly, trapped in conversation with Julie
Barnes, who talked of nothing but nappy rash and
babysitting problems, frequently turning to her
husband for corroboration of some detail: 'Isn't
that right, John?'

'Yes dear.'

At long, long last they were called in to
dinner. Brogan was seated next to Mrs Swallow
who twinkled roguishly at him, tapping his hand
playfully and calling him dear boy. She pointedly
ignored any attempt by Mary to join in their
conversation. Swallow was labouring with Julie
– they had progressed to the problems of mixed
feeding – which left Mary with the banker.
She widened her eyes and gave him a little
girl smile.

'You must be very clever, dealing with figures
all the time.'

'Oh, I don't know. It's all training.' He giggled
self-consciously.

'I just know it would be too much for . . .' she
nearly said 'little old me' but stopped herself and
substituted, 'a housewife like me.'

'I find it hard to believe you're just a housewife,' he breathed, gazing down the front of her
dress.

'Well I find it hard to believe you're a banker.
I always thought they were so dull and staid, not
at all like you.' She looked up at him through her
lashes. 'Do tell me how it came about,' she
twinkled, and tell he did, right from his years at
school to the present day with hardly a visit to the

bathroom missed out. She replied with murmurs, giggles and 'oh, how clevers' in what she hoped were the right places, drinking glass after glass of wine and letting her mind wander. At least the food was good she thought, mentally planning her menus for the coming six months. She was rescued by Swallow.

'What d'you think of the house then, Mary?' he boomed, leaning back in his enormous oak and red leather chair.

'Very impressive Fred,' she smiled. 'Suits your Henry VIII image admirably.'

Swallow roared with laughter, but his wife sniffed and rose to her feet.

'We will take our coffee in the drawing room, ladies,' she announced and they duly trailed out. Mary tried to catch Brogan's eye as she left but he avoided her gaze, tearing the remains of a bread roll to pieces and rolling a pile of little pellets.

The three women sat round the fire in silence, sipping coffee. Mary was thankful for it, her head was swimming. She tried to repair the damage with Mrs Swallow.

'Your house is really quite magnificent. Was it your design?'

'No. His second wife did it.'

Mary subsided, then tried again. 'Are you interested in showjumping, Mrs Swallow?'

The woman sighed and gave her a look of loathing. 'No, I'm not. I should tell you, miss, that if it weren't for the damned horses Fred would be abroad in the sun, where he belongs, instead of here. We could have a villa in Spain, the Bahamas, anywhere, have some fun out of life.

I keep telling him, get out of it while we're young enough to enjoy ourselves.'

'But you could go to the shows with him, couldn't you? You'd have some fun there, surely.'

The fat shoulders wobbled with emotion. 'Fun? You call that fun? Freezing cold and what do they talk about, horses, horses, horses. And the people. Paddy's a very sweet boy, I will say that, but the girls!' She gave Mary a look of scorn, saying pointedly, 'They're scheming hussies all of them, out for what they can get, hanging round the boys as if they were pop stars. Disgusting I call it.'

Mary gave up. Jean Swallow had her cast as a showjumping groupie who had seduced Brogan and might well have her eye on Fred. Julie Barnes was droning on about the symptoms of measles and she listened in virtual silence. Her smile was radiant when the door opened and the men finally returned but it faded rapidly as she saw John Barnes heading for the seat next to her.

Would this evening never end? She had looked forward to it so much and now it was like being on the rack. Brogan and Fred were talking business, a whisky bottle between them, but at last they rose, somewhat unsteadily, and the party broke up.

The night air was blessedly cool.

'I'll drive,' offered Mary but Brogan took no notice and sat behind the wheel.

Mary climbed in, saying, 'Thank you so much, it was lovely,' to a stony Mrs Swallow. She leaned back in her seat as they drove off, closing her eyes but was jerked awake by the screech of tyres as they cornered on two wheels.

'Do be careful Pat, you've had an awful lot to drink you know.'

'Shut up,' he snapped and stamped even harder on the accelerator.

Mary hung on to the seat, her foot pressing an imaginary brake as the car raced through the darkness, the headlights picking out rushing trees and hedges. When they squealed to a halt at High Wold House she was shaking and her palms were wet with sweat.

She went quickly into the house and sent Susan off to bed in the granary flat.

Brogan leaned drunkenly against the door.

'Do you want some coffee?' she asked hopefully. He frightened her, she could feel his tension. He said nothing and she tried to push past him to go to bed. It was as if she had touched a coiled spring, he pushed her back into the kitchen, hitting her hard on the side of the head. She crashed against the table, a singing noise in her ears. The world looked strangely yellow. He was coming at her again and she retreated behind a chair.

'For God's sake Pat, what's the matter?'

'You know damn well, you bitch! All night you've been at it, leading him on, how stupid do you think I am. Just waiting for the chance I suppose. When's he coming round then? Friday? Saturday? I saw you whispering to him. Didn't you?'

He made a lunge and caught her arm. She tried to speak calmly.

'Don't be silly Pat. He was the most boring man I've ever met, surely you could see that? You're just tired, you've had too much to drink.'

'Drunk am I? Not too drunk to see your little game, you WHORE!'

He started to shake her, his fingers digging into her shoulders as her head rocked backwards and forwards, until she could hardly see.

He flung her away from him, her back hit the worktop and she slid to the floor. She watched him through half-closed eyes as he hunted for the whisky bottle. Her breathing sounded loud and she tried to quieten it, he must not notice her. He was coming round to her now, she had to get away. She started to crawl towards the door but the slight movement enraged him. He kicked her viciously in the ribs and she sprawled full length, turning her head seconds later to be noisily sick on the floor.

'You bitch,' he said again, standing over her.

'Leave me alone,' she muttered. 'Please leave me alone. Please.'

He ran his hand through his hair and sank to the floor beside her. If only she could get away. She had never felt so frightened, one wrong move and he would kill her, she was sure of it. He started to cry, great drunken tears, his face twisting like a child's.

'You shouldn't have done it to me. I thought you were perfect, but you're just like her. None of you care, not really. You're all the same, cows, bitches, whores!' He aimed a punch at her but missed and sobbed harder.

She lay very still and after a long time he lolled against the wall, apparently asleep. She crawled away an inch at a time, every nerve stretched, until she was in the hall. She clung to the stair rail trying to pull herself up but her legs gave way and she crouched there trying to muffle her crying. At last she crept up, stair by stair, and into the bathroom to sponge her face and wash the sick from her hair. There was no sound from downstairs and she thought it was safe to go to bed. She pulled the bedclothes over her head and slept.

She woke to a grey dawn and lay there wondering what to do. If she had any pride she would pack and leave of course, but there was nowhere to go. What had she done to spoil it all? He should have seen, surely he must have seen, what she thought of that man at the party. Yet he had called her whore.

She sniffed and rubbed at a tear. Did he have to use that word? It was one that had often been in her mind these past weeks, selling her body in exchange for a home, but it had never felt like that somehow. He shouldn't have called her that. Tears threatened to swamp her and she sat up stiffly and tried to think. The drink was to blame, of course. But if he did this every time he had one too many she might end up dead. Odd, really, when she had never thought him a violent man, for with the children, and the horses, and up to now with her, he was gentle; kind. It just showed how little she knew him.

Oh, but she was sore. Her ribs ached and one wrist hurt when she spread her fingers. Heaven alone knew how she would milk the cow. God damn the man, she'd give a lot to make him feel as she was feeling now. But at least her face was unmarked, saving her the final humiliation of people knowing. That would be more than she could bear.

The room seemed very cold, but then she had
ice in the pit of her stomach. Her old dressing
gown was warm and familiar, and there were two
conkers in the pocket, withered with age, their
gloss quite gone. Softly, praying that he still slept,
she crept downstairs.

He was asleep on the kitchen floor, snoring, his
face blotched and slack. He still lay in crumpled
jacket and trousers, his tie cast off in the heat of
the row and several buttons gone from his shirt.
His body hair was a lovely golden colour, like corn.
Some of her rage ebbed as she looked at him for
he was Patrick again instead of the mad stranger
she had seen last night. And Patrick did not hit
people. The room stank of whisky and vomit and
she flung the windows open, careless of the blasts
of freezing air that filled the room. He woke while
she mopped up the floor, rattling her bucket in an
orgy of cleanliness. She would wash it all away,
everything, and it would never have happened.

'What in God's name are you doing?'

To her horror all her control dissolved and her
eyes flooded with tears. If she spoke she would
cry, so she said nothing and instead crashed
volubly about the floor, water and soapsuds flying.

'Mary, will you stop that? You're soaking me.'

'Go to hell.' A few tears escaped and she
brushed them away, refusing to let him see how
hurt she was.

He heaved himself up from the floor, grimacing,
and slumped into a kitchen chair. 'I'd like some
coffee if you're making some.'

'Does it look as if I'm making some? But perhaps
you think this is how you do it, the amount you
help around here. Still I don't suppose it matters,

you can always find some stupid woman to slave for you.' It was an irrelevant argument and also thin, because Patrick was quite helpful when he was there, laying tables and so on. Far better than Stephen if it came to it, for whom the kitchen had been more in the line of an alien planet.

'I'll rephrase that,' said Patrick tightly. 'Would you please make some coffee. I would like some for my headache.'

She sat back on her heels and erupted in fury. 'Your head aches! What about where I hurt? You threw me about this place like some kind of rag doll and for what? Some stupid idea about me and that creepy little man who was about as attractive as Quasimodo and a lot less nice and – and – you called me names. I hate you, Patrick Brogan.'

His face was as white as paper. 'Nobody forced you to come here. No one's making you stay.'

'You think that because I've nowhere else to go you can beat me up. You're not giving me any charity, I work for my keep, in bed and out of it.'

'I got the impression you enjoyed the bedroom side of things. You like men, Mary.'

'What's that supposed to mean? Oh God, I hurt. No, stay there, I'll make the coffee. I want some.'

They sat drinking it on opposite sides of the table. Patrick noticed Mary's hands were trembling and every now and then a tear oozed from the corner of her eye and she flicked it away. He reached across and touched her arm, but it was a sore place and she winced. He withdrew his hand.

'I'm sorry,' he said gruffly. 'I didn't mean to hurt you. I was just so angry.'

'I don't know why you were angry. Really there wasn't anything – was it this way with your wife? You were jealous of her, hit her, that sort of thing?'

He shook his head and ducked away as if from a threatened blow.

'It's nothing to do with that. I wasn't jealous of her, I never thought for a moment that – which was stupid I suppose. I should have thought.'

'What did she do?' asked Mary.

'Look, it's none of your business and has nothing to do with you. Now leave it, will you? And there's no point in saying you didn't do anything last night because whether you liked it or not you tied him in knots. God Mary, didn't you even notice?'

She sighed and watched a tear splash into her cup. Her nose was running and she hadn't a tissue but as she hunted through her pockets Patrick pulled out his handkerchief and gave it to her. Oh, it was all such a mess and it was time she did something about it.

'I think we will go, you know,' she mumbled through the handkerchief. 'I don't understand about last night and if it happened again – I couldn't bear it. It was just so awful. And I've got the children to think of, they shouldn't be exposed to things like this. No one should. If you can give us a couple of weeks we'll sort something out, I'll sell the cow and things for you. It's best.'

'Fine mother you are. Better for the kids to be farmed out to nurseries and childminders, living on chips, than to watch the occasional family row. That's all it was, you know.'

'Like hell it was! I don't know anything about you, Patrick. You could be a complete lunatic for all I know, on licence from Broadmoor. Suppose you're a child molester or something?'

'Now really, Mary, that's the outside of enough!' He was shocked rigid, the colour flooding into his face so that for a moment he looked refreshingly normal.

She choked on a giggle.'Well, you could be. I don't know. You never say.'

'Would it help if I told you?'

She nodded, slowly. 'It might.'

Chapter 8

Patrick Brogan was the eldest of three children, and the only boy. His father was a horse dealer, his mother a devout Catholic, which is to say each had their religion. Every Sunday his mother would mount her ancient bicycle long before breakfast and pedal the four miles to Mass. On the same day his father, Charlie, would prop the bar in the pub, drinking Guinness and Irish whiskey and talking horses. He was a small, weathered man with flat Irish cheekbones and a face creased with humour. When he saw a bargain or a horse came good, his eyes were a blue beacon in his smiling face, and Patrick had inherited those eyes, as well as his father's nose for a horse. Unfortunately for him he also inherited his mother's conscience. He would stand squirming with embarrassment as his father sang the praises of an aged hunter, armchair ride, jumps and stays forever, you know I'm your man Sean when you want a good horse. But somehow he would unaccountably overlook the nasty little habit the gelding had of putting his stifle joint out once a month and the knowledge bored a hole in Pat's brain. His thoughts were so loud sometimes that he was surprised no one heard them. Fortunately for his father they did not, and the family prospered.

He could not remember when he did not ride

and he was breaking horses almost before he could read. He learned early that the perfect horse has never been foaled. Horses bit, horses kicked, refused to jump or refused to leave home; sometimes they reared, sometimes they shied and sometimes – although fortunately only rarely – they hated men with such violence that they would try to kill. It was a kick from one such that was responsible for his crumpled cheek.

Since a sure way to improve a horse's price is to have him do well at a show, Pat was to be seen throughout the summer at events all over the county, in the showing classes, or preferably in the jumping. He was good, and indeed it would have been odd if his father's son had not been good, but he also had drive. He won rounds with saddles slipping, stirrup leathers the wrong length – his father would never spend money on tack – and on horses that had to be flogged into the ring, let alone over the jumps. He hated to lose and as he grew older he did so less and less. It was accepted in the family that he would go into business with his father when he left school and continue with the jumping.

The life suited him perfectly and his ambitions stretched no further than a first at the county show and girls with looser morals than the ones he seemed doomed to meet. Until that is he went to the international show in Dublin. Suddenly he saw how it could be. Men strolled about with posses of horses and strings of grooms, not to mention adoring girl followers, talking confidently of Rotterdam, Wembley, Toronto and even the Olympic Games. They had gloss and glamour, and Pat wanted to be amongst them. His imagination took off and when next he looked at the little farm with its stock of dodgy horses and the tack held together with string it was not enough.

The family rued the day that Pat had gone to the horse show. He turned their lives upside down, demanding better horses, better tack, more shows, more time, more everything. No one was left untouched and if they often cursed the effort in the end they shared the triumph, and triumphs there were. At the age of eighteen Pat was competing throughout the country. Some days he would win, but on others he did not, and with his usual honesty he faced up to the reason. He lacked the discipline and technical polish of those at the top. He would never achieve much until he acquired them, and that he could not do at home. The very things that made life in Ireland so pleasant, the courtesy, the timelessness, the art of making do, all combined to make it impossible for him to succeed there. He landed a job in England, with Tom Spence, a top class rider based in the south.

Pat's father was furious. 'How the hell d'you think I'm going to manage without you? I suppose you think it'll be all drink and women. Get out of my way boy, the sight of your face sickens me.'

He didn't mean it and if he was honest with himself, and like his son he tended to be, he had to admit that it was probably best. His wife said it was. Pat would not take second place and Charlie Brogan was in no great hurry to give up his role as cock of the midden. The rows had been getting worse and the day was coming when Pat would not back down. Yes, he was better in England thought Charlie, continuing to curse and create.

The family waved farewell on a morning of rain and wind. Charlie stayed home and felt bad about it; Patrick felt worse for the crossing was rough but whether he was seasick, homesick or just plain frightened he did not know.

He arrived at Spence's yard late at night and his welcome was uninspiring. They were polite, but by Irish standards unfriendly in that they took little interest in the new boy. It was a rather depressed Patrick who went to bed in the cold little room above the stables.

He awoke the following morning in better spirits and to the sound of buckets clattering in the yard. He dashed downstairs and was greeted with a roar of fury from Tom Spence.

'What time do you think this is, for God's sake? Six o'clock, I said and six I meant, not half past bloody seven. And wipe that smile off your face, damn you.'

Pat's incredulous grin disappeared on command and he forgot any explanations he had intended. He did not feel they would be welcomed. By the end of the day he was a very chastened young man.

The horses were magnificent, better than any he had ridden at home, but in Spence's eyes he could do nothing right. His seat was wrong, his hands were heavy, but above all he was slow. Spence wanted him working every minute of the day and even when he was running everywhere Spence accused him of dawdling. It was some months later that he realised with a shock that he had been doing just that. By then the routine was coming a little more easily and he was able to see what a country yokel he had been, mentally leaning on gates while others zoomed past, intent on their goals. He almost gave up and went home. The life there had a flavour which was lacking in this efficient, concrete world and in his rare moments of leisure he could have wept for the familiar muddle of his father's farm. But because he hated to lose, and would not admit defeat to Spence, he stayed.

One fine spring day he was working a horse over fences in the home paddock, concentrating totally on what he was doing. It was difficult, the horse was very stiff on one side, had the lightest mouth and the brain of a gnat, but its one saving grace was an incredible jump. At last he felt he had achieved something and pulled up panting. Spence walked over from the gate and Pat groaned inwardly. He had not known he was there and whenever Spence watched him there was sure to be trouble.

'Well, Pat.' The man looked at him gravely. 'You're not the boy you were when you came here, that's for sure.'

'No sir,' replied Pat with feeling. He had been a human being then, not the automaton he was now.

'I liked the way you worked that horse, he's not easy. Come over to the house, we'll look at your contract.'

With growing amazement Pat followed Spence into the luxurious sitting room, hallowed ground never trodden by him before, and drank real coffee made by Spence's wife. He emerged half an hour later walking on air. He had a new contract, he was to go on tour with Spence that summer and he had been promoted to the stable flat, which had central heating. He blotted his copy book that evening when two of the stable lads had to carry him home from the pub and he was sick in the yard, but since he was there, grey faced, at six the next morning, no one commented.

'They wouldn't notice if I bloody died,' thought Pat bitterly, splashing his aching head with ice cold water from the horse trough.

He stayed with Spence for five years, and emerged with a career and a friend. He deserved success, he worked for it unceasingly and he had undoubted talent. That Spence should have become his friend was perhaps more surprising, since on the face of it no two men could have been more dissimilar. Spence was older, quieter, more placid in every way than the volatile Patrick. He had started in the jumping world when there were no rich pickings to be had and he had made a living through perfectionism. He left nothing to chance, all that needed to be done was done and more, even if it meant they all dropped in their tracks. His influence on Pat was enormous once the boy realised that the man did not dislike him, only what he regarded as his sloppy habits. Once these were gone the door was open and on the long drives and the dark, cold evenings in strange towns they each found much to like in the other. Pat would have been very surprised had he heard what Spence said to his wife about him.

'The boy's brilliant, May,' he said, struggling out of his boots as he prepared for bed. 'You should have seen him at Cardiff, it was really stiff but he was as cool as you like. I couldn't have done it at his age, I'll tell you that. Sometimes it's as if he can read those horses's minds.'

'You've changed your tune since he first came,' smiled his wife.

'Christ, he rode like a ploughboy when he wasn't daydreaming. But he had something, even then. Now – well, he'll be heading back to Ireland soon no doubt, setting up on his own. I'll be sorry to see him go, he's a nice lad. Doesn't brood, even when things don't go his way.'

Spence had no son and he constantly had to remind himself that it did not do to get too fond of these lads. In years to come he would find it harder and harder to keep his place at the top with the Brogans of this world scrabbling for a foothold.

'I hope he marries a nice girl.' His wife was preparing to read a romantic novel, her reading glasses perched on the end of her nose.

'Yes. That could ruin him. In this game you need a special sort of lady.'

He leaned over and gave his wife an affectionate kiss on the top of the head. She giggled and blushed like a young girl.

'Really, Tom, I don't know what's come over you.'

Neither did he and he was concentrating intently on his pyjama buttons.

They settled down to sleep and in the dark she laid her cheek quietly against his back.

Patrick was also in bed, but he and his partner were not talking. They adored each other's bodies, he and Barbara, and time spent doing anything except making love was, as they agreed, time wasted. Not that they didn't have a lot in common, as he told his parents. Horses, for one thing. Barbara had an event horse which she rode when she could get away from her job as a junior with a TV company. They had met at an event, he showjumping, she completing an erratic cross-country course before going on to a party. In the end they had gone to the party together, and then on to a club, and then back to Pat's flat and the most incredible sexual experience of his life. Although by no means a virgin when he met Barbara he was still a comparative innocent, whereas she, golden daughter of a rich man, had no need of innocence. Why, they even looked alike, both tall, blond, Pat's merry blue eyes matched by Barbara's liquid brown ones. Where she was tanned with the sun of Greece he was as brown for he was never indoors. They were perfect for each other. True, her parents were a little doubtful but he was so charming and so successful that they could not quibble for long.

Everyone came to the wedding, held at a Catholic church in Barbara's parish. She was not a Catholic and had no wish to become one, but it hardly seemed to matter. Pat almost never went to Church himself. The two sets of relations mixed oddly, the Irish contingent slightly shabby and out of place when set against the expensive county perfection of Barbara's family, all pinstripe and pure silk dresses. Fortunately both families were outnumbered by the couple's horsey friends and afterwards when the drink flowed and the dancing began, it was hard to distinguish between the two.

They were to start their life in Ireland. Pat had approached sponsors there and had hopes of a place on the Irish team, while Barbara thought she might be able to get a job with Irish television.

Houses were cheap too, and when they settled on a delightful old farm some distance from Pat's parents their future seemed assured.

What was it that went wrong? In the years since Pat had spent aeons of his life trying to understand it. Money was a big problem of course, for Barbara had never been poor while Patrick had never been rich. Before they married there had been money to have fun with, but now, with horses to buy and a house to run, it was tight. They fought, bitterly, when she went to Dublin and bought clothes and when he went to a show and bought drinks. To Barbara the solution was simple. If horses did not make enough he must do something else. Predictably, Patrick was appalled. Didn't she understand, horses were his life!

Then again his view of women was different from hers. The television job had not materialised and Patrick hardly saw that it mattered. To him, a woman's job was an amusement, albeit profitable, until she had children and started real work. To realise that Barbara viewed herself as worthless without a job was something he found difficult to understand. She had been so casual about her work before, joking that in ten years' time they might let her graduate to making the tea, yet now she was behaving as if she had lost everything. And the jobs she could have, that she could do, she thought beneath her. His irritation grew and grew.

Within a year they were in deep trouble. To Barbara it seemed that Pat had everything his way, everything he wanted, all at her expense. Patrick saw only that she complained unceasingly, blaming him for things he could do nothing about.

She was a woman, he was a man, and it was a fine time now to discover you didn't like it. Yes, he knew his mother was a different generation, he didn't expect Barbara to live that kind of life, but she wanted children didn't she? No, she did not.

Patrick never really believed her. Perhaps that had been the root of it, whenever she said things that didn't fit in with his idea of the way she was, he ignored them. The real Barbara, the one Patrick hardly knew, was left screaming and hammering at a closed door.

They both tried, to the limits of their patience. He gave her treats he could ill afford, she attacked the house like one possessed. But the bank statements and the rows kept on coming and soon they had an overdraft and a houseful of unfinished patchwork and half-set jars of jam. She wouldn't come to shows any more, where she was the drudge, the moth to Patrick's flame. She stayed at home and moped.

Then even his luck deserted him. Suddenly it seemed as if he could win nothing, and the more he tried the worse it got. He was pushing too hard and he knew it. The sponsors started to mutter, as if he wanted to lose for God's sake! He was too tense, that was the trouble, coming straight from a row at home to another at the show. What he needed was a drink. For a while it helped, and he had a run of little successes, but then he began to drink after jumping as well, seriously, to give him the courage to go home. He knew how it would be when he got there. Barbara, white, drawn, her hair strawlike, the house a mess. What had he done to his golden girl? Why couldn't he make her happy?

One day he came home to an empty house. His first thought was that she had left him, but no, nothing was packed. The hours went by and still she didn't come, he telephoned his parents, the police, the hospital. No one knew where she was. He spent the night drinking and dozing. In the morning she came back, and he knew she had been with a man. It was there in the languorous turn of her head, the light in her velvet brown eyes. Someone, last night, had made love to her.

She did not trouble to deny it. He was a writer, from London, and it had been going on for weeks. What is more, she was pregnant though whether by him or Patrick she did not know, but he needn't worry because she was going to have an abortion. Their marriage was over and she for one wished it had never started. She was leaving for good.

She had stopped then, when she saw the shock and anger in his face. In her world, irreligious, rich and liberal, divorce was commonplace. In his it was not. Suddenly nervous, she went quickly upstairs and turned on the bath.

Patrick sat slumped in a chair, almost unable to think. Pictures flashed through his mind, Barbara, his Barbara, naked, laughing, while another man pressed his mouth to her breasts. Spreading herself, willingly, while the stranger filled her with his seed. And made her pregnant! The fury of it choked him, not for a moment did he think it could possibly be his child. The bitch, the whore, the cow. He burst into the bathroom like one possessed, filled with the rage and the hurt that had been building inside him for months. When he left her it was to ring for an ambulance. She was filling the bath with her blood.

* * *

Then came the time that ever afterwards he hated to remember. Barbara lay in her hospital bed, stained by bruises, drained almost of life, and her family gathered around like crows round a rabbit. No one let him come near her, no one would listen when he tried to explain. Her pregnancy had gone of course, and even to himself he would not speak of a baby. There had been no baby, just a vile, encroaching lie that spoke of failure and loss and betrayal. It was gone and he was thankful. Now, if he could only talk to Barbara, they could surely find some way to start again.

He never saw her again. One day she was gone from the hospital and when he went home they had taken her things. The house was a wreck, half of everything gone, even two pictures from a set of four. The double bed was still there though, she had taken the one from the spare room. Patrick lay on the rumpled, crumb-infested covers and wept.

There seemed to be nothing left to live for. It came as no surprise when the sponsors pulled out, and in fact he was almost grateful. There was relief in being punished. Swept by a desire to see the end of everything, Pat sold the house and was only prevented from selling his horses by his father, who whisked them off to his yard before Patrick could protest.

'Wait a while, lad,' advised Charlie. 'You'll feel different in a few months.'

All Patrick felt was that he wanted a drink. That was all he ever wanted these days.

Had it not been for Tom Spence he might never

have returned to jumping. As it was, he paid Pat
a visit just in time, he was going to sell the horses.

'Just thought I'd drop in,' he said casually as if
he habitually travelled two hundred miles for a
cup of coffee. The pale, lined face before him
looked nothing like the happy young man he had
waved goodbye to so recently. He did not seem
to be listening to what was said to him. Spence
pressed on. 'I heard about Barbara.' Still no
response. He let the silence hang, a feeling of the
futility of it all oppressing him. He noticed Pat's
hands, trembling slightly, and suddenly he was
angry.

'Do you know what they're saying about you?'
he snapped. The blue eyes looked up vaguely.

'Who?'

'Who do you think? Everyone that matters,
that's who. They're saying you're a burnt out case.
Some early promise but no grit. One little knock
and you're drinking like a fish. They're just
waiting for your horses to come up for sale,
they're all hoping for a bargain.'

He strolled over to the window. 'That's the
trouble with you Irish, of course, no stamina when
it comes down to it. Very flashy but in the end
nothing worth talking about. I'm sorry I wasted
so much time on you.'

He turned to leave, but Patrick was on his feet.
'Wait, Tom. Look – there's no way I could start
again now, even if I wanted to. I haven't the
money and there's no one willing to stake me now,
you know that.'

'Not in Ireland, perhaps. But why not come back
with me?' He spoke slowly, not sure if he was
doing the lad a favour. 'There's a man I know.

He's new to the game, pots of money burning a hole in his pocket, wants to sponsor someone. He's not stupid but he isn't in the know. He won't have heard about this recent bit of trouble, I'm sure of that. He might take you on.'

'Why don't you want him?'

Spence grinned at the suspicion in Pat's voice. 'I'm too old to be tied to someone's apron strings. But you're not, it could do you the world of good. Keep you off this stuff.' He gestured distastefully at the whiskey bottle standing on the table. 'God knows how you drink it, smells like sewer water to me.'

Pat smiled, for the first time in many weeks. 'You're right,' he said. 'I think I'll give it up.'

Chapter 9

Mary sat holding her mug, her thoughts in a turmoil.

'You don't pick your women very well, do you?' she said slowly.

He grinned, bleakly. 'What's wrong with you?'

'I thought – everything. Oh Patrick, you should have told me all this before. There was no need to be so secretive.'

'I don't like parading my failures. God, I made such a mess of it.'

An uncomfortable thought nudged at the back of Mary's mind, somewhere near the origin of her headache. When Patrick had wanted to try again he had found a woman so shackled by commitments that she simply could not pull away from him. She was perfect for him purely because of the mess she was in, she could have been anyone. Tears pricked her eyes and she sniffed and pushed at her hair.

'I didn't mean to hurt you,' said Patrick. He was staring at her and she wished he would not.

'Will you hit me again?' she asked. 'If you're drunk, or cross, or catch me talking to the postman. Will you?'

He went red and dropped his eyes. 'It sounds terrible when you put it like that.'

'It was terrible. You don't know.'

He came round the table and knelt beside her, pulling the rough wool of her dressing gown aside, discovering bruised flesh that shuddered at his touch. 'I'll kiss it better,' he whispered, and began to mouth little pieces of skin, so gently that the darts of pain might well have been pleasure. She was gasping and crying, needing him and at the same time aware that if she gave in now she would hate herself. He could do what he liked and she would still let him inside. She pushed hard at his shoulders and dragged the dressing gown round her.

'I don't want it,' she said harshly.

'Yes you do. I'll be gentle, Mary, I won't hurt you. Come on, just a little bit, I'm on fire for you and it's a lovely way to make up. Please, Mary.'

One hand crept into her dressing gown and nudged between her thighs while the other worked at his zip. That did it, he was so sure he could have her. She shoved him away and struggled to her feet, saying, 'I said no! You can't hit me one minute and screw me the next. Anyway, it's time the children were up.'

The look of torment on his face almost made her laugh. A small victory, but one that restored some little measure of self-respect.

Nonetheless he was sweet to her all that day, refusing to let her lift things and insisting that Susan milk the cow. Mary would have thought more of the gesture if he had done it himself. She was pleasant but cool, holding herself back from him. It was all for his convenience, she was sure of it. Still, it was nice to be fussed over for whatever reason, and once again she shelved her plans, such as they were, to go.

114

*   *   *

She found the letter after he had gone, it was lying on his desk with a mass of bills and receipts that he had unladen from his pockets. A thick, white envelope addressed in a neat hand, it caught her eye at once and she hesitated for only the briefest moment before opening it. Integrity was for the very young and the very secure she thought, unfolding the crisp pages. She was neither.

Dearest Paddy, she read. *Thank you for the flowers my darling, they were wonderful. I would have given anything to have stayed longer but I really had to go. Those three days – and nights – went by so quickly. I do so wish we could see each other more often, every time we meet we have to start again from scratch and there's never enough time.*

You're having a wonderful season, Paddy, I wish I knew how you did it. I'm afraid Gaytime is right off form at the moment, he doesn't seem to care what he's doing – rather like me I'm afraid. Oh Paddy, we had such a marvellous time together, didn't we? You are always so much fun, and then the nights – well, you were terrific. I'm going to Sawchester later in the month, I only hope Gaytime pulls himself together there. Will you be able to come? Please try. Yours ever, Sylvia.

Mary's heart was cold within her. She dropped the pages one by one on to the desk, screwed the envelope into a ball and tossed it on to the pile. Even he could not fail to see that she had read it. Fred's warnings and her own vague suspicions had convinced her that there was someone but for the sake of her pride, if nothing else, she had imagined a casual affair, not flowers and romance. Flowers! And all he gave her was bruised ribs and insults! He was so much fun was he? Dear Sylvia, unencumbered by house and children, was apparently worth entertaining while Mary, dowdy, temperamental workhorse, could safely be expected to endure his silences and moods. Oh, if he were here now she'd tell him just where to go.

An hour later when her rage had cooled she sipped a cup of tea and decided she would say nothing. They had made no promises to each other and as long as this woman did not threaten her home, what did it matter if he amused himself at shows? The thought of Patrick in bed with the unknown Sylvia made her swallow convulsively. Did he come home and compare performances? What did Sylvia get up to in some dingy little caravan? Once again she felt the hot, hurt anger but the memory of the sad little tale Patrick had told her returned like cooling rain. It was not a playboy she had to deal with, just a bad case of bruised male ego. Mary put her cup on the table with a bang and jumped to her feet, resolving to tidy cupboards for the rest of the day and to think of Patrick not at all. For the most part she succeeded.

When next he was home she was polite but distant. She knew he must have seen the letter for his desk was again beautifully tidy in the way he liked to keep it and the white pages nowhere to be seen, but nothing was said. Two days later he brought her some flowers, expensive hothouse blooms tied with a bow. He stood in the kitchen looking slightly ridiculous.

'Here. For you.' He held them out as if offering a baton in a relay.

'Why, Patrick, how lovely. So thoughtful.' She strolled slowly to the waste bin, took a last long breath of the perfume and thrust the flowers head first into the potato peelings and cold rice pudding. 'So thoughtful,' she said again, and slammed out of the room.

In bed that night they lay without touching, unable to sleep for the silent tension that fizzed in the air. Suddenly he reached for her and she squeaked with fright.

'I'm not going to hurt you, damn it,' he snarled, dragging at her nightgown.

'You surprise me,' said Mary shakily, trying haphazardly to fend him off, but he seemed all hands. He was determined and she gave in, resolving to lie like a log and to hell with him. He seemed not to notice, heaving himself on top of her and pressing deep hot kisses on to her throat, and by some reflex she found herself running sensuous hands over the muscles of his back. Dropping her arms guiltily on to the bed she resumed her rigid pose and then began to giggle.

'Shut up and open your legs,' he ordered but she was racked with laughter now and was shaking like a jelly.

'What the hell is so funny?' he demanded, but she could not speak, or resist as he thrust into her. The familiar warmth began to spread in ever widening circles and her giggles changed to groans of pleasure. It was only as she came to climax that she looked into his flushed, absorbed face and wondered if he was thinking of Sylvia, but the thought was lost in the moment of release.

117

In the morning he was gone again, off to another show. Their relationship puffed along like a slow train, constantly interrupted by stops at every station, never getting up speed. But after all, thought Mary, did they want to get to the end of the line?

The horses were to be rested. As Patrick said, Knight Errant was showing signs of tendon trouble and they all needed a break from the incessant travelling. It seemed quite reasonable to Mary, but not, apparently, to Fred Swallow.

'Can't think why they can't make Sawchester,' he muttered irritably to Mary as she painstakingly tried to get a new calf to drink from a bucket. The trick was to sink your hand into the pail of milk, encourage him to suck your fingers and then to withdraw them. Usually it took only seconds for the calf to empty the bucket with the efficiency of a fire hose but this one was proving somewhat dim.

'Animals are not machines, Fred,' she said firmly, 'as you can see.' The calf once again withdrew a milky nose and mooed unhappily.

'What happened to its mother?' asked Fred curiously. 'Dead is she?'

'I've really no idea, I shouldn't think so.' A thought struck her. 'Good heavens, Fred, you don't think all these calves are orphans, do you? There'd be a terrible mortality rate amongst cows if they were, the RSPCA would be up in arms and all the dairy farmers bankrupt. Calves are hardly ever reared on a cow these days. Their only mum is a bucket.'

'But that's cruel!' He sounded shocked.

'Yes, it is a bit,' agreed Mary, 'but they get used to it, you know. And jumping lame horses on hard ground is a great deal more cruel, I can assure you.' The bucket was empty at last and she straightened up.

'You might be right,' Fred admitted grudgingly and she gave him an affectionate pat.

'Let's go and have a drink, Fred. Tea.'

Mary's temperance campaign had been greeted philosophically by Fred, who merely doctored her brew with a hip flask when she wasn't looking. It wouldn't last long, he thought. He was visiting her more and more frequently, finding the casual atmosphere created by two small children a welcome change from his palatial home, inhabited only by his frosty wife and a battery of cleaners, not to mention a snappy Pekinese. His access to Anna and Ben had to be limited though, since his tolerance tended to be short-lived. Today was no exception.

'Ride-a-cock horse to Banbury Cross,' carolled Anna, 'to see a fine lady ride on a white horse.'

'What's the next bit, sweetheart?' smiled Fred, laying a hand on the golden curls.

Anna fixed him with a gimlet eye. 'And then she fell off and got all muddy and everyone said it was her own fault and went to see if the horse was all right,' she announced.

Fred recoiled and turned to the podgy Ben, lifting him on to his knee.

The baby gave an enormous belch and beamed toothily, drawing a reluctant grin from the redoubtable Mr Swallow.

'He's a grand lad, Mary,' he chuckled and she

nodded. She could take endless praise of that sort.

'Mummy, a lorry, a lorry!' shouted Anna, and sure enough the wagon was drawing into the yard. Mary wished Fred would go, everyone would be on their best behaviour until he did. It was not to be, he was paying for these moments when he could feel truly involved with the beautiful, shining horses stepping so daintily down the ramp and clattering into the boxes.

Mary uttered a silent prayer that Patrick would humour Fred today. Over the past weeks he had taken a perverse pleasure in upsetting the little man, ignoring his bouncy figure at shows and cutting him short when he did manage to buttonhole him. The trouble was that Fred believed he had bought Patrick, and true or not his tactless display of power and money was driving Pat to open rebellion.

Fred would stride over to him as he completed a disappointing round.

'Not up to standard today, my lad,' he would declare loudly. 'The money I've laid out on that horse, I expect better than that.'

It was only bluster for the benefit of the interested audience, but to Patrick it was like fingernails on a blackboard. He challenged Fred at every opportunity, making him the last to know when a horse went lame or a show was cancelled and relying on his charm to avert the resultant storm. But he was becoming less and less willing to find the honeyed words and Fred was daily more difficult to appease. Today the little man struck a confident pose in the middle of the yard, cigar in hand, and impeded everyone's progress.

Edna rushed around, more than usually poker-

faced in the presence of the sponsor. She ignored
Mary completely, rapping out orders to Mandy and
Susan in her determination to be seen to be
running a tight ship.

Brogan was in contrast alarmingly casual.

'Sorry about this, Fred,' he said, giving Mary a
perfunctory kiss and lighting a cigarette. 'Time we
all had a rest, I think. Coming in for a cup of tea?'

He strolled towards the house and Fred scuttled
along behind. Mary's heart sank. Surely it
wouldn't hurt Pat to humour him a little, to let
him feel that he was calling the tune? She noted
the angry red of Fred's neck, cut into fleshy folds
by his collar and hurried inside. Here again
Brogan, with his extra inches and calm air of
authority, was annoying Fred.

'I want you to do that show on the twentieth,'
Fred was saying.

'Can't be done,' replied Pat, throwing himself
into a chair. 'It's only small beer and I want to
keep the horses fresh for next month. Sorry,
Fred.'

'Now look here, Pat, I've got a client I want to
take to that show and I want you there. And that's
final.'

'You could take a couple of the youngsters to
Barnham, couldn't you, Pat?' interrupted Mary,
sitting on the arm of his chair. She stroked the hair
over his ear, willing him to compromise.

'Perhaps.' His tone was truculent but Mary
beamed at Fred and walked over to him, taking
his arm and leading him firmly to the door.

'There you are then, that's settled. Why don't
you come over for lunch tomorrow, Fred, we can
discuss things more fully then. Give my love to

Jean. You must bring her over sometime.' She gave him an affectionate kiss on the cheek and waved until his car drove out of the yard. Brogan's face was amused.

'You're wasting your energy, Mary. I'm not doing that show.'

'Fred will pull out if you don't, is that what you want?'

'He's a pain in the neck. I've had one or two other offers as it happens, I don't need him that much. He thinks he owns me.'

'Well, I think you should swallow your pride for another season at least. And even then, you don't have to lose him altogether. Take it steady, Pat.'

He got to his feet and took her by the shoulders, pushing her against the table, his thighs hard on hers.

'I'm boss around here, sweetheart,' he whispered and bent to kiss her.

'Excuse me,' said Edna's voice, primly. Brogan looked at her briefly, before turning back to Mary.

'What do you want, Edna?'

'It's High Time. I think he's sickening for something.'

'Damn. All right, I'm coming.' He released Mary, hitching his jeans irritably, but he had to grin as he met her eye.

'Can I come?' she asked and he nodded.

The bay gelding was standing in his box looking slightly depressed.

'He's sweating up,' said Edna and Brogan nodded. The horse's feed was untouched in the bucket and his nose was beginning to run. Mary noted the rapid rise and fall of the darkened flanks and felt a twinge of apprehension. The horse did not look well at all. Brogan felt for the pulse, all his attention focused on the problem.

'Right, Edna, get him into the far box, right away from the others, then call the vet. No one but you touches him and you don't go near the other horses without a complete change. Get on with it.'

'I'll phone,' said Mary and rushed to the house, thankful that she no longer had to race to the village to make a call. Brogan followed her some minutes later.

'What do you think it is?' she queried.

'Virus. It's bad this year, quite a few people are out with it.'

'But don't you have them vaccinated?'

'Oh yes, but there are different strains and they change, and then you catch it just the same. Not as bad, perhaps, but bad enough.'

'Will they all get it?'

'I hope to Christ they don't. You were right, I'd better be nice to Fred.'

Later that evening they all sat round the kitchen table, drinking coffee in depressed silence.

'How long would you be off if they did all get it?' asked Mary at length.

'Three months I should think. And just when we were doing so damned well.' He banged the table angrily and the cups jumped.

'By the way, Mary,' Edna sounded strained, 'I brought you something.'

Mary could recognise an olive branch when she saw one. 'Really? How lovely!' She gave Brogan a nervous glance. 'What is it?' she hissed as Edna went to fetch whatever it was. He just grinned.

Edna returned some minutes later with a

cardboard box covered with a blanket, the bottom edges dripping slightly.

'I forgot about him with all the fuss,' said Edna apologetically, setting the damp parcel down on the clean kitchen table. Mary gritted her teeth and lifted the blanket. Inside, on a bed of wet straw, sat a large, grey-haired puppy, his eyes milky-blue with babyhood and bleary with sleep. He leaped up to Mary, putting his smelly feet all over her clean blouse. She looked at Edna's anxious face and sighed slightly, then gathered the infant to her bosom.

'He's beautiful,' she said warmly. 'What sort is he?'

The girls all started talking at once.

'An Irish Wolfhound,' said Mandy.

'He's only six weeks old,' said Susan.

'I thought another Alsatian, but Paddy suggested him,' said Edna.

A warm, wet flood cascaded down Mary's front and she stared accusingly at Pat, who smiled sweetly.

'I knew you'd like him,' he said.

'What on earth possessed you to suggest something so big?' she demanded some hours later. She was mopping up yet another enormous puddle with exhausted patience. She had no idea when she would get to bed, if at all, every time she left the puppy he shrieked in anguish and woke the children.

'I was being funny,' said Brogan, moving his feet out of the way. 'I should have realised Edna has no sense of humour. But it was nice of her, wasn't it?'

'I'd be a lot more impressed if she was sitting up with it tonight instead of me,' muttered Mary sourly. 'What shall we call him?'

'He's your dog, you decide.'

'How about Paddy? He is huge and thick, after all.'

'Thanks a lot. Wouldn't Murphy do as well? Less confusing.'

'How right you are. I'd hate to see you galloping round the side of the house with your tongue hanging out every time I opened the back door and called. Murphy it is, then.'

'My tongue's hanging out now, as it happens,' he said, stroking her arm.

'Well, unless you fancy sharing a bed with Murphy I'm afraid you're doomed to disappointment.'

'Let's try. He must be tired by now.'

They had barely reached the bottom of the stairs before the volume of Murphy's cries brought them racing back into the kitchen.

'You'd think he was being murdered,' said Brogan once he could hear himself think.

'I wish Edna had ignored her guilt feelings, I really do,' moaned Mary, sinking into a chair with the orphan in her arms.

'We could drug him, you know,' said Brogan and Mary stared at him accusingly.

'Turning him into a junkie at six weeks? It's immoral, and anyway . . .' her words were drowned by an enormous yawn and Brogan went to fetch the tranquilliser they used for horses which were bad travellers. Mary did not protest.

'It will have to be a minute dose,' she warned as he stirred it into a saucer of milk. Within half

an hour Murphy was snoring happily and they
crept off to bed. Mary slept badly, dreaming of
nightmare hounds and dead puppies, with the
small round figure of Fred Swallow standing in
their midst, looking cross. But when morning came
it was clear that Murphy had survived the night
and was much refreshed by his sound sleep. He
bundled about, falling into his water bowl every
few minutes. The children loved him and Mary too
felt a reluctant affection, tempered only by the
need to follow him everywhere with a large cloth
and an armful of newspapers.

Lunch with Fred was a less sophisticated affair
than Mary had intended. Banished to the kitchen,
Murphy's wails were clearly audible as they began
their smoked salmon. Halfway through the boeuf
bourguignon Brogan could stand it no longer and
consigned him to an empty stable where his cries
could only deafen the horses, and when coffee
and liqueurs arrived the atmosphere was every bit
as mellow as Mary had planned.

'I'd be happy to do that show, I really would,
Fred,' said Brogan with disgusting sincerity, 'but
we have a problem.'

'Just tell me, lad, I'm sure we can sort something
out,' said Fred in a fatherly way. Brogan smiled
thinly.

'Well, I'm not sure there is anything we can do.
We've got the virus.'

'You're ill you mean? Why didn't you say so?'

Mary could not help smiling as Pat patiently
explained. 'So you see, we might have quite a long
lay off,' he finished.

Fred was silent for a moment, puffing on his
cigar. 'I'd better tell you what I've got in mind,

then.' He blew a cloud of smoke. 'I've thought for some time I should have more horses going, I never like doing things by halves. I'm going to take on someone else, as a second string so to speak, I'd be hard put to find anyone as good as you, Paddy.'

Brogan was not flattered. 'What do you mean?' he snapped.

'I'm sponsoring Tim Parsons, do you know him? He's got two good horses.'

'He's got two half good horses, you mean,' snapped Brogan, 'and a bloody good opinion of himself into the bargain.'

'Well, that's no bad thing,' soothed Fred. 'Anyway, I want him to move in here, though with this bug you've got the horses will have to stay with me for the time being, I suppose.'

'He's not coming here,' snarled Brogan. 'What do you think this is, a bloody hotel?'

'I think you can teach him a lot, Pat,' said Fred blandly. 'And anyway –' he paused and leaned forward, looking Pat straight in the eye ' – if you want me to stick with you over this spot of bother then you'd better cooperate.'

Brogan said nothing, but a muscle in his cheek twitched. His hand reached up in that tell-tale gesture and Mary turned and caught Fred's hand.

'I don't think I want anyone else in the house just now, Fred. It wouldn't matter who it was, we're better by ourselves. Really we are.'

Fred pulled his hand away, irritated with her for siding with Brogan. 'Tim Parsons is coming here and he's got to have somewhere to stay. I can't put him in with the girls now, can I?'

'*You* can't put him anywhere,' said Pat. 'This

is my house, my farm and the girls are employed by me.' He glared at Fred who glared back, no less eager for a showdown.

A vision of disaster appeared before Mary's eyes, Fred gone, the money gone, the house sold and she left with nothing and no one.

'I think I ought to tell you something,' she said shakily. They were hardly interested.

'What?' snapped Brogan flinging himself back in his chair, as relaxed as piano wire.

'What, my dear, what have you to tell us?' purred Fred, winning points for care and control.

'Well, it's just — perhaps you don't think it's important but — I'm pregnant. And I think it would be nice if we had the house to ourselves — for a bit.'

She stared at her hands, surreptitiously watching Pat out of the corner of her eye. The colour had drained from his face but his eyes bored into her like chips of blue glass.

'Don't pretend, Mary. Don't play games.' He was begging her to say it wasn't true. Damn him, damn all men.

'I wish I was making it up,' she snapped, hating herself for the wobble in her voice. 'But I'm not and I'm pregnant and I don't want someone else in the house.'

There was a silence. In the distance Murphy was still wailing.

'But Mary,' said Fred at length, 'you've got the wrong idea about young Parsons. He's a nice chap, friendly. Look, tell you what, I'll give him strict instructions to help out, lifting things for you, that sort of thing. He won't be any bother at all. But I'll leave you two to talk things over. Lovely meal, my dear, delicious.' He wafted out on a tide of cigar smoke, delighted with himself and with Mary's news. A bit of family responsibility would show Patrick Brogan how independent he could afford to be.

'I thought you had one of those coil things fitted,' said Patrick. He sounded quite calm, she thought.

'I did. I'm the failure rate. And do you know I never even considered it would happen to me. Damn, damn, damn. Damn it to hell.'

'What are you going to do? Get rid of it?'

She looked up at him, suddenly furious. 'Now listen here, Brogan, don't think you're sending me off for an abortion just to save you some inconvenience. This is nothing to do with you any longer, you leave me and my baby alone. We will manage.' She thought of Ben as he had been that morning, warm and cuddly, singing in his cot, and wrapped her arms protectively over her stomach.

'It's my baby too, you know.' She saw that she had hurt him and was surprised. After all, she was just one of the crowd for him.

'You don't have to bother about it. I can cope. I don't . . .' she had been about to say 'need you' but stopped herself.

'But I'm not your beloved Stephen, isn't that it, Mary? You'd rather die than depend on me.'

She said nothing because it was true. Her security lay in her independence, in her untouched heart and her building society passbook, not in him.

'You could have told me. God Almighty, I'm not some sort of ogre.'

'No, no, of course you're not.' She ran a hand

129

through her hair. How to tell him that she had needed Fred's protection, for her baby if not for herself. If Pat had taken it badly she could well have ended up like Barbara. But then she looked at him and saw that he knew her thoughts anyway.

'I'm going out to the horses.'

'Yes.'

She was left staring miserably at the polished table, awash with dirty glasses and half-filled ashtrays. She thought about her baby.

130

Chapter 10

Late summer had been beautiful, the barley rich and ripe, turning the fields to cloth of gold. She had wandered with the children down country lanes, marvelling at the bloody splashes of poppies hiding like thieves under the hedgerow, where the farmer couldn't reach. Sometimes she met her neighbour, Sam Downes, as he prowled round his acres rolling ears of corn between his fingers and muttering. It was a good year and a good harvest, so Sam was happy to chat about this and that. He was lonely, a widower with his children, all girls, grown up and gone away. She met him once when he was checking the crop and then again when she took the children to see the combines rolling through the fields like neolithic monsters, devouring all in their path.

'Been a grand month,' he commented, taking a break from the dust with his flask of tea and a sandwich. The children were playing in the straw, throwing it up in clouds.

'It's not been a month since I saw you last has it?' said Mary and he nodded. She was surprised. Time was slipping through her fingers as silently as a pure silk scarf.

Later, walking home, she felt rather sick. It was the sun, she thought, and the dust. Were it not for the harvest she would be praying for rain. But then, was it really a month since she had last seen Sam Downes? A whole month? Little things clicked into place and by the time she reached the house she was certain. The test had been a formality, she had no doubts. It was late September and she was about two months pregnant, which meant April. A spring baby.

The thought of telling Brogan had turned her cold, and she had convinced herself that she needn't do so yet. After all, he had not meant to father it and now that it was there, growing inside her, it was her own. His was the bread she ate, the bed she slept in, but the children were hers, he had no claim on them, not even on the tiny bud that hid where no one could see. She would keep it safe from him, she would keep it to herself, the pleasure, and the pain, were hers by right. It was her baby.

That he knew how she felt was something she had not bargained for. It put a wall between them though they pretended together that the child did not exist. They never spoke of it, to each other or to anyone else.

Fred told only his new rider, the ubiquitous Mr Parsons, about whom Pat said almost nothing. Mary prepared a room well away from their own and determinedly furnished it with two armchairs filched from the sitting room. The man would have to realise that he was not to have the freedom of the house, and in particular the sitting room, to witness the miserable evenings she and Brogan spent together, hardly speaking. The warmth that had crept unnoticed into their relationship was gone and she was aware of its loss as she had not been of its presence.

* * *

Susan had applied for her driving test and every breakfast was marred by her study of the highway code. She insisted that Mary test her until finally she refused to look at the book again. Really, the girl must have the mental capacity of a snail she thought, buttering toast amidst Susan's offended silence. She was a very good driver, but when it came to memorising the stopping distances or even something obvious, like the sign for a slippery road, she agonised and thought and asked for clues, before coming up with the wrong answer every time. Wearily Mary picked up the book again.

'Just once more,' she offered and Susan blossomed.

They were locked in combat over motorway hazard signs when there was a knock at the front door. This in itself was odd because no one ever went there, they always came to the back, but she seized the excuse and raced to answer it. The bolts were stiff, unused, and she wrestled with them.

A young man stood there, deeply tanned, hands in pockets. He was dressed in crisp jeans and white shirt casually unbuttoned to show a gold medallion on his smooth brown chest. Brown eyes smiled warmly at her but she did not respond.

'Well, hello gorgeous.'

'Mr Parsons I take it.'

'And you are the delectable Mrs Squires. I see what Fred meant.'

His accent was unmistakably southern and very confident.

'Do you have any luggage?' Mary was chillingly formal.

He gestured to a small red sports car obstructing the lane, being snarled at by a tractor trailing a load of muck.

'Would you please pull into the yard? And use the back door in future, we always do in Yorkshire.'

'Good heavens. Well, when in Rome I suppose.' He showed no signs of moving but just stood there staring at her.

'Quite. Well, if you don't want to be lynched by the Roman mob, namely Mr Hobson who is driving that tractor, I suggest you move your car. Now.'

She shut the door firmly in his face and raced to the kitchen. Brogan was there.

'He's here,' she squeaked, rushing to deal with the wet patch under the table. Murphy always went there and no one ever noticed until they sat down for a meal. It was most off-putting.

'Who, for God's sake?'

'The interloper, Parsons. All charm and good looks. I'm going to hate him.'

Brogan chuckled, a sound not often heard these days. 'He thinks he's one hell of a ladykiller. Why aren't you impressed?'

'Oh, he's like Gorgeous George, the tom cat in Anna's book. Why should I be impressed when he so obviously is?'

Brogan sighed. 'He's like that about horses, too. You can't tell him anything, he knows it all.' He strode angrily round the kitchen, hands thrust deep into his pockets. 'God knows why I should have to be his wetnurse. If it wasn't for this damned virus I'd tell Fred to take a running jump at himself and to take lover boy with him.'

She flapped at him. 'Watch out, he's here. Do come in, Mr Parsons.'

'Why, thank you. Hello Patrick. I'm sorry to land on you like this, old chap. Wasn't my idea as I'm sure you realise.' He held out a hand, but Brogan pointedly ignored it. Parsons was not discomfited.

'I see you're not too happy. But please don't worry, I've got strict instructions not to make any work for Mary – I hope I can call you that – now she's–'

'You mind your own business about what she is or isn't!' Brogan sounded vicious and for a moment Mary felt quite sorry for the newcomer. He wasn't to know he had entered a hornet's nest.

'I'll show you to your room,' she said quickly.

'Why, thank you.' Parsons treated her to his most beguiling smile. She stared back, blank-faced.

'You'll have to share a bathroom with the children,' said Brogan. 'Which is pretty hard on them.'

Mary was thrown off balance. 'Er – actually Pat, I forgot to tell you. The guest bathroom is finished.'

'The – guest bathroom?'

'Yes. Come along, Mr Parsons, I haven't got all day.' She scuttled out, exposed at last as the profligate she really was.

She led the way upstairs in silence. As she paused at the bedroom door Parsons caught her arm. 'Mary – I do want us to be friends, you know. This may be a little awkward at first but I'm really quite nice when you get to know me. Honest Injun.' He was all boyish charm and in fairness Mary had to admire his tactics. Pat would be a hard nut to crack so first get the women on your side. A lifetime ago she might have fallen for it, but not now. She smiled up at him.

'Of course we can be friends, Tim – I may call you that I hope? It's just that our little family does need some privacy. So I've given you some chairs up here for the evenings, although you are very welcome to eat with us, of course. Let me know if you need anything.' She walked briskly down the hall, reflecting that she might yet make a good landlady. Did she dare ask him not to bath more than once a month? That would soon get rid of him.

She was baking when he wandered back into the kitchen.

'Mary dear – I wonder if you could introduce me to everyone? I feel very much the new boy I'm afraid.'

'Of course, Tim, I'd be delighted. Sit there, I'll be with you in half an hour.' She turned the radio up and ignored him. Ben, who was playing with his bricks, hid under the table with Murphy.

'Excuse me.' He had to shout above the radio. Mary turned it down.

'Yes?'

'This child has been sick on my trousers.'

Mary hastened to look. 'Good heavens, that's just a burp, you had me worried for a minute. Wipe it up with this.' She handed him a cloth and returned to her work.

Parsons took advantage of the relative silence.

'What sort of dog is this?'

'An Irish wolfhound.'

Parsons laughed. 'Paddy's choice I suppose, he's very idiosyncratic about his origins. How do you find it living with someone so Irish?'

136

'I take it you mean "what's a girl like me doing
in a place like this?" and if so I decline to answer.
Come on, I'll show you round.'

Mandy and Susan were sweeping the yard and
stood tongue-tied as Mary introduced the
newcomer.

'I do hope you lovely ladies will give me a little
extra help until I find my feet,' he twinkled with
a grin. Susan blushed furiously while Mandy slid
her hands into the back pockets of her jeans and
looked at him under her lashes. Oh dear, thought
Mary, we shall have trouble if that girl starts
washing more often. Edna came out of one of the
boxes and they walked over to her.

'Edna my dear,' carolled Parsons, catching her
hands in his. 'How lovely to see you again.' He
turned to Mary, still holding Edna's hand. 'Edna
and I are old friends. She's often helped me at
shows, haven't you, my sweet?'

To Mary's horror, Edna gave a coquettish giggle
and turned rather pink.

'Well — I do like to help when I can,' she said
breathlessly.

'At least I have one friend in the camp,' he
replied, casting a glance of triumph at Mary. She
felt thoroughly annoyed.

'Edna's got quite enough to do for Patrick
without helping you,' she snapped and then
wished she'd kept quiet. Why was she letting him
bother her? She was tired, that was it, tired and
worried and unhappy. She managed a wan smile.
'I'm sure all the girls will be glad to help you out,
Tim,' she added kindly and was rewarded by a
look of complete bewilderment. That was the way
to handle the creature, keep him off balance.

After supper that night, a silent, difficult meal, Tim retired to his room, chased out by a coolness that bordered on the rude.

'We're being mean,' said Mary to Patrick as she cleared away the dishes. 'He's young and silly but he won't always be like that. It's not his fault he's here.'

Patrick caught at her skirt as she passed. 'Has he been making up to you?' he asked suspiciously. 'Because if he has—'

'Don't be ridiculous. No, it's simply that we ought to try and make it work, this atmosphere is terrible. Why don't you both take some of the youngsters to a show? It might help.'

'I suppose we could. The good ones that is, the others can stay and get fat.'

'Whatever for?'

'Mary love, the bad ones won't do any good but we'll let someone else find that out. We sell them full of oats and promise, say we haven't got time for them, that sort of thing. The good ones can prove themselves so we let them.'

'It doesn't sound very ethical.' She was slightly shocked. He always seemed so honest.

'That's nothing! If I told you some of the tricks my dad used to pull it would turn you white.'

But he didn't seem disposed to tell her. Wearily, she turned back to the sink, pulling at the waistband of her skirt. It was uncomfortably tight, soon she would have to go into smocks and then everyone would know. There would be winks and nudges, and conversations stopping when she came into a room, even in this day and age.

'Why the hell don't you buy some maternity clothes?'

138

Mary started, she had thought he'd gone into the yard.

'Come here.' He pulled her towards him and she stood, hands dripping, as he lifted her blouse and looked at the bulge of her stomach. He gently unfastened the pins holding the straining material and the skirt fell to the floor.

'No.' She tried to stop him as he eased her tights and panties down but he ignored her, running his hands over the firm, pale flesh of her belly.

Awash with embarrassment, Mary could not meet his eyes, but he took no notice and knelt in front of her, kissing and caressing while she tangled her fingers in his hair. She wanted him now and parted her legs, pressing his face into her. Just as she felt she could bear it no more he thrust her back against the table, his hands fumbling with his trousers. She murmured to him, for once utterly submissive, but then her eyes widened with shock. Standing in the doorway, lips parted lasciviously and an excited flush on his cheeks, was Tim Parsons.

'Patrick, he's watching us!' she shrieked and Brogan turned, in time to see the door closing.

'Who the hell cares?' he muttered and forced her now shivering body backwards. Later he said she had imagined it, but Mary suspected that he was secretly pleased, like a stallion displaying his dominance over a desirable mare. For her part, whenever she thought of it she shrivelled inside. It would only have been worse if it had been her mother, she felt.

Her mother. The guilt that had been building for weeks rose up and engulfed her. The letters kept coming, each demanding that she should telephone and explain what she was doing, and each time she wrote back, vague, non-committal, and said the phone hadn't been put in. Her thin tale about a job wouldn't survive one real conversation she was sure, already her mother made it clear that she hardly believed her. There would be such a scene when she found out the truth. Day after day she thought about phoning and day after day she put it off.

Indeed, there was so much else to think about. Within a week Parsons had the grooms in his pocket. His evenings were spent in the granary flat, with all three vying for his favours, which he allotted with undeniable skill. Edna was his prime concern for she could smooth many paths for him, but he led Mandy to believe that were it not for Edna and her jealousy they would be enjoying nights of unequalled passion. Shy Susan, for her part, needed very little more than a warm smile and the occasional arm round her shoulders for her to worship from afar, adoration mixed with terror.

He made no progress with Brogan. Pat set him to work on the horses that were intended for sale, exercising the best ones himself. It soon became obvious that Parsons did not relish the tedious groundwork that had to be done on some of the big, unbalanced youngsters that were in the yard. He soon began pushing to start fast work, but Pat was adamant.

'Another couple of weeks and that black gelding might start to be fit and might start to lighten the forehand,' he said flatly. 'If you rush him now you could finish him.'

'Well then, what about taking the bay and the chestnut mare to a show? They could both do with

an outing and so could I. You must admit there's
not much going on around here with half the nags
coughing and the other half thinking about it.'

Pat shook his head. 'Those horses are for sale.
They are not going to any shows.'

'You must be mad,' fumed Parsons, ill temper
getting the better of him. 'If they weren't so fleshy
and were given a bit more work they'd be first
class. A show or two would do them good.'

'Which is what we want the buyer to think.' Pat
stared hard at him, cool blue eyes meeting hot
brown ones. 'It's time you learned some patience,
Parsons. Your own two nags could do with some
of your time, instead of bribing Edna to go and do
it. You can't just pull them out at a show, blast
off and win, not unless you want to be a nine days'
wonder that is.'

'I've been doing all right up to now.' Tim's voice
had become slightly shrill, he was losing his
accustomed confidence in the face of Brogan's
greater knowledge and experience.

'You've done fairly well at County shows with
two very expensive horses bought ready-made,'
replied Brogan. 'The horses are worse now than
when Daddy bought them for you and you haven't
learned anything.' He looked at the furious young
face opposite him and relented somewhat. After
all, as Mary said, everyone had to learn and God
knows what Tom Spence had had to put up with
from Patrick himself. He resolved to be patient.
'You've got talent, Tim, but you're wasting it. If
you want to be good you've got to work. There
are no short cuts, not doping or rapping, none of
the little tricks you've heard of. You've just got
to work.'

Parsons coloured slightly, confirming Pat's suspicions. His mare had been that much too keen at the August show. Fred had no idea of course, and wouldn't have cared even if he had known. His only yardstick was the rosette which the mare had won after a round three parts out of control. She had almost reared over backwards in the paddock afterwards and came out the following day lethargic and drained.

Tim went sullenly back to work, but continued his campaign behind the scenes. Edna asked Pat about the black gelding.

'I think Tim may be right, Paddy, the horse is better than we think. Perhaps he should do a show or two.'

Brogan stared at her in amazement. He knew he was no longer the brightest star in her sky but he had never expected it to cloud her judgement of horses.

'Damn it, Edna, you know as well as I do the horse is the biggest coward ever foaled. Show him anything over three foot, and quite a few things under it for that matter, and he goes to pieces. I'll admit he's good looking but he's useless.'

'But are you sure, Paddy? I mean if I spent more time with him, built his confidence more. Tim says . . .'

'Oh yes, I'm sure he does. Well, lover boy might thrill you but he doesn't do anything for me. Or Mary for that matter, she calls him Gorgeous George.'

Edna looked at the floor for a moment. 'Paddy, about Mary – is she pregnant?'

He cleared his throat noisily. 'Yes. I suppose it's obvious. I should have told you.'

142

'I saw her without that overblouse thing she's been wearing. Do you think she ought to be doing the calves and things?'

He turned to look out of the tack room window. It was raining, a thin, persistent drizzle that might go on for ever. 'She never complains, but then she doesn't say much at all nowadays. And she's so damned independent she won't let anyone help.'

'Yes, isn't she though? She's the sort of woman who'd kill herself changing a wheel rather than ask for help, even though a dozen lorry drivers would stop if she just winked. Stupid, really.' Edna looked ruefully down at her strong, large hands, roughened by work that no man ever felt moved to help her with. Brogan heard her sigh and felt a sudden warmth towards her. It was odd how their relationship had improved since Parsons had arrived. Sex complicated so many things.

'Looks aren't everything, love,' he comforted, unwittingly plunging her still further into depression. 'But you don't want to get too keen on Parsons, he's only amusing himself.'

Edna nodded and made for the door. She felt like crying, but large, bony women only looked ridiculous when they cried and embarrassed everyone.

'I must go and see High Time,' she muttered, and tripped over the doormat.

Of the three horses that had contracted the virus, High Time was by far the worst affected. Secondary infections had set in and they had serious doubts about his lungs. Despite all their care he could still end up with broken wind, puffing and coughing at the least exertion, his magnificent promise come to nothing. They would simply have to wait and see, and in the meantime he was put on a long course of vitamins and medication. He received two injections a day, and the poor lad was beginning to feel like a pincushion. Whenever anyone approached the box, for whatever reason, he retreated to the farthest corner and stood there trembling, sweat forming visibly on his neck, his eyes showing white. As he gained strength boredom became a problem and he would stand for hours, idly kicking the heavy woodpanelling. The dull thumping became the accepted accompaniment to work in the yard. He started to worry Brogan.

'Mary,' he said one day, 'don't let the children anywhere near that horse, will you. I don't like the look of him.'

'He's not infectious any more, surely.'

'No, but he reminds me of a horse I knew once.' His hand strayed to his cheek.

'Was it a kick?' she asked and he nodded.

'He was a funny animal, not at all like High Time really. Very placid most of the time but he'd been laid up for a while after a bad fall. It turned him in some way. He'd come at you suddenly, for no reason you could see, ears flat, head like a snake. But he was a good horse.'

'Oh yes,' said Mary feelingly, 'now I suppose you're going to say it was your fault he kicked you.'

'Well, it was really. I only went in for a second, I should have tied him up but it didn't seem worth it. He reared on me. They fended him off with pitchforks and dragged me out, all very dramatic.'

'My God! And High Time reminds you of him?

I hope you've told Edna, she's doing him, isn't she?'

'Oh, she can cope, she always does. But watch the children.'

Mary nodded. It was just one more thing to be kept constantly in mind. Sometimes she felt like a juggler desperately trying to keep a dozen balls in the air at the same time. Before her pregnancy she had revelled in it, always occupied, always interested, but now she longed to crawl into bed and stay there for ever.

Apart from the rest it would have kept her away from Parsons. Often she would turn and find him watching her with an expression that was almost wistful. He was like a winter-starved wolf looking at food, longing to take it but fearful of the consequences. He made excuses to be alone with her, standing too close, but not so close that she could legitimately complain. In lighter moments she could see that Parsons was only young, self-opinionated and over-sexed, as even Ben might be one day, but somehow he bothered her. In self-defence she took to smocks at last, the bigger the better, and kept the children by her as much as she could. Since they usually dogged Brogan's footsteps Patrick assumed that she had decided to keep them away from him, but he would not challenge her and she could not explain, so it only added to the chill. She so much wished Tim had never come.

Chapter 11

Autumn was upon them, its first sign in those high hills not the changing leaves, nor the evening chill, but the wind. They would lie at night and listen to its howl amongst the chimneys, roaring in the trees and gusting softly in at ill-fitting windows. Odd bangs and tinklings punctuated the night and in the morning they would find doors pulled from their hinges and the cats' bowls smashed in the yard. It rained a lot that year and the stock poached the fields but at High Wold House all was bustle as the virus burned itself out and the hunting season began. Young horses, unsure of themselves and their role in life, grew up in the excitement and company of a day following hounds. Twice a week Mary would wave goodbye to Brogan and Tim Parsons as they set off, looking immaculate, only to return hours later covered in mud, exhausted and in rare good humour. They would flop down by the Aga, a whisky in hand, and tell Mary the story of the day.

Sometimes it would be a blank, trekking coldly from covert to covert without a sniff of a fox, but occasionally it was perfect. Hounds would find almost at once, their snuffles and whines deep within the trees and brambles turning to the cacophony euphemistically called 'music' as they found the line. They would pour from the wood, a river of brown and white, flowing over fences with scarcely a pause. A ripple of excitement would pass through the field at the sound of the horn and the horses would start to sweat. This was the time of greatest strain for Brogan and Tim, both mounted on youngsters already overcome by the unaccustomed company and the chill open air. Tension was released in a series of bucks, an attempt to bolt or sudden switching into reverse, to the fury of anyone standing behind them. Everyone cursed and swore.

At last, at long last, they were off and fighting to prevent the horses going flat out. There was a long day ahead and exhausted horses make mistakes. They made mistakes anyway, too green and excited to negotiate fences as wiser horses did, slowly and with care. They would race towards them, get too close, have a moment of indecision and then do a last minute scramble. It took a very good horseman to keep his nerve and let the horse work it out when at any moment he might be turned upside down in a ditch. In the end it was worth it though, to see excitable babies turned into keen, competent performers.

Mary always wanted to know if they caught anything.

'Don't think so,' Brogan would reply, time and again.

'I can't think why they call it a blood sport, it's more like jogging for foxes,' she commented, having stood and watched a fox emerge calmly from a wood, yawn and saunter off unconcerned as the hounds hunted madly for his scent.

'I think it's the followers who bleed,' muttered Brogan, nursing a knee rammed against a tree.

'But you want to go, the fox doesn't.'

'Come off it, you'd go too if you weren't pregnant. I've seen you, little orphan Annie with her face pressed to the window.'

She had to laugh, it was true. He ruffled her hair. 'Next year,' he said and she looked at him in surprise. She never thought further ahead than tomorrow.

Hunting mornings were very hectic and it was on one such, with haynets, rugs, bandages and hoofpicks scattered everywhere in a turmoil of horses and people, that Mary's mother arrived. Brogan looked up irritably as the car drove in.

'Oh Christ, some damned sightseer no doubt. Edna!' he bellowed, 'go and see what they want.'

Sighing, the girl left her bandaging – it had taken her half an hour to do three legs as it was – and marched over to the car, as welcoming as an angry hornet. A trim, elegant lady with silver hair, dressed in a navy blue suit, smiled charmingly up at her.

'I'm looking for my daughter,' she said, forestalling Edna's aggressive questioning. 'Mrs Squires.'

'Oh. Well – er – you mean Mary, I suppose.' She looked round wildly for support but no one was taking any notice.

'Yes, indeed. This is the place, I take it?' Her fastidious gaze took in the blowing straw and snorting horses. 'Yes,' she mused, 'it's just the thing Mary would like.' She looked expectantly at Edna.

'Well – er – that is, I don't know . . . if you'll excuse me!' She turned and ran towards Brogan, feeling more than usually big and clumsy in the face of such fragile elegance.

'Paddy!' she hissed. 'It's Mary's mother!'

'You deal with it,' he said abstractedly, sorting through a pile of bits.

'For God's sake Paddy, will you listen! It's Mary's mother!'

'Indeed it is,' said a cool voice behind them. Brogan stood up slowly, wiping his hands on his trousers.

'Er – how do you do, ma'am. I'm Patrick Brogan.'

'And I am Mrs Bennett. I would like to see my daughter, please.'

'Yes. Well. I don't really know . . .' his eyes met Edna's in desperate entreaty. No amount of disguise could hide the fact that Mary was nearly five months pregnant. The coming scene appalled him.

'I think she's out,' he said desperately.

'Then I will wait in the house.' She opened her Italian leather handbag and removed a pair of suede gloves which she put on with elaborate care, stretching and smoothing the fingers. It was a gesture Mary would have recognised. Her mother always put on her gloves when preparing for battle, once, incongruously, whilst wearing her dressing gown.

'I don't think – perhaps you could come back this afternoon? We're very busy, as you can see.'

'I shall get in no one's way, Mr Brogan. I merely want to see my daughter.'

'Oh God.' He ran a hand through his hair. Panic must have improved his hearing, as above all the clatter of the horses he heard the back door open and Mary's light step across the courtyard. She appeared round the corner, pretty and healthy in a dark brown smock with cream lace at neck and cuffs, but unmistakably pregnant.

'Mummy.'

Her mother turned. 'Oh Mary. Mary, my little girl!' Her voice broke and she clung to her daughter, giving little sobs.

'Come into the house, Mummy.' She looked over her mother's shoulder and held out a packet to Brogan. 'Your sandwiches,' she said matter of factly.

He took them and stood turning the bag in his hands. As the two women moved away he leaped into action, racing round like one possessed. Edna looked at him blankly.

'Let's get out of here,' he yelled urgently, thrusting a bucket into her hands, 'before she gets over the shock!'

The wisdom of this was immediately apparent and within ten minutes everyone except the unfortunate Susan was in the horse box and speeding towards the meet, an hour early.

Mary would have given anything to be with them. Instead she installed her mother in the kitchen rocker and made tea. Anna and Ben hid shyly, taking cautious peeps at this unknown woman.

'The children have grown so much,' gasped Mrs Bennett, striving to regain control, 'I hardly know them.'

'I'm sorry it's been so long,' said Mary, aware that this was but the first of many apologies she was going to have to make that day.

'Yes. Well, now I see why. Oh Mary, how do you

151

manage to get yourself into so many muddles? Look at your sister, she manages to get along quite well with Humphrey and nothing more dramatic than the occasional scratch on the car.'

'It wasn't my fault Stephen died.' She could feel her voice rising, why was it always this way when they talked?

'Oh, I don't mean that. Even before then you never once had a sensible boyfriend, always ton-up boys or racing drivers. Even then you could have married a rich one, but no, it had to be Stephen, full of ambition and not a penny to his name. You can't tell me you enjoyed grubbing away on that miserable patch of earth all that time.'

Mary sat at the table. 'We were happy, Mum, we really were. That's what makes it so hard.'

'Don't call me Mum, dear, it's vulgar.'

'Yes, Mummy. Sorry.'

'What about this latest man. Head of the provisional wing of the IRA, no doubt.'

'Not quite. He's in showjumping. Divorced.'

'Really, Mary, I honestly don't know where you find them. When you were young and silly I might have understood, but darling, there are the children. And now there's another on the way.' She fiddled with her gloves and then in a rush said, 'Why won't this man marry you? I take it he is the father?'

She was fighting embarrassment and Mary felt a sudden rush of warmth. She bent and pressed her cheek to her mother's. 'Of course he is. And he's a nice man, really. It's just that – he was very hurt before, you see. And we didn't plan this baby, it was an accident. I think we're better off the way we are, for the moment anyway.' She did not want to say that Brogan did not love her.

'How you can possibly have an accident, as you call it, in this day and age is beyond me. Still, at least you've been sensible about it. No — operation — or anything.'

Mary looked at her curiously. 'I thought you'd have been all for that. No scandal or anything.'

Her mother waved an impatient hand. 'In the end what does it matter what people think? But I do so want to see you with someone who will take proper care of you, darling. He does look after you, doesn't he?'

Mary giggled. 'Since he's just run out on me as fast as he can go I think you can draw your own conclusions.'

'That doesn't count, men can never stand scenes. But you have help in the house and so on?'

'Well — I manage, Mummy. The place looks all right, doesn't it?'

Her mother cast a distasteful glance around the muddle of jars, pot plants and cookery books. Her own kitchen was a stainless steel operating theatre, a pristine environment where food seemed an alien presence. 'You always were untidy, darling. It will be all right if I stay for a few days, won't it? I've brought the children's Christmas presents and so on.'

'Yes, of course. I'll go and make the bed.' Mary congratulated herself on a hurdle safely negotiated, little knowing that her mother had at once decided to do battle for her daughter with this unknown Mr Brogan.

Lunch was a gossipy affair, full of giggling reminiscences.

'Do you remember your father's face when you brought home that boy in all his leather gear?' chuckled Mrs Bennett.

'He wasn't that bad! I was terribly impressed anyway and I bet I can still strip down a motorbike. That was all we ever did.'

'I wish you'd told me that at the time, I was worried to death.'

They were just finishing the washing up when the horse box drew into the yard. 'They're early,' said Mary worriedly. 'I hope nothing's gone wrong.'

She dashed into the yard to meet Brogan.

'Why are you back so soon?' she asked.

He looked slightly discomfited. 'I thought the horse might be going lame. Seems all right now, though. And anyway – I felt a rat running out on you like that.'

She was touched. 'There was no need to spoil your day. She's been very good about it really. She's staying on for a day or two, is that all right?'

'Holy Mother of God. Does she have to?'

'Well, I daren't tell her to go, but if you –'

'No, no, no, she's very welcome I'm sure. Come on, let's go and meet her.'

Mrs Bennett was busily wiping worktops. When Brogan entered, she greeted him with a smile that turned Mary cold.

'Did you have a nice time, Mr Brogan?'

'Tolerable, thank you. I gather you will be staying for a few days.'

'Just until I can assure myself that my daughter is well cared for. Is she, Mr Brogan?'

'Well – er – I'm not sure what you mean.'

'I was a little surprised to find that she has no

154

help in the house. And yet she has to cook, and clean and wash not only for you but for–'

'Mummy, please–'

'Are you telling me that I'm exploiting her? Because let me tell you–'

'Patrick!' He looked at Mary's anguished face and stopped.

'Look, I've got things to do outside. I'll be in later, Mary.' He flung out into the yard, leaving Mary to stare reproachfully at her unrepentant mother.

At five o'clock he reappeared in time for the children's tea, outwardly sober but smelling of whisky. They sat round the table listening to Anna crunching ginger nuts and Ben slurping orange juice, picking their way through a conversational minefield.

'I saw a strange bird today,' commented Mary hopefully.

Brogan looked morosely at her mother. 'So did I.' Mary choked on her tea.

'It was a penguin, Mummy,' said Anna.

'I don't think so, darling. We don't have penguins.'

'It was a penguin, I sawed it, and it got eaten by a lion. A big, huge, 'normous lion. It ate Murphy too.'

'What's he still doing here, then?' queried Brogan, intrigued by the sudden advent of a safari park on the doorstep.

'He didn't taste nice,' replied Anna inconsequentially, her mind on another piece of cake.

'Talking of that dog, dear, don't you think he ought to be in a kennel?' said Mrs Bennett, pouring herself another cup of tea with neat, decisive movements. 'He is rather large for the house, after all.'

'But he's very good-natured, and anyway I don't think Edna would like it.'

'Is Edna that tall, plain girl? Well, I don't know what she's got to do with it. It seems to me that everyone's feelings are being considered before yours, Mary, and I find that quite unforgivable.' She directed a meaningful stare at Brogan.

'Patrick!' warned Mary, her voice tinged with panic. He was almost grinding his teeth with rage but with an enormous effort which was obvious to everyone, remained silent.

'You've gone all pink Daddy,' said Anna.

'Anna,' thundered Mrs Bennett. 'That man is most definitely not your father!'

The little girl burst into frightened tears and Mary rushed to comfort her. When she looked up Brogan had gone.

'Mummy, you're driving him mad!' burst out Mary, who felt quite sure that she was going mad herself.

'I'd rather have him mad than you worked to death,' snapped her mother. 'I will not stand by and see you turned into a drudge!'

The next two days were a nightmare for Mary. Tim took refuge in the granary flat during the day, sneaking up to bed like a thief late at night. His absence was the one thing Mary could be thankful for. She found it surprisingly easy to tolerate her mother's criticisms of her housekeeping, letting her scour wastebins and tidy saucepan cupboards to her heart's content, but her attacks on Brogan she was less able to bear. Her theme was that he was taking shameless advantage of her daughter and that he ought to be made to do the right thing. When she discovered Violet and the calves she trembled with outrage.

'Does that man have no conscience?' she cried. 'Allowing a pregnant woman to struggle with these beasts like some Indian peasant?'

All Mary's protests were ignored and Mrs Bennett spent the rest of the day fuelling her rage. When evening came she was ripe for battle and when the unhappy threesome was seated round the fire in the sitting room she decided the moment had come.

'Mr Brogan,' she began, fingering her rings, 'you will be happy to hear that I am leaving in the morning, but there is something I should like to say before I go.'

'Now, Mummy, please behave,' cried Mary despairingly, but her mother rushed on.

'My daughter has been through a very difficult time and her judgement cannot, I feel, be relied on. I had hoped that people would be sympathetic and understanding towards her but this has not been the case. Her husband was an exceptional man and we can't expect another like him, but this! I find her a virtual slave in your home, pregnant, a fact which you seem prepared to ignore, working as a farmhand in the little time she has free from the house, and left alone for weeks at a time. It is simply not good enough!'

Brogan sat quietly smoking as she raged at him, his face very pale.

'Mary has everything that she wants,' he replied stiffly.

'I suppose she wants to bring a bastard into the world!' declared Mrs Bennett and gave a frightened gasp as Brogan leaped to his feet. He towered over her, shaking with fury.

'Mary wants that baby,' he hissed, 'and if people like you will just leave us alone we might manage to be happy here. We want nothing from you.'

'I find that a rather odd statement from someone standing on my Persian rug,' replied Mrs Bennett.

Brogan swore violently and wrenched at the carpet, pushing chairs away and knocking over tables as he tore it up. A table lamp crashed to the floor in his path and he kicked it aside. Under the amazed gaze of Mary and her mother he dragged the ungainly bundle into the kitchen and threw it into the yard.

'You can take it with you,' he panted, 'now!'

'It's far too late for her to leave now,' protested Mary but her mother stopped her.

'I will go, darling, but I would like you and the children to come with me. I can't leave you here, I just can't. I know it will be difficult, your father and I – well, we don't like change, but this man is impossible, not at all like Stephen. You simply cannot stay.'

'She is staying with me,' snarled Brogan and Mary looked miserably from one to the other.

'Yes, Mummy,' she whispered. 'I'm going to stay with Patrick.' She went to stand next to him and heard him give a long sigh.

'Well,' said Mrs Bennett, gathering up her handbag. 'I'd best go up and pack. Keep the rug, Mary, I don't want it.'

'I'll not have it in the house,' said Brogan and

neither woman felt disposed to argue with him. In virtual silence they loaded it into the car, next to the matching set of tan luggage.

'You won't be able to see out of the back,' said Mary anxiously.

'It doesn't matter.' Her mother gave a rueful smile. 'There's no need for you to worry, I do quite enough for both of us.' She gave her daughter a swift hug. 'Take care.'

Mary nodded, fighting tears, and stood waving until the car was out of sight. Shivering, she turned to go back to her decimated sitting room.

Brogan watched in silence as she righted chairs and picked up broken glass.

'Leave it to the morning,' he said at length. She shook her head, not trusting herself to speak.

'Come on.' He took her gently by the shoulders and with a sob she turned and buried her face in his jumper. 'I tried to keep my temper, love,' he said softly.

'It wasn't your fault, she was impossible. But all the same I do wish she hadn't gone like that. You see, it's just that she worries, that's why I didn't want her to come, I knew it would make her miserable. She was like that when Stephen was alive too, every time she came she'd go on about how hard I had to work, why didn't I have help with the housework, it was awful!'

'She's right you know, you've got to have some help. The kids alone are a full time job at the moment.'

'I can manage.'

'Damn it all, you'd say that if the house was four foot deep in water and the roof had just caved in.'

'Judging by this room I think it has.'

He chuckled and they stood silent for a moment, enjoying the rare privacy.

'Your bump is kicking me!' He was incredulous. Mary pulled away, very pink. 'No, no, come here, I want to feel.' They stood motionless, waiting.

'It never does it when you're waiting,' whispered Mary, as if it could hear them but then, gentle as a butterfly, came the soft pressure against Brogan's hand.

'Well behaved already,' he crowed. 'Do you think it's a boy or a girl?'

'You're supposed to suspend a wedding ring over it and see which way it turns but it doesn't work. Or at least, if it does, Anna is a hermaphrodite.'

'What the devil's that?'

'Oh you know, worms and things. Or is it snails? Come on, let's go to bed.'

Chapter 12

They were leaving for the big Christmas show. Parsons was delighted to be up and doing at last, sure that he would show Brogan, and the impressionable Fred, just what he was really worth. He had been vastly amused by the sudden departure of Mrs Bennett and Mary was convinced he had been upstairs listening on that last evening. He leaned nonchalantly against the horsebox, his boots gleaming, courtesy of Susan, jodhpurs skintight, with a fashionably huge dark blue sweater to complete the ensemble. All around was bustle.

'For Christ's sake, Parsons, get your finger out!' bawled Brogan and Tim went, sighing, to help load horses. He, at least, was one person Mary would be glad to see the back of. The other was someone who, it seemed, was going to stay however much she resented it. That was Mrs Harding, Brogan's idea of the ideal cleaning lady. Certainly she looked the part, in her flowered overall and headscarf, but she was more inclined to lean on a broom than wield it; apart from the time she used it to attack the kitchen table as the best way of removing the crumbs, following which she was barred from the kitchen. Still, all would have been well if she had held her tongue.

'See it's all at the front,' she started one morning.

161

'I beg your pardon?'

'The baby. The way you're carrying it. Sure sign of a bad time that is.'

'Oh. I hope not.'

'Your third too, them's often the worst. Dorothy Matthews was forty-eight hours with her third. They said you could hear her screams halfway down the street.'

'Well, I'm going to Beverley and it's a very good hospital. I don't think things like that happen there.'

'Oh, you'd be surprised! Knew one woman, drugged to the eyeballs she was, they just took a knife to her. All because the doctor wanted to go home early. Forty-three stitches she had.' She dropped her voice. 'Down there!'

Mary swallowed convulsively. 'I think I'll go and sort the washing Mrs Harding,' she muttered and scuttled off down the passage.

'I'll get going with the vac then, love,' carolled the pet vampire. 'Pity there's no carpet in the lounge or I'd a done that 'n all.'

She began to think of excuses to go out on the mornings when Mrs Harding cycled up from the village, exertion from which it took her at least three-quarters of an hour to recover. She knew she was being cowardly but Brogan was not there to see. One day she took the children to see Father Christmas in York, a treat which aroused as much excitement in her as in them.

Mist lay heavy in the lanes that autumn morning, leaving a clammy chill in the air. The van crept along, the lights bravely battling against the fog and the passengers singing as much of 'Jingle Bells' as they could remember. The weather must have discouraged all but the hardiest because when they finally arrived they were the only customers for Cinderella's coach to Santa's Fairy Grotto. The ride started up with much whirring and grinding before plaster horses, dimly seen, bore them off through magical snowy woodlands. The children sat silent and unsmiling, eyes wide in amazement. Journey's end was signalled by a dull thump and they all shuffled out to confront the great man, seated amidst jerking puppets which were all, as a small notice informed them, available in the toy department.

'Look children, here is Father Christmas,' declared Mary ecstatically, gently pushing them forward. Ben let out an ear-splitting wail and Anna took a dive under her mother's skirt, revealing Mary's knickers. No amount of persuasion would induce either child to go within five feet of the red and white horror, so Mary collected their presents and made a rapid exit. All this effort to frighten them to death.

They repaired to the cafeteria for orange juice and cakes. Ben was in seventh heaven, smearing synthetic cream from ear to ear, but Anna was more thoughtful.

'Will Father Christmas bring me a pony?' she asked plaintively and Mary caught her breath.

'I don't know dear – are you sure you want a pony?' Surrounded by horses as she was the child had never before asked for one of her own.

Anna nodded firmly. 'I wants one lots. I can be like Edna, I can gallop. And jump, 'normous jumps. Will Father Christmas bring me a pony?' Mary considered. There was really no reason why he shouldn't, one small pony would go almost unnoticed in the equine throng at High Wold House. If she could find one before Christmas it just might do something to improve Santa's image and indeed to put some sparkle back into a Christmas without Daddy. Last Christmas was one she never wanted to think of again, a travesty of merriment.

'I think he might, darling,' she said at last. 'We shall have to see if he can get it in his sleigh.'

A week before Christmas she was in despair. Anna talked constantly of her pony and Mary could find nothing. She would rather risk her daughter's heartbreak than let her mount any of the headstrong, temperamental and above all huge ponies being advertised as 'ideal for small child'. It was Sam Downes who came up with Moonlight Matador, a name so unpromising that she would not have bothered to go and look but that Sam would have been offended. He was owned by a distant relation of Sam's, a farmer near Garrowby, a youthful, chatty man as Mary discovered on an afternoon of rain and wind. The exotic sounding Moonlight Matador stood on his little black hooves four square against the elements, raising his head at the sound of their voices to come trotting to the gate, eyes bright, ears pricked. Mary studied him as he gently nosed for titbits. He was a dapple grey, his coat thick and shaggy as befitted the outdoor life he was leading. His head was small and intelligent, hinting at a Welsh cross somewhere about and he was narrow, an essential for a child's pony. Two of the farmer's children had learned to ride on him and he was obviously the family pet. Mary had no hesitation in paying over the odds for him but she used her own hoard; she could hardly expect Brogan to pay for this. The farmer promised to deliver him on Christmas Eve, when he would be smuggled into a loose box.

She drove home in high spirits for Brogan would be back later that evening and she was looking forward to boasting of her find. At least he would be interested, Stephen had never cared much for her horses, corn and cattle were his delight. In the event when the travellers did return it was late and they were tired, cold and hungry and once thawed out had far too much of their own news to tell to be interested in the minor events on the home front. Patrick had done well, a win and two seconds, all against good competition. He was elated but was doing his best not to show it in front of Tim. That was the worst of having a stranger in the house, Mary thought, you could never fully relax. Parsons had had what everyone assured her was the worst possible luck. One of his horses had gone badly lame halfway through a competition and the other had unaccountably taken to putting in a stop when asked to jump at speed.

'We should take Fred's advice,' said Tim pointedly and Edna looked embarrassed.

'Any more tea, Mary?' asked Pat and Tim slumped back in his chair. Mary made a mental note to grill Pat on that at the earliest opportunity.

Her moment came as they were undressing for bed, no longer a mad scramble to beat frostbite but a luxurious ritual cushioned by thick carpets and central heating. She often felt guilty as the boiler roared away, heating the whole house when only she and the children were home, but since Brogan had omitted to tell her how to alter the timer and she was certainly not going to ask, she was happily impotent. Nonetheless she hurried into her nightdress, hating Brogan to see how huge she was getting and tonight he seemed not to notice, flinging himself on the bed with a contented sigh.

'God, I'm tired. Everything OK?'

She nodded. 'What did Tim mean? He was a bit cheesed off, I thought.'

'You can say that again. He came to grief through his own stupidity and now expects me to lend him one of my novices so he can ruin that as well. I told him where to get off.'

'But he's not that bad a rider, is he? Would it hurt?'

'Not the horse perhaps but me, certainly. Anyway Fred's on his side so I'm damned if I'll give in.'

Mary sighed. They were heading for big trouble with Fred and she was not looking forward to the explosion. She felt that when the split came Pat would pack his bags, up stakes and depart for Ireland leaving her – where? She preferred not to think of it.

'I've got some news as it happens.' She perched on the edge of the bed, unaware of how pretty and feminine she looked in her pink, high-necked nightie, its folds falling softly over her enlarged breasts and swollen body. 'I've bought a pony!'

'You've what?' It was almost a roar.

'Oh, don't worry, I used my own money. It's for Anna, for Christmas and you've no idea the trouble I had, I've looked at dozens . . .' she trailed off worriedly as he leaped to his feet and strode round the room. He seemed almost speechless, clutching his hair and mumbling, turning several times to say something only to clutch his head again and continue his pacing. Finally he halted in front of her.

'Patrick . . . what is the matter?' she asked faintly, expecting at any moment to be knocked to the floor.

'Mary. Dear Mary.' He was all patience. 'There is one thing at which I am an expert. You may be able to beat me hollow on everything else under the sun but in this one thing you don't stand a chance. What is that one thing, Mary?'

'Horses, Patrick.'

'Correct. And what have you just bought?'

'A horse.'

'Correct. And how much did you pay?'

She told him.

'Jesus Christ!'

'Well, I know it was a lot but he really is a lovely pony, you've no idea – well perhaps you have some idea but – anyway, I don't care what you say, I like him.'

'Do you realise I could have borrowed a perfect child's pony indefinitely from at least a dozen people?'

'You never said!'

'I never knew you wanted one!'

They were silent for a moment. Brogan sighed heavily and collapsed on to the bed. 'Why don't you talk to me?' he asked, forcing his voice to deliberate calm. 'In future, damn it, you will tell me what the devil you're doing, or else. And when I'm away I will telephone daily and be told the truth, not just yes Patrick, thank you Patrick, everything's fine Patrick, I can manage. Do you understand?'

'Yes, Patrick. Thank you, Patrick. And while

we're being honest, Mrs Harding has got to go.'

'What's wrong with her?'

'The woman's a ghoul, that's what. Her entire conversation is breech births, forceps deliveries and days of anguish, I can't stand it! Also she's filthy. And lazy.'

'Anything else?'

She shook her head.

'Then I'll tell her tomorrow.'

'I feel a coward, don't you think I should?'

'No, I'll let you off. Fred might know someone better, he's got to have some uses I suppose.' He turned off the light and they were silent. Mary could not get comfortable and scrabbled around, finally sleeping curled close to Brogan's back.

Christmas Eve's muddle offended even Mary's less than ordered soul. The grooms were all going home for Christmas, as was Tim Parsons and everything had to be left ready so that Brogan could manage with the help of a couple of girls from the village for two or three days. Mary gave presents to the grooms, perfume for Edna, make-up for Susan and, pointedly, soap and bath essence for Mandy. In return she received a book on bloodstock, a horse brass and a tea towel with a picture of Red Rum on it. No one could say the girls were not dedicated she thought, resolving not to tell Brogan in case he was preparing to give her a horsey headscarf. Tim Parsons cast her into confusion by presenting her with a beautiful, expensive and totally desirable cashmere shawl. Thankfully she had not yet given him the small box of cigars intended for him and could substitute the silk tie destined for Fred. She then had to race off in the protesting van to find something else for

Fred, not an easy task in a village with three shops on Christmas Eve. When she returned, with an over-priced copper kettle, Moonlight Matador had arrived.

He stood quietly, dwarfed by the vast loose box, apprehensive yet more than hopeful of good things to come. He seemed very scruffy, mane and tail tangled and mud in the long winter coat, and for a dreadful, disloyal moment Mary felt ashamed of him and quailed before the expected criticism. The pony remained quite self-possessed, stepping forward daintily to sniff at Brogan's pockets.

'Well, little man, looking for sweeties are you?' He stroked and patted the little animal, paying particular attention to his belly and back legs. Then, with a swift movement he picked up the metal water bucket and dropped it with a loud clang. The pony jumped, snorted and went to sniff the bucket.

Brogan laughed. 'Takes more than that to upset you old stager, eh? We shall have to see about smartening you up.' He marched off to get brushes and combs, leaving Mary staring. Grooming horses, even the superior Knight Errant was, in Brogan's opinion, a job for women. She returned to the house to finish stuffing the goose.

By evening the children were beside themselves with excitement. They had helped to decorate the Christmas tree, holding each glass ball and tinsel garland with reverence. Pat put the plug on the lights and they all stood round in the gathering dusk for the lighting up ceremony.

'There you are – Christmas!' he declared.

'Oh Mummy, it's like stars,' breathed Anna.

'Mum, Mum, Mum!' bellowed Ben, hands

reaching and clutching for the sparkling jewels. In the end they made a barricade from the clothes airer, an obstacle which Ben viewed as an assault course provided by kind providence entirely for his amusement. He was carted bodily off to the kitchen to eat fish fingers and prepare for bed. The tension of the night was beyond him but his sister was in turmoil. By seven o'clock, the ritual of hanging the stocking completed, she was in tears.

'I don't — I don't — I don't want Father Christmas,' she sobbed and Mary started to laugh. Seen from her daughter's viewpoint Father Christmas must indeed be a shady character, creeping into people's bedrooms in the middle of the night. He was only one step removed from a burglar and yet, it seemed, her parents were powerless to keep him away, in fact they encouraged the rascal.

'Never mind darling,' she soothed, unpinning the sock, 'we'll leave this downstairs for Father Christmas to fill and then Daddy will bring it up here. Will that do?' She smoothed the tangled curls, plumped the pillow and switched off the light.

The grey dawn, so cold that there was ice on the insides of the windows, saw a very different Anna, racing through the house in her thin nightie clutching an armful of knobbly parcels.

'He's been, he's been!' she shrieked and Mary opened half an eye. She was tempted to order the little girl back to bed but one look at the flushed cheeks and delighted grin and she heaved herself up. She heard the boiler gurgle into life as she lifted a bewildered Ben from his cot and by the time she returned Patrick was awake. They tucked themselves beneath the covers in an uncomfortable row, elbows and heels poking painfully as excitement mounted. All was over in a sticky, noisy half hour, leaving a tide of paper lapping round the bed.

'But, Mummy,' queried Anna combing the hair of a new doll, inexplicably christened Tango, 'where has Father Christmas put my pony?' She looked worriedly around as if it might somehow be hiding beneath a toy engine or inside one of her plastic saucepans.

'If he's brought one I should think it would be in the stables,' mused Pat.

'Tell you what, I'll go and have a look while you get dressed.' He scrambled into some clothes and rushed off, leaving Mary to persuade two wriggling children to stand still for at least the time it took to put on jeans and a jumper.

The wind caught them the moment the door was opened, worrying them like a wild dog with a lamb, glad to have something to chew. The pony gazed at them enquiringly; red ribbons decorated his mane and tail and a tinsel garland hung round his neck.

'Oh Pat, he's beautiful!' gasped Mary.

'Grand little chap, isn't he?' agreed Pat.

'Oh, Mummy, is he all mine? Father Christmas doesn't want him back?'

'No, he's all yours,' assured her mother, 'provided you let Ben have a turn now and then.'

'He can have turns when I'm tired,' declared Anna. 'Stand up, old lad.'

She walked confidently to the pony and gave him a slap, a miniature Edna.

Once round the yard and they were blue and

gasping with the cold. Only Anna wanted more and she could hardly close her gloved fingers round the reins. She was summarily removed from her perch and thrust into the kitchen to recover next to the Aga.

'Do you think it's going to snow?' asked Mary. The tales of streams frozen solid and drifts higher than a man had seemed laughable in the milk and honey days of summer, but not today.

'Too cold perhaps. I don't know.' Their eyes met over steaming mugs of tea. 'Here. For you.' Pat was holding out a small parcel.

She unwrapped it with stiff fingers, wondering how to feign pleasure if it was a horse's head brooch. It was not. The dim morning light gleamed on silver and sapphire blue. Silent, she slid the bracelet on to her wrist, an incongruous sight next to the thick ribbing of her sweater. She tried to speak but the tears came.

'Don't you like it?'

'It's the most beautiful present I've ever had,' she whispered. Sniffing, she tried to smile. 'And I've got something for you.'

It was with some trepidation that she gave him a shooting waistcoat and a book called *The Amateur Gun*. He was a keen shot but rarely managed to accept any of the invitations he received. Nonetheless he seemed pleased.

The snow came on Boxing Day, huge wet flakes whipped into swirls by the wind, blotting out the sky in minutes. Work outside was a battle against the cold, doors frozen shut, metal catches burning fingers. Mary milked in the quiet barn, comforted by the small noises of the cow cudding, jumping involuntarily when she coughed. The snow cast an eerie white light over the steading, making it appear fragile and impermanent. It was hard to believe that the grey walls had withstood hundreds of years of the worst that the hills could provide and had been there still to welcome each spring. It was harder to believe that there would be another spring. The world would be cold, wet and white for ever.

'Thank God we've no stock in the fields,' gasped Brogan, bringing a rush of cold air into the kitchen. His coat and boots dripped pools on to the floor.

'I've made some soup,' said Mary, handing him a mug. It was thrilling to see how hard it was snowing. She secretly hoped for it to be feet deep, but in the evening it stopped and the frost came. Nonetheless the road was impassable and it was clear that it would be some days before anyone could get through to them. The snow had drifted, cars had become trapped and until these were removed the snow plough was useless. They settled down to days of isolation and found it surprisingly enjoyable. Once the stock had been fed – there was no question of exercise – they were free to do exactly as they liked.

On a clear, cold morning they went sledging in the snowy fields, sliding down sitting on plastic sacks. Brogan and Anna were typically reckless, not braking until the last minute, often with disastrous results. Time and again they hurtled head first into the hawthorn hedge, crawling out bruised and prickled only to pick up their sack and do it again.

Mary and Ben, in silent agreement, made a ponderous descent at halfspeed. Afterwards they sat in the kitchen drinking hot soup and wondered whether to spend the afternoon playing Ludo or watching old films on television. Mary sighed in content.

'This is lovely, almost like when Stephen was alive,' she said without thinking. There was no reply. She glanced at Brogan and saw that he was staring fixedly at his mug. 'I just meant – like a proper family. No Tim or anyone –' She had the feeling she was only making it worse.

He rose to his feet. 'By the way, I shall be going to Ireland for a few weeks. Fred wants to buy some horses and I can see my family at the same time. I might ask Tim to come along, it might amuse him.' He went out into the yard, not bothering to find a coat.

Mary mentally cursed her stupidity, she should know by now that he hated her to talk of Stephen, however obliquely. It would be so much easier if she knew what his feelings for her were. As time had gone on, they had become comfortable together and sometimes even friendly, but too often they turned to claw. Not in bed of course but she discounted the sex, it deceived. For her part she knew much of the conflict was rooted in her own insecurity, but for him – there was a hardness she could not penetrate. He had loved Barbara with a youthful passion that had turned bitter and he could never hope to regain that, nor would she wish him to. She and Stephen had travelled that road together and had come through to the wide and sunny plains of friendship, understanding and accord. This was what she sought to recapture, but Patrick? He seemed more inclined to demand devotion in return for supporting her and the children, but to give nothing of himself. He would probably like her to be madly in love with him so that he could gaze upon her fawnings with Olympian detachment. You'll wait a long time for that, she thought fiercely, fastening Ben's nappy so tightly that it was almost a straitjacket. He went pink and patted worriedly at his bottom, saying 'Mum, Mum' in a bewildered way. She relented and let it out.

Did Brogan think she would beg him to stay, she fumed?

'I will manage,' she announced, somewhat to Anna's surprise. After all the girls would be there, the baby would wait until April and the weather man had forecast a thaw. She did not need Brogan.

Sure enough, it was raining when she woke the following morning, a drizzle that turned the snow's magic into grey, slushy reality. Life returned with the rivers of mud that flowed into the yard. The road was flooded near the village and it was mid afternoon before Edna and then Susan appeared.

'Er – I don't think Mandy's coming back,' said Susan shyly.

'What? Why ever not?' Edna had lost none of her sharpness over Christmas.

'She rang me. She's got a job with a racing stable. Thinks it'll be more fun.'

'More boys you mean,' snarled Edna and Mary had to agree. Racing stables tended to be somewhat lusty; Mandy would be in her element.

The rain continued that night and all the next day as Brogan and Tim prepared to leave. Everyone sloshed about looking bedraggled with the exception of Tim, who was immaculate in bright yellow sailing oilskins.

'Thinks he's at bloody Cowes,' muttered Brogan,

but Mary ignored him. She was getting quite good at it.

'Do I detect a frost?' cooed Tim into her ear as she stood at the sink.

'Go to hell.'

'Oh dear, we are touchy today. Is the nasty man being horrid to you?'

'Thank God you're going to Ireland. Perhaps the boat will sink.'

'We're flying actually.'

'Even better, I can pack a bomb with your socks.'

'What, and lose dear Patrick too? Things must be bad.'

She did not reply and pushed past him to the table. He hung around whistling for a few moments before going into the yard.

'See you in three weeks,' said Brogan awkwardly.

'Is that all?'

'Oh, for Christ's sake. Look Mary – you'll be all right, won't you?'

'Please don't worry. No doubt we shall survive.'

'If you didn't want me to go you could have said so! But it would have choked you, wouldn't it?'

'Yes, it would,' said Mary, meeting his eyes for the first time. 'I can manage perfectly without you, thank you. Goodbye.'

He stood for a moment, then swore violently and stormed out, slamming the door. All the plates on the dresser trembled and chinked. She sank into a chair, ashamed to find her knees weak and her eyes wet with tears.

Chapter 13

Things began to go wrong almost at once, starting with a telephone call from Susan's widowed mother. She had fallen on the ice and cracked her ankle and she wanted Susan at home to look after her. Mary was dubious, feeling that Brogan would have been firm in a refusal, for Susan was not an only child and she was needed here. But in the face of tearful distress she gave in and Susan was despatched to the bedside. Edna was scathing.

'How are we supposed to manage?' she demanded. 'Are you going to muck out, work horses, clean tack? Well, are you?'

'I'm sorry, Edna. Perhaps we can get some help from the village. I'll do what I can, you know that.'

'You'll do nothing of the sort, you work too hard as it is,' relented Edna. 'I'll cope.'

'We always seem to be saying that, you and I,' sighed Mary. 'Women's Lib has a lot to answer for.' Edna nodded despondently and they sat together in a moment of rare harmony.

The weather became bitter and Mary and Edna slithered around all day on the icy ground. Ben and Anna fell over so often that they refused to go out and Mary had to do all her outside work in short snatches interspersed with dashes to the house to see what havoc the children had wrought. Once she found them merrily crayoning on the walls and she was suddenly so angry that she rushed out again and went to talk to Violet. She dropped hot tears on the cow's back and felt bereft. When she returned the mural was even more extensive but this time she could be rational. After all, it was hardly their fault when she left them alone so much. Susan had spoiled her, always willing to look after the children at a moment's notice, fitting in her other work as and when she could. It had not seemed such a luxury at the time but now she saw it for what it was.

Once again, the horses could not be worked.

'We should have a covered school,' fumed Edna, as they sat together in the kitchen one evening.

'He won't spend money when he doesn't mean to stay,' said Mary flatly.

'What? You mean he's going to move?'

'I should think so. Back to Ireland probably. That might be what this trip's about, I don't know.'

'But what about . . .?' Edna met Mary's stony glare and subsided.

'I shall have to think about another job, then,' she said at length.

'Oh, I should think he'd take you with him. But you could always work for Tim, you'd like that wouldn't you?'

Edna coloured and looked confused. 'I don't think so,' she muttered. 'I'm not so stupid I can't see what he's like. Buttering me up suits him, that's all.' Her misery was obvious and pathetic.

'Edna, please don't be upset about him, he's a conceited worm. There'll be someone who'll see how nice you really are.'

The girl sniffed. 'Who's going to fall in love with someone like me? I'm too big and clumsy, I don't know the first thing about clothes, in fact all I do know about is horses. Men fall for you so easily, you don't know what it's like to be me.'

'I'm not doing so well either,' sighed Mary and went to put the kettle on. 'Let's have some coffee and talk about something more cheerful.'

Another batch of calves was ready for market but Mary felt too tired and ill to go. She had not felt like this in either of her two previous pregnancies and it worried her. She lay at night waiting for the baby to kick, sure it was dead, then filled with short-lived relief when the movement finally came. Third time unlucky she thought, running through the various deformities the child might have. Spina bifida seemed most likely with Down's syndrome a close second. She mentioned her fears to no one and was not comforted by the doctor's bland assurance that all was well. If it was, then why did she feel so ill? He was only being kind, she would know the truth soon enough and he did not want to worry her.

Eventually she asked Edna to take the calves. They were getting far too big for the little pens and had voracious appetites, besides which they set up a hideous bellowing whenever Mary came into view.

'All you think about is food,' she grumbled as she piled yet more hay into the boxes. 'I wish I was a cow.'

Edna loaded them into the wagon without complaint, which only added to Mary's guilt.

'I do hope it's not too much bother,' she quavered for the third time.

'Go and lie down, do,' said Edna firmly, and Mary went.

Shortly after Edna left for York market it started to snow, at first just a few flakes blown by the wind but gradually increasing until the day became a mist of whirling white. Mary stood at the window peering out into the blizzard, willing it to stop. Edna must get back, she must. By half past three it was dark. Mary jumped as the phone shrilled and ran to answer it.

'Edna? Edna, is that you?'

'Yes, it's me.' The line crackled and buzzed.

'You sound very faint. Where are you?'

'I'm at Sam Downes's. I can't get through, the road's solid. The drifts are really deep, I've never seen anything like it. Will you be all right tonight? I might make it in the morning.'

'Of course I'll be all right. I'm just so relieved you're safe, I had visions of you being stranded. Come back when you can, I'll manage.'

She hung up and went again to the window, feeling none of the confidence she had tried to send down the phone. The voices of the children drifted from the sitting room and she gave herself a mental shake. What was a little snow, after all, it would be gone in a day or so. As she had said, she would manage. She went to fetch her boots, for animals must be fed whatever the weather.

Edna sat in Sam Downes's big, stone-flagged kitchen and shivered. The miserable fire in the old-fashioned grate made almost no impression on the dank air and her breath rose in clouds.

'Bit nippy I'm afraid,' apologised Sam.

'Oh no, no.'

'Perhaps you'd like a drink.'

'Coffee would be nice.'

'Oh. Yes. Now, where's that jar.'

'I'll do it if you like.' At least it would stop her freezing to death and her lack of domesticity was as nothing compared to Sam's incompetence. He meekly accepted her brew and made appreciative noises.

'I'm sorry to land on you like this,' she said.

Sam spluttered into his cup. 'Only too happy. Not everyday I get a lady like you on the doorstep. Thing is – what will people say?'

'What do you mean?' Edna's bossy manner was returning.

'Well – your reputation.'

She was cast into confusion. No one ever thought of her as a real, live woman with a reputation to lose, it was always only Edna, and she didn't count. She looked up at the burly farmer and blushed a deep, rosy red.

'I'm sure I don't mind about that,' she said gruffly and jumped to her feet. 'Let's see what I can do about that fire.'

When she went to bed that night Edna felt as if she were in some incredible dream. Sam hovered about her, snatching coal scuttles from her hand as if they were poisoned, rushing to open doors and pull out chairs. So unused was she to this that they frequently wrestled with door handles and chair backs, each jumping dramatically if their hands so much as touched. He accompanied her to the door of her room and said goodnight so formally that she was tempted to laugh.

'May I – may I call you – Edna?' he said hoarsely.

'Oh. Well yes, if you want to – Sam?' She swallowed convulsively, went hot all over and turned to dash into her room. The door was stuck but she gave a mighty heave and forced it open so violently that she fell in a heap on the floor.

'Edna – my dear – are you all right?' Sam was bending over her, lifting her as if she was the most fragile porcelain.

'My big feet. I'm so clumsy!' wailed Edna.

'You? Big? I never saw a more handsome woman. The first time I saw you on a horse I said, there Sam, there's not many like that these days, more's the pity. That's a really fine woman, that is. Hardly had the courage to speak to you, I can tell you.'

'Shouldn't have thought you'd notice me with Mary around', said Edna with an embarrassed laugh.

'Mary? Well she's nice looking in her way, I suppose. Bit scrawny for my taste though, all big eyes and hair, looks as if she could do with a decent meal. Wears all those floaty bits and pieces too.'

Edna could hardly believe it. Here, in real life, was a man who thought she was beautiful, enormous hands, beaky nose and all. Odd that she had never really noticed Sam before. He was very – comforting. She sighed in content, casting a last look round the grim little bedroom with its brown paint and faded wallpaper before turning out the light. A true Yorkshire farmer, Sam's money never showed. Not everyone's idea of heaven perhaps, but enough for her. More than enough.

During the night the wind rose again, bringing with it further snow and biting cold. By morning the earth had lost all sign of man and had become supernatural, the thin light sparkling diamonds from the blanketing white. Roads and hedges had ceased to exist and the isolated steadings were reduced to insignificant huddles of snow-spattered stone, hardly noticeable. Edna scratched at the ice on a window and gazed in amazement at the scene. There was no way she could return to High Wold House today and she felt a tremor of anxiety as she thought of Mary alone there.

A knock came on the door.

'Edna – I've – er – I've brought you a cup of tea. Thought you might like it.'

'That is kind of you. Just look at the snow!'

'Aye. Be with us a fair time this will.'

She nodded, touched to see that Sam had abandoned his ancient green sweater in her honour and was looking uncomfortable in his go-to-market tweeds. Her own choice was limited to the jeans and jumper she had come in, but she rummaged in her bag for a lipstick. She rarely wore make-up but today, she felt, was special. Dancing downstairs she felt light-hearted and for once irresponsible, pushing away the tiny niggle of doubt. Anyway with snow this deep there was nothing she could do. This was to be her day and she intended to enjoy it.

There was a very different awakening for Mary, although the scene from her window was much the same. Loneliness had never frightened her before but then, she thought, she had never been truly alone. Friends and neighbours had always been within reach, albeit at the end of a ten-minute drive but there should she need them. No amount of need would bring them now. Her eye lighted on the telephone and she smiled in relief.

How stupid of her to panic like that, if anything went wrong she had only to lift the receiver and they would send a helicopter; she had seen it on television, fit young men in combat jackets rushing to the aid of stranded farmers. Comforted, she dressed and began the day.

The work was unending, and made so difficult by the snow that she had to force herself only to concentrate on the immediate task, refusing to think of all that was left to do. If she allowed her mind to jump ahead she simply ground to a halt, defeated by the enormity of it, and she could ill afford such wasted moments. January days are short at the best of times and if the snow came again she would have to retreat inside. The leaden sky spurred her on and she struggled round the boxes, up to her knees in snow, throwing great bundles of hay to the animals. The water pipes in the yard were frozen and she spent hours lugging bucket after bucket of water from the one working tap. When she came to High Time he rushed to the door, trying to bite, but she waved and shouted, driving him away so that she could thrust a bucket in. By two o'clock she was exhausted but she had finished, and she went inside to make the children some lunch. They were not hungry having spent the morning stuffing chocolate biscuits and she was too tired to eat. What would happen tomorrow, she thought, when there are no more chocolate biscuits? She was dropping to sleep in the chair, giggling at the thought of summoning a helicopter for an urgent consignment of sweets, when the lights went out.

At intervals over the next two days she found

herself muttering 'I will manage' and 'I can cope' in an attempt to strengthen her resolve, but the words had an increasingly hollow ring. No electricity meant no heating, no lights, no television, no radio. Fortunately they had the Aga and the coal fire in the sitting room but that was all, and the hours between darkness and the children's bedtime, lit only by the flicker of candles, were a triumph of playacting.

'I'se frightened, Mummy,' Anna would wail, struggling to climb into a lap already occupied by Ben.

'Good heavens, why? Look what fun it is, having candles. I'm not frightened and Murphy isn't either, are you, Murphy?'

The dog gave her a sideways look and crawled under the table.

'Thank you, Murphy,' she murmured. 'I don't think the wolves would have had much to fear from you.' She wished she hadn't thought of wolves, the night was tailor-made for red-eyed, slavering brutes to appear out of the dark to scratch at the door.

'Let's play trains,' she cried, too loudly, but the children jumped up in excitement. Twenty minutes of chuff-chuffing and it was tea-time. 'Baked beans, your favourite.'

Even Ben looked askance, for this was the fourth time in three days, but there was nothing to be done. The freezer was clamped firmly shut and she dared not open it for fear of ruining the entire stock of food. She might have to tomorrow, but for tonight it was baked beans or starve.

When the children were in bed she sat huddled by the Aga and admitted her defeat. Perhaps if

Edna had come back, or if the electricity had not failed, or if she had not been pregnant, then it could have been all right. But it was not all right and she was increasingly anxious. This morning she had slipped in the barn and banged her head. What if she had been knocked unconscious, what would have happened to two small children left alone, up here, in the worst winter the country had seen for years? She wished she could blame someone for her plight, but the only name that came to mind was her own. Brogan would have stayed if she had asked him. It was time to ask for help.

As she lifted the phone her thoughts were on the conversation she was to have and it was seconds before she realised it was dead. It could have been like this for days but she had been so immersed in the struggle to keep going that she had given no thought to the lack of calls.

'Just as well I didn't know before,' she said firmly, trying to calm the flutter of her heart and the sick churning of her stomach. 'After all, the snow can't last for ever.' Neither can we, murmured a small, insistent voice.

Always before in times of strain she had found comfort in her possessions, the hand-knitted tea cosy or the print of York Minster bought on a rare family outing with Stephen when Anna was very small. Tonight even these deserted her, looking alien in the yellow light of the candle. Stifling sobs of panic she rushed to the stairs, desperate to hide beneath the bedclothes and shut out the world. The banging of a door broke the silence and her mind froze. It came from the yard. Who – or what – was out there?

'Do be sensible,' she whispered severely to herself and tiptoed to the window, dragging a reluctant Murphy with her. He was if anything more miserable than she, but at least he was warm and alive.

The yard was brilliant with moonlight and there, stark against the snow, huge and unreal, was a horse. He stood proudly, sniffing the air, his breath curling in plumes from his nostrils. Mary giggled with relief for escaping horses, if not exactly common, were at least usual enough not to occasion terror. She was halfway to the back door when a thought struck her. The horse had no rug on, in fact he was unclipped. Her thoughts whirled madly and then crystallised, for there was only one horse it would be. High Time.

Wrapped in a blanket she sat at the window and watched him as he circled the yard, tramping the snow at a walk only to break into a brief, plunging gallop which ended abruptly as he met the deep drifts at the entrance.

'Why can't you run away somewhere,' she hissed, but she knew he would not, preferring to stay with the other horses in the comparative shelter of the buildings. She contemplated leaving him there and staying safe in the house until someone came, but she knew she could not. It could be days and the very thought of Violet's pain if she was not milked upset her, let alone the lines of patient horses waiting trustfully for food that would not come. It was her fault High Time was out and she would have to put him back.

She rose purposefully to her feet and fetched the large stiff broom from the cupboard, not much as a weapon perhaps but the best she could do.

When the horse was rummaging in the farthest corner from the house she opened the door and crept silently along the wall to his box. Once there, she pinned the flapping door back and crept on her way, fetching hay and feed as quietly as she could. The horse knew she was there of course, she had no illusions about that, but as yet her presence had not alarmed or annoyed him. Having made his stable as inviting as possible, she resumed her cautious progress until she was behind him and could drive him towards it. The night was so quiet that she could hear the flutter of birds roosting in the warmth of the barn and when she spoke her voice startled even her.

'Come on lad, move along there.' As she said it she knew he was coming for her and she dived for the nearest door, flinging herself inside only to hear him thud against the wood, squealing in fury. A soft nose touched her and she leaped, but it was only the little pony, welcoming an unexpected visitor. The huge head of the gelding loomed over the half door, peering at them, and the pony snuffled in disapproval. Mary rubbed his neck affectionately. 'I wish it was you out there, pony. If you'll excuse me?' She picked up her broom and thrust the bristles into High Time's face, roaring at him to go back. At first it only seemed to enrage him but a particularly determined thrust drove him back and he careered off to the far wall, kicking up fountains of snow.

Quickly Mary slipped from the box and followed him, always prepared to dive into a doorway if need be, but the bait of food and warmth were too strong for the animal's confused fury. After endless moments of indecision he picked his way

188

into the stable and began to eat. Mary covered the
five yards in a second, slamming the door hard,
too hard, for the horse came for her as she
struggled with the bolts. Once again she wielded
her broom, dealing a vicious crack across the nose
for this time there was to be no slipped catch. She
could not go through this again. So tired she was
drained of all feeling, she staggered to the house.
The stairs might have been Everest for all the
chance there was of climbing them and she sank
with her blanket to the floor in front of the Aga.
Sleep came as the first hot tears of reaction
scalded her cheeks.

'What's the matter, Mummy?' Anna was
standing over her, brow furrowed and the blue
eyes anxious.

'Nothing. Nothing. Just tired. Be all right.' It was
impossibly hard to get to her feet and the baby in
her womb was a dragging weight. She leaned
against the Aga but there was no warmth. The fire
had gone out.

The coke was frozen together and the metal
handle of the shovel burned her hand but she
laboured on, some part of her mind watching
amazed at the struggles of this pathetic woman.
When she saw the man coming towards her it
occurred to her that she might stop, but she kept
on in case she had imagined him. He looked quite
unreal, vast in his layers of clothing, frost caking
several days' growth of beard.

'Patrick?'

'I came as soon as I could. Are you all right?'

She put a hand to her head. 'No. No, I'm not all
right at all. Oh Pat, I'm so glad to see you!' Under
other circumstances she might have hugged him,

but strength had deserted her. She merely leaned against him letting the relief flow through her.

She slept as never before, without dreams, never wanting to wake. In the evening Brogan brought her some soup and she dragged herself to the surface. The food revived her.

'High Time got out.'

'Oh my God. What did you do?'

'Chased him with a broom. Can we get rid of him, Pat, he – he frightens me.'

She lifted her eyes to his face and it seemed so dear, so familiar with its odd lopsided cheek that she started to cry and to talk at the same time, telling him just how bad it had been and how much she wished he had been there. At last, when there was nothing left to tell and his jumper was sodden with tears she said, 'Do you think the baby will be all right?'

A finger stroked her cheek. 'Why are you worried?'

'I don't know, I just feel so tired all the time, even before all this, and the doctor never says anything, just see you next month Mrs Squires, take your iron pills, and sometimes at night I think about it and I've been lucky twice after all so perhaps the third time . . .'

His arms were round her and her face was buried in his shoulder and none of it seemed quite so bad. After a time he said, 'Next time you see the doctor I'll come with you. OK?'

She nodded sleepily. 'How did you know to come?'

''My dear girl, news of the worst weather for over fifteen years even filtered through to Ireland. When I couldn't get through on the phone I rang

Sam Downes and Edna was there and she told me you were on your own. I'd have been here days ago but the airport's closed, I had to come by sea, and then the motorway's blocked. I walked from the village, of course. Can't think why Edna didn't call for help though, I shall have a few words to say to her. She must have known the power was off.'

'It wasn't too bad until then.' A thought struck her. 'How did you manage with Violet?'

He laughed and gave her a shove. 'Move over, I'm freezing. Well, I tried but she made it pretty clear she thinks I'm an idiot. Still, I got enough to make the kids some porridge.'

'Is that all? She's giving three gallons!'

'She kept knocking the bucket over.'

'Sounds like Violet. If you're coming to bed hurry up, you're letting the cold in.'

'Stop grumbling woman, I thought you were glad to see me.'

Mary gave a contented sigh 'You could very well be right,' she murmured.

The thaw came suddenly in a deluge of cold rain that reduced the white mountains to muddy little hills overnight. The snow plough made a belated appearance, thundering past majestically and deluging the unwary.

'I don't know why he bothered,' said Mary, 'another two hours and you could have wheeled a bathchair up the lane.'

But the children were thrilled and rushed about being 'snow ploughers' and throwing things at people. At lunchtime the lights came on and in mid-afternoon Sam Downes's Volvo drove in.

'Hello, Edna,' said Patrick pointedly.

'Hello, Paddy. I didn't know you were here.'

'And where the hell have you been for the past week?'

'At Sam's. I couldn't get through, you know that.'

'You didn't damn well try, you mean. Have you any idea what Mary's been through up here alone? Now you may have had your differences in the past but leaving her in a mess like this was damn nigh murder!'

Edna stood before him, head bowed, fists clenched. Brogan drew breath for another onslaught but before he could begin Sam Downes stepped forward, placing an arm protectively round Edna's bony shoulders.

'Now see here young man, Mary's your responsibility, not Edna's. It's you who should never have left her here, baby coming and all. And it so happens that Edna was taking Mary's calves to market that day, which is why she was stranded and might have frozen to death for all you care.'

Brogan's blue eyes took in the spectacle of Edna's head resting on the shoulder of the burly farmer and his lips twitched. Rubbing his mouth he said mildly, 'And where is the wagon? Or is that too much to ask?'

'It's in my yard,' snapped Sam. 'Diesel's frozen. And what you can be thinking of getting a lady like Edna to drive that great thing I do not know, the steering's far too heavy. You've been taking advantage of her!' Sam brandished a thick finger under Brogan's nose and he took a pace backwards.

'Er – I can assure you I've never – well, let's talk about this another time, shall we?' He made as dignified a retreat as he could, well aware that he had been routed.

'Did you see that?' he chortled to Mary.

'I thought I was imagining things. Sam and Edna!'

'I thought he was going to challenge me to a duel. He says I've been taking advantage of her.'

'Oh dear. Well, I suppose he only means work and so on, and anyway that's true.'

'Like hell it is. Look, he's going.'

They watched in fascination as Sam plonked a large kiss on Edna's waiting lips and turned to go. But passion was too strong and he returned to clasp her once again in a lingering farewell before finally steeling himself to leave. Edna went into the house, flushed but triumphant. No one knew what to say.

'Did you have a nice time at Sam's?' asked Mary innocently and Brogan succumbed to a fit of coughing.

'Yes, thank you,' said Edna primly. 'Oh, by the way Paddy, I shall be out tomorrow night. Sam's taking me to dinner.'

'Oh. Good of you to let me know.'

'Well you've been taking it for granted that I'll be around most of the time and I think I should warn you that it's not going to be like that in future. Now, what is there to do?'

Within a week of Patrick's return High Wold House was in full swing once again. One cryptic phone call brought Susan rushing back and Tim had returned from Ireland with the dozen or so horses Patrick had bought. These were careering round the long meadow and Mary could make nothing of them.

'You can't see anything for hair and mud,' she complained.

'They've all got four legs, if that's what you mean,' replied Patrick, lighting a cigarette. 'We'll smarten three or four up and sell them on, the rest will just have to hang around until we've time to do something with them.'

'But that could be months!'

'You know that and I know that, but Fred wants to be a horse trader, thinks it's easy money, the silly sod.'

They were preparing the jumpers for the start of the season but they were beset by problems. The weather was cold and wet and the horses worked reluctantly, laying back their ears and clamping their tails against the wind. A constant interruption was the procession of girls for Mandy's job, mostly inexperienced, idealistic and unsuitable. Patrick eventually took on Carol, just out of school and appallingly shy but from a farming family and with some real idea of what the work entailed. She was very pretty, with auburn hair, freckles and a creamy skin that turned scarlet if anyone spoke to her. She was happiest with the horses and for once Edna did not take it upon herself to lick her into shape. Indeed, Edna was altogether changed and lived only for the moment each evening when Sam arrived to collect her. She was allowing her mannishly short hair to grow and took to wearing tweed skirts and boots in place of the ubiquitous jeans. Whenever she thought of the affair Mary mentally crossed her fingers, for the new Edna, if more glamorous, was also more vulnerable.

Chapter 14

Doctor Bateson looked up in surprise as Brogan accompanied Mary into the consulting room.

'Oh. Good morning, Mary. And Mr er . . .?'

'Brogan. Mary asked me to come with her.'

'I see.' He was distinctly chilly. But then he turned to Mary, his face softening, and said, 'And how are you today, my dear?'

'Very well thank you, doctor.' As always when she was in the surgery the little speech she had rehearsed deserted her and she told the meaningless lie. Brogan stepped in, his manner brisk and determined.

'Rubbish Mary, you're not at all well. She's very tired, Doctor, feels sick and faint. And she seems to think there could be something wrong with the baby, for no real reason. It's worrying her and I – I don't like to see her so upset. I want you to reassure her.'

The doctor stared at him over his spectacles for a long moment.

'We shall do what we can, Mr Brogan.' His tone became gentler. 'Why have you not told me this before, Mary?' She shook her head and mumbled something.

'Well, let's have a look, shall we?' He ushered her to the couch and pulled the screen, shooting Brogan a look of dislike before he disappeared behind it. If the man was so worried about her he could marry her, couldn't he?

The examination was long and thorough but the doctor made no comment until Mary was dressed. He looked thoughtfully at their tense faces.

'As far as I can judge,' he said slowly, 'there is a healthy but rather large baby in there. Now, if you wish I can make an appointment at the hospital for further tests but I really see no need. You are feeling tired, Mary, because you are working too hard and if you remember I had to speak to you about that when you were pregnant before.' He waved an admonishing finger at her and she blushed. 'The prescription is a few days' holiday and at least two hours rest each day. Now be off with you.'

They rose to go, laughing with relief.

'Oh Mary,' added the doctor, 'I take it Mr Brogan will be present at the birth?'

'Yes, doctor, of course,' said Mary blithely and skipped out.

'I will not!' declared Brogan as soon as they were outside, and watched the happy glow die from her face. 'I mean – do you want me there?'

'Of course I do! You've no idea, you need someone on your side in these places or they bully you to death. Please Pat – will you?'

'All right. If I'm home.' He resolved to make quite sure that he was not.

'You can come to the February show,' he said cheerfully as they drove home.

'Is that the holiday?' She should have seen this coming.

He nodded. 'Two days in a hotel. Want to come?'

'I don't have to cook or anything?' He shook his head. 'Then, yes please.'

It was only later that she became dubious, thinking of the curious stares of all Patrick's friends. It was the hotel that decided her, two days when she would have nothing to do. She pushed her doubts away and thought of the clothes she would pack instead.

According to Patrick it was a small indoor show but the lines of expensive wagons gave Mary pause for thought, as did the prize money set out in the programme. Even Patrick looked surprised when he saw the huge television vans parked near the entrance but after some enquiries came back with the news that they were filling in here because the football had been rained off.

'You'd better ring Fred, he'll want to watch,' said Mary and Patrick looked sour.

Pat and Edna knew everyone and once the horses were stabled they lost no time in catching up on the gossip. Mary felt out of it and mooched around disconsolately hoping no one would notice her. Suddenly Pat remembered she was with him.

'Mary – you're there are you, trying to hide or something? Come on, I want to introduce you to Tom Spence, I used to work for him.'

'How do you do.' She was immediately attracted to the small man with the weathered face and saw with horror that he was looking unashamedly at her bump.

'You never said you were married, Pat. And going into production too, you don't waste your time, do you?'

Mary licked dry lips but Patrick merely laughed.

'You can come to the christening, Tom,' he said easily and Mary felt a spurt of annoyance. He had it all ways, for as long as he wanted, for he knew she would not stand up and declare the truth in front of everyone.

'Come round for a drink,' Pat was saying, 'we're staying just down the road.'

She felt happier when they reached the hotel. It was small and cosy, with a log fire burning in the hall and pot plants at every window.

'Name of Brogan,' said Patrick and Mary once again ground her teeth. He was too good at this. She noticed a tall woman standing staring at them, beautiful in narrow velvet trousers and suede jacket, her honey blonde hair caught in a heavy bun at the nape of her neck.

'Paddy,' she said softly, and he turned at once, the colour draining from his face.

'Barbara.' They said nothing for a long moment.

'I didn't know you were married.'

'I'm not,' said Patrick.

Mary supposed she was in shock. She had asked for the key to the room, requested that tea should be sent up and had told Patrick with a brilliant smile that she was sure he and his ex-wife had much to discuss and she would go and lie down. He did not appear to have heard her. She climbed the stairs on legs that did not tremble and sat calmly on the bed waiting for the tea. After all, she told herself, this was bound to happen sooner or later. But why, oh why, now? Once the baby was born she was sure Pat would feel tied to her by more than the bonds of convenience, but these were slim threads when Barbara was here looking so wonderful and she was so huge and unlovely. There was a knock at the door and the motherly proprietress brought in the tea.

'Now dear, you put your feet up and have a little rest, I know how tiring it can be. Is it your first?'

'No, my third.'

'Ah, then you do need a rest, I'm sure. Is there anything else I can get you?' She withdrew and Mary sat and wondered how much she knew. Surely she would have given some sign if there was a passionate reunion taking place downstairs? The tea was scalding hot but she drank it in furious sips. The second cup was almost finished when Brogan came upstairs.

'Is there any more tea in that pot?' He was a little pale but otherwise quite normal.

Mary pushed the tray towards him. 'She's quite a stunner, isn't she?'

Brogan nodded. 'I've asked her to have dinner with us tonight.'

'You've what?' shrieked Mary, forgetting all her carefully planned restraint. 'With me in this condition and her looking like a fashion plate? You must be joking.'

'She is bringing her husband,' said Brogan mildly and Mary's mouth formed a round 'Oh' of astonishment.

She dressed for the evening with exaggerated care but the final result depressed her.

'I look like the side of a house,' she sighed. She was wearing a deep blue floor-length caftan, braided at sleeves and hem, which usually made her feel relaxed and feminine. Tonight she just felt huge.

'Come on, you look super,' said Brogan, taking her arm. He was very cheerful, which only depressed Mary further. It was what she would expect of someone fanning the flames of a broken romance.

Barbara and her husband were waiting in the bar. She was exotic in a plum-coloured woollen catsuit, gathered at the ankles, with a gold slave collar round her slim throat and gold bracelets on her wrists. Her husband was as tall as she and very good looking with an aquiline nose and piercing brown eyes. He was wearing a white polonecked jumper and collarless jacket, making Brogan's suit and tie look staid in the extreme. Barbara slid sensuously from her stool and took Brogan's hand.

'Paddy, I'd like you to meet Darrell.'

They were treated to a flash of white teeth before Darrell ordered champagne cocktails, much to the consternation of the lady behind the bar.

'You've forgotten where we are, darling,' sighed Barbara and he reluctantly changed the order to brandy and Babycham for Barbara and himself, beer for Patrick and gin and tonic for Mary.

'Bitter lemon,' said Patrick sternly and Mary gave him a weak smile. Pregnant or not, tonight she needed a drink but she was not up to a fight.

The conversation was stilted. It seemed that Barbara and Darrell had been married for a year. They both worked in television and led a life centred around London, seemingly an endless whirl of parties and film premières. Not a single domestic detail was forthcoming.

'Do you have any children?' asked Mary and at

once could have bitten her tongue out. Barbara gave a merry laugh.

'No, thank goodness. I'm not the maternal type.'

Mary saw Patrick take a desperate gulp of his beer.

'Is this your first?' asked Barbara sweetly.

'My third,' said Mary, and left her to make of that what she would.

At dinner Darrell pushed the food around his plate and complained about the poor choice, the plain cooking and the service from the single, well-upholstered matron with a frilly apron pinned to the twin mountain peaks of her bosom.

'If you think this is bad, darling, you should see Ireland,' said Barbara, stroking Pat's hand with a long finger. He did not move away.

'Do you ride at all now, Babs?' he asked.

'I've grown out of that. I do yoga now, and meditation, of course. You're doing quite well though I see. You're with that funny little man Swallow, aren't you?'

Mary noted that she still took quite an interest in Patrick's affairs. They talked of showjumping for a while and Barbara and Darrell spoke of the problems of fitting it into a television schedule when you never knew how long it would last. They became very technical and Mary's thoughts wandered. In all the fuss she had forgotten to phone home, she really must do so first thing in the morning.

She realised everyone was looking at her. 'I'm sorry, I wasn't listening. Did someone say something?'

'I asked how long you had known Paddy,' said Darrell with a twinkle.

'Long enough,' said Mary, and caught Patrick's eye. They both laughed.

'What are you going to call the baby,' asked Barbara and Mary looked blank.

'Attila the Hun,' suggested Patrick, 'it kicks hard enough.'

Mary felt that she was giving an impression of a meek, baby-orientated housewife and she decided to give the conversation a new turn. 'Are you interested in cows?' she said.

'You mean for sailing? Yes, we have a friend with a yacht down there, go quite often in the summer as a matter of fact. When we can get away. Do you sail?'

'No. Actually I meant cows that you milk.'

'Oh.'

'Do you do any shooting, Darrell?' asked Patrick valiantly.

'Good heavens, no. Personally, I can find no pleasure in the slaughter of innocent creatures. I'm considering becoming a vegetarian.'

'Oh.' Patrick cut thoughtfully into his rump steak.

'I do believe in muesli,' said Barbara, 'so good for the bowels.'

'I beg your pardon?' Patrick was looking slightly taken aback.

'She means uncooked porridge with raisins and things, you know; we bought one packet and fed it to the dog and even he wouldn't eat it.'

'Oh.'

'What sort of dog do you have?' Barbara's social conscience was working overtime as she struggled to find some kind of common ground.

'An Irish Wolfhound.'

'How lovely! They are such courageous, majestic animals I always think.'

'Murphy's an abysmal coward, I'm afraid,' sighed Mary, aware that she was once again pouring cold water on the conversational spark. 'But he may improve,' she said hopefully.

'Would you like anything else?' asked the waitress.

'Brandy,' said all four in unison.

At midnight Mary yawned ostentatiously and declared that she simply must go to bed, pregnancy was so tiring. Patrick leapt to his feet with ill-concealed relief, saying that he, too, had a busy day tomorrow, but what an enjoyable evening it had been; Barbara and Darrell must come to see them in Yorkshire some time.

Neither spoke until they reached the bedroom.

'Holy Mary Mother of God,' said Mary, borrowing one of Pat's phrases and sinking on to the bed. 'What an awful evening.'

Patrick chuckled, tugging at his tie. 'We're a pair of country yokels and that's for sure, compared with those birds of paradise.'

Mary eased her shoes from her feet and wriggled her toes luxuriously.

'She makes me feel dowdy and boring.'

'That makes two of us. I can't believe I was ever married to her; the whole, miserable episode feels like a dream, or something I read. God, what a mistake that was.' He flung himself on to the bed and lay, hands behind his head, staring at the ceiling. 'If they ever come and visit us we'll have to have smallpox or something. This civilised restraint is a very bad idea.'

'Unzip me please,' said Mary, turning her back. He did so, running a slow finger down the warm flesh and neatly unhooking her bra.

'I can't wait for you to have that baby,' he said softly and she turned to look at him.

'Come on,' she whispered, 'let's go to bed.'

He needed her that night, he was hard with desire long before he held her in his arms. Was it really Barbara he wanted? Or Sylvia? Or any other woman who was slim and pretty and didn't cry out in pain as he tried to make love to her? In the end he held her close, his face in her breasts, and satisfied himself, murmuring that it didn't matter, he didn't mind. But Mary minded.

She lay awake in the night, thinking about Patrick and Barbara and the many, many times they must have loved. He was a good lover, tender and patient, with no sense of shame. Had Barbara taught him that? What had they done together? Stephen would never have done as Patrick had tonight, he would have burned and endured until at last she was properly available again. Stephen had been so very gentle. She wondered what Patrick thought of her performances, substandard surely when compared with the gorgeous, glamorous Barbara.

With a sigh she struggled to find a position that eased her back, her thoughts again straying to home. Would they remember to shut up the geese? The foxes were very daring after the hard winter. She had once had some ducks slaughtered by a fox and she had walked amongst the blood like a stretcher bearer in the trenches. Only one had survived and he was so badly shocked that he refused to leave the hut. They wrung his neck in the end, it seemed kindest. Odd that she should still remember his fluffed up feathers and miserable quack after so long. She turned over once again and slept.

Chapter 15

'This kitchen is a disgrace,' declared Mary. It was mid March and an early spring sun shone dimly through windows blotched with winter grime.

'Looks all right to me,' said Brogan, reading the post and eating breakfast at the same time. He had not yet noticed Ben's careful pile of alternate toast and letters, so Mary quietly removed the mess and wiped off most of the marmalade with the dish cloth. Tim grinned. He was in a rare good humour, for lately he had been moody and irritable, bending under the weight of Brogan's criticisms.

'Nesting instinct,' he said sweetly.

'And you're the cuckoo,' replied Mary.

Brogan got up. 'Don't you do it, get the cleaning woman in.' He gathered up his papers. 'My God, this lot only arrived ten minutes ago and it's already covered in jam. The place is bewitched.'

Left alone, Mary sprang into action, dragging the table into the hall and piling the chairs on top. The cleaning lady, Mrs Dobson, a dour efficient woman, was due tomorrow but it was her day for the bedrooms and she was apt to turn nasty if asked to deviate from her chosen path. She had once been asked to do the stairs on her sitting room day, simply because they were covered in bits of hay and straw, and it was three weeks before she could be prevailed upon to so much as open the sitting room door, let alone polish anything. No, if the kitchen was to be done Mary must do it herself.

She spent a busy morning scrubbing, polishing and tidying cupboards and at lunchtime was able to serve soup and sandwiches in surroundings that sparkled. No one noticed.

'Are you ready to go?' she asked. They were leaving for a show early the next morning.

'Just about,' nodded Brogan. A heavy sigh turned all eyes to Edna.

'What will Sam do without you?' teased Tim but Edna was too miserable to respond. She stared glumly at her plate.

'Can you spare Susan this afternoon?' asked Mary. 'I need some shopping.'

'She'd better get enough for a week, I don't want you left alone here,' said Brogan. He was becoming neurotic on this point and perversely Mary found it annoying.

When the dishes were done she sat down to read to the children. Her back ached and the gripping adventures of *Desmond the Donkey* did nothing to alleviate it.

'Come on everyone,' she announced. 'Let's go and watch the horses.'

Tim and Brogan were trying two of the Irish horses and the afternoon, though cold, was bright and springlike. Snowdrops were out in the orchard and the few daffodils that Murphy had omitted to dig up were coming into flower. She felt lighthearted and hopeful as she strolled to the paddock fence. Only four weeks to go and she would be thin again, perhaps able to climb the stairs without panting. Sometimes she felt she would stay like this for ever.

Brogan was lunging a big, unbalanced four-year-old and was having trouble steadying him. The horse was belting round the circle, apparently tireless, but at last he began to slow. Within minutes Pat had him trotting and walking on command and Mary wrinkled her nose. His horsemanship always impressed her.

'Oh dear,' she said suddenly and put a hand on her stomach. Was that, or was it not a contraction? She put it down to imagination and turned again to watch the horses, unable to suppress a slight tingle of excitement. If only it could be today! Refusing to think of it she turned her thoughts to Tim, who was for once showing patience with the reckless little mare he was schooling. It was the type of horse he loved, all fire and no brakes and it brought out the best in him. Mary leaned on the fence, enjoying the entertainment, but she tensed again suddenly. Another contraction, only minutes from the last.

'Patrick,' she called, 'could I have a word with you?'

'Wait a minute, love,' he said abstractedly, not turning his head. Mary shifted uncomfortably.

'Please Pat, it's important.'

'Five minutes . . . steady lad, steady.'

Another contraction was on its way. She took a deep breath. 'Patrick, the baby's coming. Now!'

The reaction was all she could have wished. 'What!' yelled Pat and his horse took off down the field at a flat gallop, alarming Tim's mount which promptly bucked him off.

'Well, not right this minute,' she said apologetically as Brogan thundered up to the fence.

'Are you in pain, look lie down, I'll fetch the car – or something. No, I'll ring the hospital, I'm sure that's what you're supposed to do. Er – you can hang on, can't you?'

'Relax Pat, things are only just starting. I'd better . . . oh!' She clung to the fence and puffed her way through the contraction. 'The house,' she gasped, 'I haven't packed my case.'

They made stately progress across the yard, stopping twice while Mary leaned on Pat and breathed hard. He was starting to look panicky and she began to giggle. She always felt unnaturally calm when she went into labour, a feeling which seldom survived the first real pain.

'Mummy's going into hospital to have your baby brother or sister,' she told Anna.

'But who will look after us?' asked the child, her eyes huge.

'Susan,' grunted Mary and sank into a chair, striving to look normal.

When she could move again she raced upstairs and burrowed for towels and nighties. Patrick trailed in her wake.

'Where's my sponge bag?' she demanded.

'I can bring it later, look we must go, it's a half-hour drive!'

'I must have everything or they'll be cross. My God, I haven't anything to take the baby home in.'

Patrick barred her way to the attic. 'It doesn't matter, I will bring it. Now come on!' He propelled her to the head of the stairs.

'Wait a minute, I think . . . oh!' She was standing in a puddle. Foolishly she blushed. 'I think the waters have broken,' she apologised.

'So get a move on! The baby could arrive at any minute.' His voice rose hysterically.

'Oh, it's not coming yet,' said Mary casually. 'And I must clear this mess up, Mrs Dobson will be furious.'

'Bugger Mrs Dobson,' roared Patrick and dragged her downstairs.

Tim was standing in the kitchen, his face streaked with mud.

'You have ruined my kitchen floor,' said Mary accusingly, 'so clean it up.'

'I only wanted to wish you luck,' he said in a hurt voice and today Mary was powerless to see beneath the little boy charm.

'Oh. Thank you. And leave the floor it doesn't . . . Oh God!' It was a vicious contraction that went on for ever. When at last it subsided she clung to Patrick, gasping.

'Was it bad?' he asked unnecessarily.

'The worst one is the one you think you're going to have,' she said with wry philosophy. 'We'd better go.'

The drive to Beverley was misery for Mary, the seat was too upright and she felt acutely uncomfortable. Absurdly, when they turned into the hospital gates she felt an urge to turn and run.

'Let's not bother,' she said suddenly.

'What on earth do you mean?'

'I won't have the baby today, I don't feel brave enough.'

He grinned, then saw from her white face that in some weird way she meant it. He took her hand. 'Be a brave girl,' he said softly. 'I'm here.'

She smiled wanly.

A contraction seized her as they approached the reception desk. The nurse took no notice.

'You are Mrs . . .?' she enquired brightly.

'Brogan,' said Pat and the woman looked puzzled.

'No it's Squires, gasped Mary, 'that's what it's booked under.'

'Oh yes, I suppose it is,' said Pat vaguely. 'Mrs Squires.'

'If you're quite sure,' said the nurse acidly, 'there's nothing else you'd like to choose?'

'That will do for now,' said Pat coldly. 'And if you'd hurry please, my wife is in pain.'

'I'm not your wife,' said Mary crossly as she was led across the hall. Several heads turned in surprise.

'This is hardly the time to argue about it,' he insisted.

'Well, we don't do weddings, I'm afraid,' said the nurse cheerfully. 'People usually try and fit those in before they get here. I take it you are the father?' He nodded. 'Just you go and sit down over there and we'll call you.' She ushered him through a door. Feeling excluded, Pat went to sit down, trying to ignore the interested stares of the other anxious relatives.

'Get undressed and someone will be with you in a moment,' the nurse was saying to Mary.

'Please . . .' she cried, but the door had closed and she was desperate to go to the lavatory. She looked wildly round the room for a bell and noticed another door, it was indeed a loo. With a sigh of relief she sat down and then felt very odd indeed, almost as if the top of her head was about to blow off. She took a gasping breath and started to push, leaping up the moment she realised what she was doing.

212

'NO!' she shrieked and staggered back into the examination room. Hurriedly she scrambled into a nightgown.

The door opened. 'Now dear, let's have all the details shall we?' said a large lady in a blue sister's uniform. 'Full name?'

'Please, I think . . .'

'Come along, dear, we've no time to waste.'

'But . . .'

'Full name?'

'I want to push, the baby's going to be here any moment!' she shrieked.

The sister sighed and put down her clip board. 'Is it your first?'

'No, my third.'

'Oh. Well, perhaps we'll have a look then. Lie down please.'

One swift feel and all was changed. 'Nurse,' called the sister, 'Mrs Squires to delivery at once, please. She's left it very late, I'm afraid she has missed her enema.'

'Shucks,' murmured Mary but was silenced by a basilisk stare.

'And I don't want to hear any foul language,' said the sister.

'But I only said . . .' she tailed off miserably as they forced her into a wheelchair. The speed of their passage down the corridor blew the hair back from her face.

'I want – I want Patrick,' she wailed as they flew through the doors of the steel and tile delivery room.

'I'll go and get him, dear,' said a small nurse with a kind smile. 'I'll only be a moment.'

The kindness unnerved her as the sister's

brusqueness had not and she felt tears rising in her throat. The delivery table was high, narrow and horribly precarious and she huddled miserably on it in her short white nightgown, longing for it to be over.

Every head lifted as the nurse came into the reception hall.

'Mr Squires?' she called and at first Patrick did not respond. Then he jumped up.

'Oh, you mean me I think. My name's Brogan but I'm the father.'

'Never mind, dear, we have lots of those,' said the nurse helpfully. 'Your – er – wife wants you. She's about to deliver, come along.'

She gave him no chance to refuse, whisking down the corridor in a swish of starched apron. Mary's strained expression dissolved into a beam of relief as he entered the room. She clutched his hand tightly.

'What do I do?' He felt feeble and inadequate.

'Just be here,' she said.

A contraction seized her.

'Deep breath, chin on chest, bear down,' intoned the sister and Mary struggled to obey, feeling the veins on her forehead bulging with the effort. She fell back with a gasp as the contraction passed. The room was filling up, presumably little else of interest was going on. Another contraction, and another, oh God how many more, she was so tired.

'Soon be over,' said Pat, reading her thoughts. Again the incredible pressure and this time the throng round the bed entered into the spirit of the thing, yelling 'Push!' as if watching rugby. If she could have found the breath she would have laughed at the indignity of it all, but instead she

214

leaned her damp forehead against Pat's arm. Again.

'I can see the hair,' yelled Pat suddenly. 'It's got black hair!'

'Just take it gently, dear, little pushes,' said the sister. 'Five minutes and it's over.'

Mary pushed and pushed again, in pain but caring nothing for it, anxious only to have it over. Suddenly, with a slip and a slither, it was there. She fell backwards, not giving it a glance.

'It's a boy!' yelled the crowd in unison, almost drowning the first, choking cry.

She opened her eyes to ask Pat if a boy was acceptable and was amazed to see his face wet with tears.

'Is it all right?' she asked worriedly and he clutched her to him.

'Oh darling,' he sobbed, 'everything's wonderful. Just wonderful.'

'What does he think you are, baby?' grumbled Mary, watching him flap tiny arms in a Babygrow three sizes too big.

'It was all I could find,' apologised Pat, 'all the smaller things were dresses and my son's not going to be a pansy.'

'All babies wear dresses at first, boys or girls.'

'This one doesn't.'

'I don't suppose you brought a horse for him to ride home, did you? We want to start as we mean to go on, after all. Come on, let's go.'

The sister was in the hall dealing firmly with a girl on the verge of hysteria. Under her iron gaze the sobs became quieter until the girl was sitting silent, her eyes wide.

'That's better,' admonished the sister. 'I won't have you upsetting everyone. There is nothing to be frightened of, as you'd know if you had attended our classes. But you girls always know best. Ah, Mrs Squires, going home I see.' Mary froze to attention. The sister drew back the shawl and looked long at the sleeping face. 'He's a beautiful baby, my dear,' she said softly. 'Enjoy him.'

'Thank you, sister.' She scuttled out to the car.

'Do you think she's human after all?' she asked Patrick.

'Hewn out of solid granite, more like. Is John all right in the carrycot?'

'Thomas is fine,' replied Mary.

'Not Thomas, I knew a creep called that at school.'

'Well not John either, it's such a stolid name.'

'What about Daniel?'

Mary was silent, turning it over in her mind. 'I like it,' she said at length. 'Daniel Patrick Squires, it's nice.'

His foot stamped on the accelerator. 'Daniel Patrick Brogan you mean,' he roared, overtaking a lorry on a blind corner.

'No I don't. And please be more careful, he hasn't got a charmed life. He's my baby and I'm Mrs Squires, so there you are.'

'He's my baby too, goddammit! Anyway, I've been thinking about that. It's time we got married, this situation is very bad for the children.'

Mary's breath caught in her throat. If she had been driving she would have aimed the car straight at a wall.

'I think I am the best judge of what is right for my children,' she said icily. 'Daniel will be registered

216

as Daniel Stephen Squires and you can go to hell.'

Patrick shot her a look of bafflement. 'You bitch!'

Mary met his gaze with a bland stare and then turned her attention to the scenery, seething with repressed rage.

In bed that night she lay and listened to the snuffling sounds coming from the cradle and wept silent tears into her pillow. Suddenly the form beside her erupted and switched on the bedside light.

'For Christ's sake, I can't stand the sniffing. What's the matter?'

Mary sniffed. 'Look, love,' he said gently. 'It's not my fault I'm not Stephen, you know. You've got to live with things as they are. If you want to call him Squires then OK, but please not Stephen. Please.'

A thin wail came from the cradle and Mary managed a wavering smile. 'Daniel Patrick wants me,' she said and swung her legs out of bed. In her absorption with the baby she never remembered to say that it was months since she had thought of Stephen with anything more than fleeting regret.

'I thought I'd come and look at my horses,' declared Fred Swallow, striding briskly from his Daimler. 'You've been taking things a bit too easily up here Paddy, my lad.'

Patrick stiffened as every head turned. 'What makes you say that?' he asked tautly.

'Missed the show last month, didn't you? With not a word to me. And you've done nothing with the horses you bought, nothing at all, and it's my money standing idle. I like my people to work, none of your Irish dawdling in Yorkshire, thank you.'

'Let's discuss this in the house, shall we?' snarled Pat, aware of Tim Parsons's smirking face.

'Nay, we'll see the horses,' rapped Fred.

They stood at the paddock fence in silent contemplation. Fred could not tell one from another and always before Pat had been prepared to give him an informative commentary, but today he said nothing.

'When will they be ready for sale?' demanded Fred. 'We made good money on the last lot, what's the matter now? They look really well, they do.'

Patrick shrugged. 'When I'm away at shows I can't be working horses.' Suddenly all his pent up rage at Mary, Tim, the lovelorn Edna, rose up and engulfed him. He swung to face Swallow, his voice low and furious. 'You're the one that wants me at every show, large or small, week in and week out. It's bloody stupid, the horses get stale and so do I. And then you want to start horse trading, and want to tell me how to do it. Christ, you can't tell a horse's arse from its ear!' He spoke with real venom, towering over Swallow's self-important little figure.

The man swallowed hard. While he wanted Pat to heel he had no wish to finish with him yet awhile. Success like his was hard to find, however much you were prepared to pay. 'Now look here Pat, I don't want to quarrel with you over this.'

'Is that so? Bawling me out in front of my staff, telling me I don't know my job, that's all touch your cap and pass the time of day, is it? Since I came in with you I've put you on the map, Swallow, but the more you get the more you want. You're a bloody vampire.' He turned and strode back to the yard, the shorter man almost running to keep up with him.

'Now, Paddy, I can see you're under strain,' he soothed as best he could while trotting. 'It was tactless of me to bring this up when you've a new baby in the house and everything. Why don't we forget it for now and look at the jumpers shall we?'

Patrick stopped and turned to face Swallow, so suddenly that Fred nearly bumped his nose on his chest.

'And let's pretend we're friends. Right, you pay the piper as you're so fond of telling me, so let's all dance to your tune. Come on.'

They began with Knight Errant, the wise old horse lifting his head with interest as they entered his box.

'Why are his legs bandaged like that?' queried Fred and Pat snorted.

'Because he's been pulled out at every tuppeny gymkhana for the past six months.'

They continued the round without speaking, finishing with Tim's two mounts. One started nervously as they approached and began to sweat while the other slunk away into the farthest corner in case they wanted him to come out and do something.

'Pretty pair aren't they?' asked Pat with heavy sarcasm and Fred innocently agreed.

'What about the horse that was ill?' he queried and Pat moved on to High Time. He paused to light a cigarette while Fred continued to the door of the stable and blithely opened it.

'No!' bawled Pat, extending a long arm and hooking his fingers in Fred's collar. The horse was taken unawares by Fred's rapid entrance and equally speedy exit and relieved his frustrations by squealing and thundering round the box. Fred adjusted his tie and cleared his throat.

'That horse is dangerous,' he quavered.

'Yes, isn't he just?'

'You're going to get rid of him I hope!'

'Good God, no. He's got real promise and I know how keen you are on winning, Fred. Couldn't waste a horse like that. He's starting work tomorrow, why don't you come and watch?'

'No, no thank you, Pat, as you know I like you to handle the practical side of things, it's my job to put up the money. Let me know if you've any problems, I'm always glad to help. Love to Mary.' He walked quickly to his car, his stride no longer a jaunty bounce.

Pat went to talk to Mary. 'He was scared witless,' he said with contempt.

'Not surprised, you frighten everyone at the moment.' Mary heaved yet another load of nappies, sheets and babyclothes out of the washing machine and sat down at the table. She yawned capaciously.

'Bad night again?'

She nodded. 'He had wind. At least I suppose it was that, sometimes I think he just likes watching me stagger round the floor at two in the morning. The others were never like this.'

'You should leave him to yell, you're too soft,' said Pat irritably. She did not bother to reply, he would never understand the invisible cords that bound her to the baby, pulling her to the cradle even before she was properly awake.

'If he wakes tonight, you leave him,' warned Pat. 'This is wearing you out.'

In truth he was jealous thought Mary, thinking of his set face as he watched her breastfeeding. She would be absorbed in the baby, crooning to him as he struggled to find the nipple, laughing as he guzzled away and she would feel Pat's eyes on them. The moment she looked up he would make some excuse to leave for he could not hide what he felt. He gave nothing yet demanded her all.

'Are you going to keep High Time?' she asked, changing the subject.

'Now I am, yes. He's my anti-Fred insurance, I only have to pull him out and Fred'll be gone.'

'He's not the only one. Anyway if he does get to a competition he'll be too busy savaging the audience to bother about the jumps. They mightn't like a horse that eats people. And what a job for you.'

Brogan leaned back in his chair, putting booted feet on the table. Mary did not dare protest. 'More fun than bawling Tim out night and day anyway.'

'What for now?'

He avoided her eyes. 'Oh, you know. Any more tea in the pot?'

That night Daniel woke at eleven, only an hour after he had been fed, and began to scream. They had just gone to bed and Brogan wanted to make love.

'Leave him,' he whispered, his lips travelling from shoulder to breast to plum-coloured nipple. Mary lay rigid, her mind filled with the baby's cry. Pat's hands were caressing her thighs and she pushed him away with sudden impatience.

'I must go,' she insisted, grabbing her nightgown, but a strong hand dragged her back to the bed.

'I said leave him,' he hissed, forcing her on to her back, her wrists held above her head. He rolled on top of her and thrust between her legs, making her cry out. He vented his anger on her with every brutal stroke until at last he was finished and lay panting beside her. Mary knew she should have felt ravaged and yet somehow she did not. She caressed his cheek with a gentle hand.

'That bloody baby's still crying,' she murmured and pulled the sheet over her naked shoulder.

He sighed heavily. 'I'll go.' He swung his legs out of bed and reached for his dressing gown.

'Mary. Mary, wake up, you've got to feed the baby.'

She clawed her way out of sleep to find a grey morning and Patrick standing over her, holding Daniel. The screams ceased the moment her breast touched the baby's cheek, his mouth searching for the milk. Pat got back into bed.

'Did you manage him all right last night?' she asked. 'I'm afraid I went to sleep.'

'I walked him up and down a bit and he went off.'

'Perhaps you've got the magic touch.'

He gave her a sideways look and grinned. 'Don't think I'll do it every night.' But in fact from then on she had only to lie still and he would go, quietly and without fuss. Once she went to offer help and found him downstairs in the rocking chair, crooning Irish lullabies. She felt an intruder and withdrew, leaving him alone in his private world with his son.

Chapter 16

Reluctantly and with much grumbling Fred approved Patrick's schedule for the season. It irked him to surrender but at the same time he had to acknowledge that unless he gave Pat more rope he would leave. It made Fred feel powerless, which he hated, and in retaliation he came back again and again to the subject.

'I don't see why you can't do more shows,' he insisted and then held up a restraining hand. 'I know your views but look at Tim, his horses come out twice as often as yours.'

'But they don't win twice as often, do they Fred?' Patrick sat on his temper, determined to retain control. He would choose his time to go and it wasn't yet.

'Aye, you're right there,' agreed Fred, for once in the mood to compromise. He had scored a little victory that day and could afford to be mellow, eating Mary's fruit cake and drinking Pat's scotch. They had sold two Irish horses to another stable, against Pat's advice but the price was good. Patrick wondered how pleased he would be if either of the nags started winning, as well they might. Damn Fred, for a clever man he could behave like a fool.

'Tim's settling down nicely then,' said Fred.

'No he is not,' replied Mary sourly. 'Look, I'm

sorry Fred, it would be different if he wasn't living in the house but I would like you to find somewhere else for him. We have little enough privacy as it is.'

'Complaining about me again, Mary?' said a lazy voice from the doorway. 'If you will make love here, there and everywhere you're bound to have some uncomfortable moments.' He tweaked her cheek to show that he was joking.

'It's you and your sneaky ways, Tim dear,' she said thinly.

'I think we've got a grand little team,' said Fred cheerfully, 'so let's drink to a good season.'

Mary sighed but obediently raised her glass. The constant bickering exhausted her, she was always waiting for the final bang, like a member of CND.

Patrick was approaching content. The travelling got him down of course but he loved to come home. There was peace in the house, a feeling of common purpose that had at its centre a small, pink baby. Life was never simple and the problems never went away, but when in the evening he sat and looked at Mary, and knew that overhead there slept three healthy, happy children, the emotion of it caught in his throat. If only he could hold on to it, this time of grace, and keep them all safe in the circle of his arms. But Mary did not want it. His happiness was tinged with foreboding.

He began to do a lot of work with High Time, almost to the exclusion of everything else, and it began to pay dividends. At first Pat simply tied him up and groomed him for long hours, until the horse was forced to relax in his presence. Once he could get a saddle on him he took him to the

farthest field and went right back to basics. The
slightest noise would send the horse into a
paroxysm of rage which he vented on the nearest
available object. As long as Pat remained on top
he was safe but on more than one occasion he had
hurdled the hedge, closely followed by a furious
horse.

But gradually things improved until grouse
flying up from under the horse's feet or the shout
of a farmer in a nearby field occasioned no more
than a shudder. His ability was undoubted and if
the aggression unleashed by his illness could be
harnessed Pat was sure he had a winner. He said
as much to Mary.

'Stephen used to say the same sort of thing
about our bull, and it nearly killed him,' she
replied and then winced as Patrick slouched out,
slamming the door. She should not have
mentioned Stephen now, especially since her
mother was coming to stay.

Brogan was away when Mrs Bennett arrived and
she and Mary spent a peaceful two days together.
The relationship seemed to function best when
they resumed their well-tried mother and
daughter roles and rejected any attempt to
communicate as one adult to another. The
children in no way impeded this since they were
subordinate to Mary and she was under her
mother's direction. It was Brogan who added the
unstable element.

'Mary, it is time Anna was in a dress, she wears
trousers far too much,' Mrs Bennett stated.

'Yes, she has some very pretty dresses too,'
Mary replied meekly.

'Trousers are the only practical wear for the

country,' broke in Brogan, casting a withering glance at Mrs Bennett's pale blue jersey suit.

This was a declaration of war and over the next four days Anna was whisked in and out of clothes like a Paris fashion model, into dresses by grandma and into trousers by Mary, who had to endure Pat's sarcasm every time he saw the child.

Then, there was Mrs Bennett's attitude to Daniel. 'You poor little thing,' she crooned, not specifying exactly what he was suffering from. 'What has he done to you, then?'

'Just what am I supposed to have done to him?' rapped Brogan.

'Oh! I didn't hear you come in.' Mrs Bennett tried never to be alone with him, but Mary was upstairs bathing Ben and Anna and there was no escape.

'Have you had a good day?' she tried feebly and he sneered.

'You're not so brave to my face, are you? Go on, what have I done to Daniel?'

Mrs Bennett took a deep breath and clasped her hands. 'If you must know you've made him illegitimate and in my day that was a dreadful thing for a child to be. I only hope things have changed.'

Brogan gave a hard laugh. 'So Mary hasn't told you, then? She's the one who's made him a bastard, not me. Madam likes her independence too much and after all, as you so often say, I'm not a patch on Stephen.' He almost spat the name and flung himself into a chair.

Mrs Bennett said nothing for a long moment. 'You're wrong Mr Brogan,' she said at last. 'I feel sure you would never let Mary down as Stephen did, leaving her destitute. Sometimes I just don't understand her.'

'That makes two of us,' said Brogan morosely. 'Would you like a drink?'

When Mary returned she found her mother decorously sipping gin and tonic and discussing bridge.

It was Mrs Bennett who first noticed that Carol was unhappy. The girl was always so quiet that Mary tended to overlook her but when her mother found her sobbing in a corner she was perturbed. The grooms were Edna's province but she was taking less and less interest and Mary felt guilty. She should have noticed.

'It's not the first time she's been crying,' said Mrs Bennett as she prepared to leave. 'Her eyes have looked very red several times. But she wouldn't tell me what was the matter, it's probably nothing, you know how things are at that age. But I think you should know.'

'Thank you, Mummy. I'll have a word with her today.'

They kissed and Mary stood waving until the car was out of sight.

She cornered the girl in the tackroom and saw that she did indeed look peaky, tired and strained with violet shadows beneath her eyes. But she insisted that nothing was wrong.

'Well, has somebody upset you, Carol?' Mary demanded at last. 'It's no use saying there's nothing the matter because I can see there is. Is it a boyfriend?'

Carol's huge brown eyes brimmed. 'He doesn't love me any more,' she wailed, and cast herself into Mary's arms.

'Who doesn't?' insisted Mary, mentally running through the contenders and finding only the butcher's boy, who had acne and was surely beneath even Carol's notice.

'Him! Tim! Mr Parsons,' sobbed Carol, and cried harder.

A horrible thought occurred to Mary. Carol's father was a strict, rather stupid man who had uttered dire threats about 'getting into trouble' on the only two occasions Mary had met him.

'You're not pregnant are you?' she asked, her voice squeaking with fright.

The girl shook her head. 'But he doesn't love me any more,' she said again and choked into her handkerchief.

Piece by piece the story came out. With Edna in love and Susan too cautious, Parsons had been without admirers and he had turned to Carol for company. Young, pretty and impressionable, she had fallen for him with an ease that he had found amusing at first, and then plain tedious. She would have died for him, and in return he exploited her, making her groom his horses and clean his tack for the scant reward of a few breathless kisses and easy compliments in the hay barn. If he had left it there Mary would have thought nothing of it, but he didn't. He borrowed money off her, although she earned a pittance, he made her clean his boots, sew on his buttons, cook meals for him at midnight. It was almost as if he was seeing how hard he could kick his dog before it no longer came when he called. Then he made her sleep with him. She was afraid, a virgin, and didn't want to, but Tim plucked her like a ripe plum. There was nothing to worry about, he'd be careful, and besides, he loved her. Didn't she love him? In a fever of love and self-sacrifice Carol stepped out of her jeans and let him use her as he liked. He pushed her back on the hay, forced himself between her virgin thighs and when she cried out told her to shut up or someone would hear. It was over in seconds, he zipped up, patted her cheek and told her to hurry up and get dressed, she had work to do. His parting gift was the used condom, with instructions to dispose of it.

Since then he had virtually ignored her; when she spoke to him he pretended not to hear, when he looked at her it was if she wasn't there.

'It's awful,' sobbed Carol. 'I don't know what to do. I love him!'

'Still?' asked Mary incredulously and Carol nodded, pushing strands of wet hair aside with grubby fingers. Mary stamped on the impulse to shake some sense into the silly child, and tried to find words of comfort. There was nothing that would console. At last she said, 'Do you want to leave, Carol? You could you know, if it would make you feel better. What do you think?'

The girl caught her breath and tried to stop crying. 'I'd like to go home. I want me mum.'

Filled with guilty relief Mary agreed that she should leave at the end of the week.

She marched back to the house imagining what she would like to do to Tim, and for that matter all men who took what they wanted from women and then abandoned them. Susan had taken the three children for a walk, since bouncing Daniel along country lanes in his pram seemed to soothe him, and Anna and Ben enjoyed the exercise. The kitchen was quiet and still, with only the usual puffing of Murphy keeping vigil at the fridge door. He had not gone on the walk because Susan said he ran away and refused to come when she called, which he did when Mary took him as well but she hated to admit it.

Tim came in. Mary jumped and glowered at him, her body rigid with loathing.

'What have I done now?' he queried with his special, charm-laden grin, usually reserved for Edna when he brought a horse in filthy.

'Where's Patrick?' snapped Mary, determined not to answer him. She didn't trust herself to speak with control.

'He's gone to the village I think. But come on, Mary, you've been nice to me lately. Tell me what I've done and I'll say sorry. Go on, you know you'll feel better.' He slid an arm around her waist and she pulled away from him, flouncing over to the sink and starting to dry dishes. She was wearing a pale pink short-sleeved T-shirt tucked into an Indian cotton skirt. Her anger had stiffened her nipples and they were clearly outlined against her thin top. Tim leaned on the draining board next to her and slipped a finger inside the waistband of her skirt.

'Three children and a figure like this. No wonder Paddy can never wait to get home, I'd break a few records if you'd give me a cuddle.'

Mary turned and glared at him. 'I'm not Carol,' she said slowly. 'You may be able to convince sixteen-year-old virgins that you're the greatest lover there is, and even she thought your performance pretty substandard, but I am a different proposition. I don't like men who are vain, selfish, lazy, opinionated, mean, greedy and seducers of children. I don't like you, Tim.'

The young, tanned face before her flamed scarlet and then paled. 'She's been lying to you. I never touched her, not once.'

'I think you are the liar, Tim. But don't worry, she's leaving at the end of the week and if I have any say in the matter so will you.' She didn't think for one minute that she could get rid of him, for she suspected that Fred, and possibly Brogan, would think she was being hysterical. Still, it alarmed Tim and that was worth doing.

'You bitch! You would, wouldn't you, all for the sake of some stupid kid who'd let anyone crawl all over her. And who the hell are you to be so high and mighty, your husband wasn't dead five minutes before you were letting Paddy stuff you.'

'God, but you're revolting! Get out, Tim, I don't want you in my house.' Two high spots of colour stained Mary's cheeks and she trembled with rage that owed something to the realisation that Tim spoke the truth.

'Like hell I'll go,' said Tim, and grabbed her by the shoulders. Mary hit him, hard, across the face, intending to wipe that smirk away once and for all. 'You bitch,' said Tim again, and reached for her breast.

Mary screamed, and the sound echoed in the empty house. There was no one to hear. Her T-shirt ripped beneath Tim's iron hands, she felt him clutching at her flesh and as she pushed him away she felt his teeth in the skin of her neck. She gasped, her hands flew up to strike and in that instant he tore at her panties, thrusting stiff fingers into her. She kicked and her sandalled foot met the muscles of a leg made hard by riding, and this time the mount would be her. Fear seemed to refine her senses, and she could feel every bevel in the sink edge pressing into her back and at the same time seemed only conscious of Tim's hands, probing and clutching. She could feel herself losing this fight. She thought herself strong, but against Tim she was a butterfly. Murphy was barking, hysterical yaps from underneath the table. Again she screamed and began to claw at Tim's face, leaving the marks of her nails in bloody furrows on his cheek. He hit her then, hard, rattling her teeth in her head and she slipped and almost fell, clutching at the sink for support. Her hand closed around a pan and she hit him with it, without strength, knowing that she was lost. The face above her was mask-like, absorbed, she was nothing now but a body to be used.

And then the door opened and Patrick came in. The struggling couple froze, a tableau of conflict. There was a long and terrible silence. Tim's hold on Mary slackened and she sank to the floor, shaking with sobs that she struggled to contain.

'I'll kill you,' said Brogan, and he meant it.

Tim backed away, his hands feeling the work surface behind him for a weapon that was not there, the blood from his cheek running down his neck like a network of arteries. 'She asked for it,' he muttered. 'She plays you like a fish but she's nothing but a whore. Leads men on and then says no, she gets what she deserves.'

'I'll kill you,' said Brogan again, as if surprised that what is often said so lightly should now be so much intended. Then he lunged, catching Tim unawares, hitting him so hard in the gut that the younger man doubled over in agony. He tried to straighten but Brogan was on him, his blows falling with the sodden sound of boots on wet earth.

'No! Patrick, stop it!' The words came from far away, they had no meaning until repetition caused him to listen. 'Patrick! Stop!'

He looked down to see Mary clutching his legs, struggling to stand. 'Just – just make him go away,' she said shakily. 'Please Pat. Just – away. Please.'

Tim groaned. Had he really a moment ago been going to destroy him? As if in a dream, all sound muffled, Patrick dragged him to the door and out into the yard. Mary stayed where she was on the floor, and after a while there was the sound of a car. Patrick came back. He was pale, he had never before shown such emotion and it embarrassed him. Sober, aware, he had known himself capable of murder. He had not believed it possible to feel such rage and now that it was gone he felt drained, exposed and raw. He took off his jacket and draped it round Mary's shoulders, turning his eyes from the bloody gash on her neck. If he looked he would choke on fury.

'What happened?' he asked bluntly, and because of what he felt it came out sharp and accusing.

Mary shuddered and looked fearfully up at him. He was going to blame her, she knew he was. 'I was cross because of Carol,' she said shakily. 'He's been horrible to her and she was so upset. And she's leaving, it seemed best . . . and when he came in, all smarmy charm, I lost my temper and said things – and he said things – and then he grabbed me. It wasn't my fault Pat, I didn't lead him on!'

Patrick looked at her, tearful and bloodstained,

her skirt torn, one breast showing its pink and tender nipple, and thought that women like Mary never had to lead men on. That she was unconscious of her attraction was part of it, she walked like a child amongst men's thoughts and never knew.

'Get washed and put some clothes on,' he said abruptly. 'There'll be hell to pay when Fred hears.'

'He won't think I – good God, Patrick, it wasn't my fault! Except that I didn't take enough notice of what was happening to Carol, and neither did you . . .'

'Of course I knew what was going on. It wasn't important. The girl asked for it, she couldn't have been more of a bleeding doormat if she'd tried. I did tell him to make sure he didn't get her pregnant which I hope to God he hasn't, and with any luck she might show a bit more sense in future. It wasn't anything to do with you.'

'Patrick! This place isn't a brothel! Her father trusted us to take care of her.'

'Neither is it a convent, as you should know,' snapped Brogan. 'So he was a bastard to her, if it was my daughter I'd be livid, but I hope any child of mine would never be that stupid. Oh for God's sake go and get washed, I don't want the children to see you like that.'

It was a difficult evening. Mary felt shocked and betrayed, her head ached and there was skin under her fingernails. She scrubbed her hands until they were red. 'What's that funny mark on your neck, Mummy?' asked Anna and Mary turned, too quickly.

'Nothing, darling – I scratched myself.' She saw Susan's wide, disbelieving gaze. However little she said everyone would know what had happened.

Brogan was whitefaced and withdrawn. 'Put the kids to bed, Susan,' he ordered and she went at once to do so. He met Mary's eye. 'You too. Bed.'

'I'm all right.'

'Like hell you are. He's gone, he won't come back. You're quite safe.'

'Of course I am. After what you did to him I should think he can hardly stand anyway. Pat – you don't think I led him on, do you?'

He sighed. 'Mary, Mary, sometimes you are so bloody stupid. Go to bed. I'll bring you some cocoa.'

She went, sinking into the pillow with relief. Sometimes Patrick was impossible to understand.

Sharp at nine the following morning Fred Swallow drove into the yard.

'I want a word with you Paddy,' he said darkly. Without speaking Patrick led the way into the sitting room. The door closed. Trembling, feeling physically sick, Mary stood outside. She could hear every word they said.

'You've gone too far this time, Paddy. You and women. But I didn't think you'd soil your own nest.'

'What's the slimy little bastard been saying?' Patrick almost sounded amused.

'The girl, Carol. Pretty little thing I admit but for a man like you to get involved –'

'It isn't true, Fred.'

There was a silence. 'So? And what's your story?'

'My story is my business. I don't seduce stable girls.'

'Must be your only scruple then. I was warned when I took you on but I thought you'd settle down. Then there was that Sylvia creature and God knows who else, and now this –'

Mary could bear no more. She fled upstairs and sat frozen on the bed until after a long, long time Fred's car drove off down the lane. Patrick came to find her.

'I didn't tell him.'

'Are you finished? You and Fred?'

'Probably. The contract runs out at the end of the year anyway and I don't think I'll renew. I'd better put out some feelers for someone else to take me on. Look, are you all right? You look like a ghost.'

She was shaking too, like a woman in shock. She longed to scream at him, demand to know if Fred had been telling the truth. Were there other women? Still? But what right had she, a woman who had allowed yesterday to happen. When Patrick slid his arms around her she lay and shuddered, flinching involuntarily as he touched her. But afterwards, despite herself she took comfort in his warmth. Faithless or not, she needed him.

The headline jumped out at her in letters three inches high: 'SEX SPLIT IN JUMPING STABLE'.

'This is about us, Jim?' She looked at the farmer in bewilderment. He nodded.

'Thought you wouldn't have seen it, it's not the sort of Sunday paper you take. This un's Mrs

236

Milne's, she buys a bit of milk off me and I saw
this on the step. Couldn't miss it really.'

'No. Just a minute, I must read this properly.'

*'Scandal hit the world of showjumping today
with revelations from one of its rising stars,
twenty-three-year-old Tim Parsons. In an
exclusive interview he has detailed the bizarre
lifestyle of Patrick Brogan, the top flight Irish
born rider now based in Yorkshire. Parsons,
son of wealthy stockbroker Sir Roderick
Parsons, left the stable last week after a row
over riding practices and Brogan's seduction
of a sixteen-year-old stable girl. Brogan is
divorced but lives with his mistress, a young
widow by whom he has a son. "I wouldn't like
my daughter to work there," said Parsons,
refusing to say more. He also attacked
Brogan's treatment of his horses, which are
jumped to the point of lameness and then
dosed with the controversial painkiller
butazolidin. "One animal has turned
savage," says Parsons, who has now joined the
Leicestershire stable of Mark Felton.'*

There was a blurred photograph which Mary now
saw was of Patrick.

'Come on, love, sit down,' soothed Jim, 'no one
will believe it.'

She swallowed hard. 'Yes, they will. We can't
prove it isn't true, one of the horses is savage, one
of the girls was seduced, by Tim as it happens but
we can't say that, and she won't tell. No one will
care about the truth. Oh God.'

Patrick came in, whistling cheerfully and

stopped in surprise as he saw the elderly farmer. 'Mr Pearce isn't it? What brings you up here?'

Jim turned his hat in his veined and freckled hands. 'Mary'll tell you. I must get back, cows to see to.'

Mary tried to smile. 'Thank you, Jim, it was kind of you to come up so early. Give my love to Betty.'

'Yes. Well. Thought you should know. Be seeing you.'

His little car coughed its way down the lane as Brogan read the article.

'He's getting his own back and no mistake,' he said thoughtfully.

'What can we do, Pat? Can't we deny it?'

'The only thing we could do is tell the truth, and I won't do that. Imagine, everyone staring at Carol, wondering who she did sleep with, everyone leering at you, thinking perhaps he did rape you after all? And we'd end up in court, his father would sink us. We can't do a damn thing.'

'It seems so unfair. Why should we suffer from Tim's spite?'

He put an arm round her shoulders. 'It'll blow over, you'll see. No one will believe it.'

The telephone rang and he went to answer it. From then on the calls were almost non-stop, from newspapers, television programmes and concerned friends. The one notable omission was Fred.

'He must have heard by now,' said Mary, chewing on tough roast beef. She had been unable to concentrate on cooking this morning and the meal was a disaster. She miserably turned singed carrots on her fork.

'I think he's left the sinking ship,' said Pat philosophically. 'Anna, eat properly please, stop feeding it to Murphy.'

'I don't like it,' said Anna with a defiant pout.

'I'll get the pudding,' said Mary and went to the oven. The rice pudding was a skinless, watery mess which also went to Murphy. They ate tinned peaches enlivened by Violet's cream.

'Why can't we have this more often, it's nice,' said Patrick and Mary looked at him sourly. She prided herself on her puddings. The phone rang again as they finished. It was Fred.

'You'll never believe it.' Patrick stood in the doorway looking stunned.

'What? Tell me, Pat, what did he say?'

'Not all that much. He didn't have to, I could tell he was hugging himself.'

'You mean he's pleased? He doesn't mind?'

'Oh no, he doesn't mind. Why should he, he's got me right by the balls. I ought to have seen this coming I suppose, after all it's publicity and it's all the same to him, good or bad. As he says, who's going to take me on now this has blown up. I'm stuck with the bastard. Stuck with him!'

Mary blinked, unable to take it in. Her world, that minutes before had been lying in pieces around her, reformed and took shape within her head.

Chapter 17

The garden was warm in the early morning sun, and a few butterflies danced in the undergrowth. Mary had cleared the long herbaceous border in fits and starts over the past months and today she began to weed round the huge clumps of peony and lupin that she had uncovered. The task satisfied her because it gave her the feeling that things would carry on. For her, gardening was an act of faith.

Patrick was due back today. It was over two weeks since Tim had left and nothing had been resolved, Pat seemingly content to weather the storm without a single word spoken in his defence. It was not good, they received sheaves of abusive letters with every post, Pat was booed at shows and an RSPCA inspector had come to prowl round the yard. Murphy had lifted his leg against his trousers and High Time had tried to bite him.

The wagon arrived home in time for lunch. Brogan jumped out at once and strode into the house.

'Well?' asked Mary, putting her face up for his kiss as she always did at meeting or parting. It was a little ritual they had lately drifted into and neither ever mentioned it, although neither ever forgot. He sighed and slumped into a chair.

'Won one, but there were boos all round. Nearly

241

a riot on the way out as well, they had to call the police. Still, it's bound to die down.'

'What do the other riders think?'

'Mostly that it's just Tim's spite. One or two are looking at me sideways though, and at the girls. It's rough on them.'

'I'd like to see any of them say anything to Edna,' laughed Mary and Patrick grinned.

'Yes, but much more of this and Susan will quit.' He lifted the baby on to his knee and then disappeared under the load as Ben and Anna claimed their right to a place there too. Eventually he gave the baby to Mary and tickled the others until they squealed. 'Upstairs to get washed you horrible brats,' he urged and chased them giggling from the room. Mary put Daniel in his bouncing chair and began to pour out the soup for lunch.

There was a sudden, thunderous knock on the door, causing Murphy to creep from his place in front of the Aga and under the table.

'You miserable coward,' said Mary automatically as she went to answer it.

Sam Downes stood there, his shoulders hunched aggressively.

'Sam! How nice to see you, come in. Have you seen Edna?'

'No. She's to keep out of this, it's between me and him. Now you take the children out the road and leave this to the men.'

She blinked at him. 'Well, I don't know . . .'

'Sit down, Sam, I'd like to talk to you.' Patrick was unconcerned, a look of amusement on his face.

'This is no laughing matter,' roared Sam, barging past Mary who dashed into the yard to find Edna.

Someone had to stop her jealous lover from creating mayhem.

'What's this I hear about orgies,' bellowed Sam, waving a newspaper.

'Ancient history, Sam, the paper's two weeks old at least. I thought you'd have heard long before now.'

'That's got nothing to do with it. I knew you'd been taking advantage of a sweet, good girl and now there's proof. I'm going to make you pay, that I am and I'm taking Edna away from here. I'll not leave her in this – this – knocking shop!'

Patrick gave a guffaw which ceased abruptly when Sam lunged at him across the table. He leaped to his feet and began to circle the kitchen, Sam lumbering after him like a bear wakened from hibernation.

'Now, Sam, let's talk about this, you don't believe everything you read in the papers do you –' he dodged a haymaker of a punch '– for God's sake Sam, I wouldn't touch Edna with a barge pole.' This was not well received and he retreated behind the table. Sam seized it, gave a mighty heave and threw it to one side. Murphy scuttled away.

'That's our table! Now enough is enough –' Pat watched amazed as Sam hurled a chair across the room to crash against the Aga with the noise of splintering wood. 'You bastard,' roared Pat and seized Sam by the lapels, slamming him against the wall. He was about to knock his front teeth out when Edna hurtled into the room like an avenging spirit.

'How dare you touch him! Leave him alone!' she cried.

'Look what he's done to my home,' complained Pat, retaining his hold.

'Please put him down, Pat, he's older than you,' gasped Mary breathlessly.

'And should know better,' grumbled Pat, reluctantly releasing his victim.

Sam stood in front of Edna, somewhat downcast. 'I told him you were leaving and you will,' he said, trying to regain his impetus.

'And why, may I ask?'

'Because of what he is, that's why! It's in the paper, look.'

Edna seized the offending sheet and tore it into shreds with her firm, brown fingers. 'If you believe that you're a fool, Sam Downes,' she cried. 'What sort of woman do you think I am? You don't own me and I make my own decisions. If you think you can walk in here and order me around you're very much mistaken.'

The colour was draining from Sam's face. He stood looking at Edna for a long minute, his shoulders drooping. 'Yes,' he said quietly. 'Perhaps I was mistaken. About a lot of things. Goodbye Edna.' He walked slowly to the door and was gone.

The girl stood looking after him, her strong hands twisting together, a dirty mark on the side of her bony nose. A sob shook her, and then another, and Mary was about to go to her when Pat caught her arm.

'Don't,' he urged. 'You're not the only person who likes to cry in private.'

'But if she went after him –' hissed Mary, but he glared at her.

'Keep out of it,' he insisted. 'She can manage it by herself.'

Mary shot him a look brimming with doubt. To her mind if Edna ever needed guidance it was now. But she and Patrick had known each other ages before Mary came on the scene, so he could be right. She stood helpless as Edna's lanky, jean-clad legs galloped across the yard into the solitude of the granary flat.

Next day Edna was still in hiding. When lunchtime came and went without any sign of her Mary decided she had to do something. Fortunately Patrick was out so she had only herself to convince. If she was rebuffed then so be it, but Susan's reports of silence interspersed with groans were alarming to say the least. She crossed the yard with all the trepidation of a paleface making overtures to the Indians.

The granary flat was steeped in the squalor of girls living together. Dirty plates littered the table, underwear hung in garlands from the fireplace and a stray cat slept in a straw-filled box. Mary picked her way across the room, her nose wrinkled in distaste, and knocked on Edna's door.

'Edna, it's me, can I come in?' There was no reply and she turned the handle. The room was in semi-darkness and smelled of stale perfume and misery. She touched the huddled form on the bed, for one terrible moment thinking she was dead.

'Edna! Are you all right?' There was a muffled sob and Mary breathed again. 'Come on,' she said, flinging back the curtains, 'you can't stay there forever, there's work to be done. Have you eaten anything?'

'I want to die!' wailed Edna, surfacing from the tangle of bedclothes. Her face was blotched and swollen, large nose gleaming, eyes hardly visible.

Mary sat on the bed, taking one of the big, rough hands in hers.

'Everyone has quarrels, love,' she comforted. 'It'll pass.'

'Edna shook her head. 'It's over,' she sobbed. 'I should have known it was too good to last, he won't want me any more. Why am I always so stupid, that terrible, terrible row!'

Mary choked back a laugh. 'Really, you call that a row? My good girl you ain't seen nothing yet. I well remember Pat flinging me round the kitchen like a rag doll when he'd had one too many. And we're still together.'

'But you're not married,' sniffed Edna, 'and Sam and I – it was going to be wonderful.' She flung herself on Mary's shoulder, awash with grief, and Mary soothed and patted as best she could. Comforting the afflicted seemed her role in life these days, yet there was no one to comfort her.

'Edna you really must stop this,' she said at last, giving her a little shake. 'There's no reason why you can't drive round and apologise, now is there. In fact,' she added, inspiration dawning, 'I think you should go at once, heaven knows what Sam may have done. He really is desperately in love with you, poor man. It could be The Worst!'

'You mean . . .?'

Mary nodded. 'So hadn't you better go and see?'

She struggled to prevent Edna rushing off there and then, blotched face, winceyette pyjamas and all, and it was an almost presentable figure that drove out half an hour later, still tearful and red nosed but washed and dressed.

She almost collided with Patrick who was driving in at his usual breakneck pace.

'Where's she going?' he demanded. 'You haven't been getting at her have you, Mary?'

'Good heavens, Pat, as if I'd dare. But I think you should start looking for a new head girl. Edna's off up the aisle any minute.'

'Bloody hell, I hope not. Surely I don't deserve that as well as everything else.' Mary sniffed and turned away. Perhaps he did deserve it. After all, she would be the last one to know.

Fred called in at around nine that night, and Edna was still not home. Mary was worried, suppose it hadn't gone well with Sam, it might be Edna that ended it all. Suppose at this moment she was lying amidst the crumpled wreckage of her car, bleeding to death with no one even looking for her –

'– isn't that so, Mary?'

'What? I'm sorry, Fred, I was miles away.'

'We can go on as we used to, the three of us, a united, close-knit little team. Almost a family, really. Eeh, I'm glad we're staying together, what a waster that lad turned out to be. Still, we live and learn.'

Mary opened her mouth to say that he could afford to be philosophical since he wasn't suffering but then met Patrick's eye and said instead, 'I'm so glad you see it like that, Fred. It is nice to be friends again.' Then, because it still sounded a bit cool she added, 'You are like one of the family, Fred dear.'

He beamed and gave her a hug, but she dared not look at Patrick. Anyway, Fred did resemble a cantankerous old uncle, so rich that you dare not

upset him in case he changed his will. There was
the sound of an engine far away down the hill. At
night you could hear cars coming for miles,
grinding their way upwards. They always sent
policemen in person for fatal accidents, thought
Mary; with Edna gone they'd never persuade
Susan to do High Time. It was an odd repercussion
of Stephen's death that she now saw dying as a
distinct possibility, no longer did it seem
unthinkable that people close to her should die.
Morbid of course, for they very seldom did.

It was Sam Downes's big Volvo, with Edna in
the passenger seat. Patrick went to the door and
there was the murmur of voices before they all
came into the sitting room, Edna blinking in the
light.

'Like a drink?' offered Patrick, anxious to
cement relations with Sam.

He and Edna both accepted a beer and sat side
by side on the edge of the sofa, their knees
touching. Edna had a love-bite on her neck. Mary
saw Pat follow the direction of her eyes, and then
they glanced at each other, not needing to speak
to know what each was thinking. From Pat, 'Good
God, can you imagine those two –' to which Mary
replied, 'I think it's sweet.'

Fred was feeling jocular. 'Well then, Edna,
when's the big day?'

The girl's face flamed and she slopped some beer
on to her knee. Mary passed her a tissue, saying,
'Don't be premature, Fred. We don't want to lose
Edna just yet.'

'You can say that again, it took us hours to get
finished tonight,' complained Pat. 'You might tell
me when you're –'

'Pat!' warned Mary, seeing the telltale flush on Sam's neck.

' – and as I was going to say,' continued Patrick smoothly, 'we'll have to get someone else pretty quick. Ye Gods, with all the horsemad girls in the world you wouldn't think it would be this hard to get someone to stay.'

'That newspaper might have something to do with it,' said Sam Downes and Pat turned on him, waving an admonitory finger and saying, 'If you think that the rubbish in there is true – '

'Of course you don't, do you, Sam,' urged Edna. They all looked at him.

'Well – no, no I suppose I don't. Though why you put up with a rapscallion like that beats me, why in all my years of farming I've never had back word from someone as worked for me, not once.'

'It's your lovable nature, Sam,' snarled Brogan and Mary looked pleadingly at him. He was being very good under the circumstances, but she sensed the anger that boiled beneath the surface. It would be good to have him to herself. Since the episode with Tim they had made love only the once and she had been tense and unable to enjoy it. Now, tonight, she had drunk a little and relaxed a lot and she needed him. She stretched, her leg firm against her skirt and felt Pat's eyes on her.

'Been a long day,' said Patrick loudly. 'I shall sleep well tonight.'

Fred had been looking for another drink, but as Pat yawned capaciously and glanced at the clock he sniffed and got to his feet. After all, he could afford to be tolerant. Equally obedient, Sam and Edna hastily downed their drinks and made for the door, Edna nervously avoiding Patrick's eye.

Mary set about clearing glasses and ashtrays, aware of Patrick leaning against the fireplace. She made her movements slow, she bent so that he could see down her blouse. Oh, how she wanted him.

'Put those things down,' said Pat and she turned to him, laughing. He was a wonderful man to love. He entered her as she lay on the thin rug and she complained that it hurt her back but he nibbled her ear and told her that she should have thought of that before. So she wrapped herself around him and cried out as he thrust into her, but there was no pain in it. At last her body exploded in a giant convulsion of pleasure. Then they lay side by side, panting and exhausted.

'You're wonderful,' murmured Patrick and bent his head to her lips.

There came a knocking on the door. 'Who on earth is that?' said Mary, frantically searching for her knickers.

'God knows. Stay here, I'll go.' He stepped into his trousers and went shirtless to investigate. He came across Edna hovering uncertainly.

'Paddy. I heard noises. Someone screamed, I thought – is Mary all right?'

'Oh for Christ's sake, Edna, what did you think I was doing to her? I don't give her a nightly beating whatever you may think.'

'No, but – you're not the calmest person in the world, Paddy, and you seemed in a bit of a temper. Is Mary there?'

Mary emerged from the sitting room, her shoes in her hand, her buttons half undone. 'It's kind of you, Edna, but I'm quite all right. We were just –'

'Talking,' said Patrick.

'Talking?' Mary shot him a look of surprise.

'Yes, talking, and if you'd take yourself off to your lonely couch, Edna, you can safely leave us to our discussion. Nuclear disarmament. Mary gets very heated.'

'Well,' said Edna, pink with embarrassment. 'It was very noisy, you know.'

'We'll be quieter, I promise,' said Mary and Edna was ushered into the night.

Patrick and Mary collapsed with laughter. When he could speak Patrick said, 'Come on to bed, though you're a shameless bitch and noisy. I think I liked it better when Edna was on my side.'

'I didn't,' yawned Mary and wandered off upstairs.

Mary was happy the next day, larking with the children as she dressed them and changing all the sheets with feelings of energetic virtue. When the phone rang she answered it hurriedly, sure it was yet another newspaperman wanting some meat to flesh the bones of the story. Without any facts to go on the papers were delving into showjumping generally, searching for signs of cruelty and dope. Mary never told them anything but it didn't stop the calls. She had ceased even to be polite.

'Hello,' she snapped aggressively. There was a pause.

'Could I speak to Patrick Brogan, please?' said a very Irish voice.

'He's not here.'

'Oh. This is his mother speaking. Would you be Mary?'

For a desperate moment Mary considered

hanging up, or saying she was the cleaning woman. 'Er . . . yes,' she said eventually.

'Oh,' the voice said again. 'Patrick tells me you have a new baby.'

'Er . . . yes, we do. Daniel Patrick.'

'My third grandchild and the only boy, his sister has two girls, you know. I should love to see him. Have you never thought of visiting Ireland?'

Mary ran a distracted hand through her hair. This was purgatory.

'No, no I haven't,' she managed, and there was again a pause. 'Do you – ever think of coming to England?' she asked and the response was immediate.

'Oh my dear, how kind of you to invite us, sure and we should love to come. October would be our best time, I'll telephone with the arrangements though I do hate the instrument.'

'Yes. Of course. How nice,' said Mary feebly and after a few more pleasantries, entirely mechanical on her side, she hung up.

Wandering through the kitchen she wondered what on earth she was to say to Patrick. He wrote regularly to his parents but she never asked about them and he never volunteered any information. From casual remarks about his father she thought he sounded a complete rogue, and some of his dealings almost criminal. For his mother she imagined a quiet countrywoman of deep religious conviction, but now she endowed her with diabolic purpose. She wanted Daniel Patrick. Pat's divorce was not valid in Ireland so any second marriage would be considered void. For a wild moment she envisaged this mad Irishwoman bearing off both Patrick and the baby to some

Catholic stronghold where she, a loose woman and a Protestant, would be forbidden entry. And she had invited her to stay! She felt near to tears and went for a walk round the yard to calm herself.

She stopped near to High Time's box. The horse still resented any sudden movements and was particularly sensitive about his stable, allowing no one but Pat to touch him whilst he was in there. Once outside however, any of the girls could groom him although it usually fell to Edna, as long as they tied him up short and were quiet and careful. He was to go to a show in a fortnight and they would see what he could do. It was not far and Mary was considering taking the children and making a day of it. She wondered if Patrick could stand the strain. Thinking mundane thoughts of house and family she clutched at her security, standing there in the sunshine. Happiness was so fragile and could be broken so easily, however careful you were. She took a deep, restoring breath. October was a long way away.

Chapter 18

August. The vale of York was hot and dusty, the greens no longer fresh and the roses overblown. High in the hills the breeze was light and cool at this early hour of the morning and the trees that sheltered the house whispered. The clatter of buckets and the banging of doors signalled the start of the day at High Wold House and soon a plaintive moo was heard as Violet ambled in from the field for milking. She was heavily in calf and objected to the walk.

Mary milked at the double, which exhausted her and took just as long, but today they were going to a show. She tried to revert to the slow, rhythmic squeeze that paid dividends but she was soon racing again, sending little sharp jets fizzing into the pail. Brogan met her as she ran to the house, closely followed by a posse of cats.

'Aren't you ready yet?' he enquired. 'We're leaving in half an hour.'

He resumed his leisurely progress round the yard while she fought her way into the kitchen, ignoring the outraged mews of the cats deprived of their usual warm milk.

They thumped the closed door softly with their paws and Anna, disconsolately stirring her breakfast cereal, obligingly went and opened it. The feline flood swept across the floor and over the table, making short work of Anna's leavings, and cats shot everywhere like rogue fireworks as Mary tried to shoo them out.

'Aren't you ready yet?' enquired Susan, cool and casual, a cowboy hat balanced on the back of her head. She wandered out to the wagon. Mary ran a hand distractedly through her hair and wildly threw knives and forks, feeder cups and chocolate biscuits into a hamper. The butter would be liquid by the time they got there but she was past caring.

She ran upstairs to assemble Daniel Patrick's travelling kit of nappies, bibs, bouncing chair, carrycot, sunhat, blankets and toys. A voice floated up from the kitchen. 'Aren't you ready yet?' called Edna. 'We're leaving.'

She raced to the bedroom, throwing clothes in all directions, and fell into a blue linen shirtwaist dress, intended to look cool and relaxed. Grabbing her make-up bag she thrust her feet into rope espadrilles and flew downstairs. Panting, she handed bag after bag into the wagon and finally climbed in herself.

'Where's the baby?' asked Edna. He was asleep in his pram. Out again to fetch him, on the way noticing a cat under the dresser gnawing a piece of toast. She left it there and struggled back to the yard. The wagon pulled out.

'You do look hot,' commented Edna, 'and your buttons are all done up wrong.'

'Beautiful morning,' said Brogan conversationally, changing gear. 'And no need to rush, we've hours to spare.'

Mary gave a low, anguished groan and they all looked at her in surprise.

It was a County show which had sprung from small beginnings to become something of a major event, with livestock classes, parachute jumping and a Women's Institute tent. The sun blazed upon the showground and Patrick sniffed disapprovingly, he hated jumping his horses on hard ground. But they had come, and he manoeuvred the wagon over the bumps and into the field.

'I want a wee wee,' announced Anna at once, and eyeing the miles to the nearest tent Mary directed her to a suitable patch of turf.

'Well, really,' declared a lady in a flowered hat who stalked past complete with shooting stick and fat labrador. Mary poked her tongue at the retreating back.

When the ramp was let down, out bounced not only Susan but Murphy, delighted to be released.

'Who brought him?' demanded Mary and Susan looked big-eyed and innocent.

'He would have been lonely at home,' she wailed.

'Down Murphy, down!' exhorted Mary trying to preserve the blue linen dress at least until lunchtime and fortunately he suddenly sighted the waddling rear of the labrador, making slow progress.

'What is he doing?' asked Patrick in amazement and Mary scuttled into the wagon.

Murphy had lately developed an unhealthy interest in sex and was inclined to practice on any dog he met, male or female. Susan was despatched to collect him.

They had only brought two horses, High Time and a youngster called Swallow, in honour of

Fred. It had been Pat's idea because the horse was barrel-shaped with short, bouncy legs but Fred had been thrilled, seeing it as a mark of the esteem in which Patrick had come to hold him. It was the only horse he did not talk of selling at least once a week.

Patrick went off to collect his numbers and Susan and Edna, for whom this was largely an outing with little to do, went in search of their cronies in the other wagons, obligingly taking Anna and Ben with them. Mary was left in blessed peace, seated on a rug in the shade, the baby asleep. She was nearly asleep too when someone spoke to her.

'Mrs Brogan – Mary? I thought I recognised you, my name's Spence, you remember we met before?' She looked up at the man through half-closed eyes, dazzled by the sun.

'Oh – oh yes, of course I remember. Sit down, would you like some lemonade?' He accepted a paper cup and sat down with a sigh.

'Don't know what I'm doing here, really. I don't usually bother with the shows this far north but the prize money's good this year. Is Paddy somewhere about?'

She nodded. 'We're all having a day out but I'm beginning to wonder if I'm up to it.'

There was a wail from the carrycot. 'May I?' asked Spence and she handed Daniel to him. He was one of those men who can sit for hours with a baby, enthralled by the barely focused eyes and waving fists, making faces and burbling nonsense. Mary went into a peaceful daydream.

'How long have you been married now?' he asked and she sat up with a blink.

258

'We're not married,' she said awkwardly. 'I'm sorry – I know it's rather misleading, with Daniel and everything. My name's Squires, Mary Squires.'

He looked most upset and she almost wished she had lied.

'But Paddy's got his divorce, hasn't he?' It was plain that Tom Spence still felt a fatherly concern for Pat and Mary could not feel offended.

'Oh, there's no real reason,' she said hurriedly, 'it's just that – well, Patrick doesn't – he isn't – in love. I don't think. It's better this way.' She gave a shaky smile and then started. Pat was standing by the wagon, but he could not have heard, she felt sure.

'Hello Tom,' he was saying, 'what are you doing here?'

Her embarrassment was lost as the two men talked horses and she began to set out the lunch. As she had predicted the butter was a yellow pool, but it had confined itself to a bowl with rare consideration. And she had remembered the corkscrew. Tom accepted her invitation with alacrity and they all sprawled on the grass eating pork pie and hard boiled eggs washed down with warm wine.

'Anna will you please eat something,' exhorted Mary for the child seemed almost to live on fresh air. Murphy was always sure of a friend in Anna and haunted her at mealtimes. He left Ben strictly alone for anything he refused was inedible.

'Be a lion,' suggested Pat and with roars and lion-like grunts coaxed some pie into the little girl. Ben was delighted and he and Anna ran round and round, roaring and pouncing, until High Time began to stamp nervously.

'I'd better get him warmed up,' said Pat and Edna obediently rose.

'Take the kids for an ice cream, Susan,' he suggested. 'Give Mary some peace.'

Again everyone was gone and she was alone with the baby. Feeling carefree, she popped an enormous floppy sunhat on his head and strapped him to her front in a babysling. Now she could look round the show.

Flowers, vegetables, cakes, handicrafts, fences, machinery, it was all there. Daniel's head lolled against her in sleep as she plodded round, one of many country ladies urgently gleaning ideas and information from the displays. She hitched Daniel to a more comfortable position and went off to watch the spinning demonstration. So interested was she that she almost missed the showjumping and she arrived at the ringside in a fluster.

There was a big entry but the course was difficult and there had only been three clear rounds. The problem fence was a combination, the first element a big spread, which tended to land the horses too close to a parallel, and if they scrambled over that they fell foul of the upright at the end. The course builders hovered there as horse after horse brought it down, one sliding to a halt on his bottom and demolishing one of the ornamental trees. Mary found a seat and prepared to enjoy herself, showjumping was too often tedious with nothing more than the occasional fallen pole. This was spectacular.

The arena had been watered and was a brilliant green in the afternoon sun.

'And the next to jump – Patrick Brogan on High

Time.' A buzz of conversation rose from the audience as Patrick appeared.

'I think he's horrid,' piped a girl of about twelve and Mary gave her a furious stare. High Time was clearly upset by the noise, dimly heard through his cotton wool earplugs. Sweat was forming on his neck and his tail thrashed angrily. She could hardly bear to watch and clutched the sleeping Daniel with a fervour that drew surprised glances from the woman sitting next to her.

They began the round. At each fence Pat had to fight for control, the horse slewing sideways and refusing to go straight. As they approached the combination Mary could see nothing but disaster and began praying that if he fell off Patrick would not let go of the horse, he would be sure to eat someone. High Time pricked his ears as he saw the fence and his headlong pace slackened as he wondered what to do. Sensing his indecision Pat forced him on and for once the horse listened to him. They sailed through without a touch and the crowd applauded, so upsetting High Time that he seemed not to notice the last fence and completely flattened it.

Rising from her seat Mary hurried to the wagon, prepared for despondency. Patrick radiated cheer.

'Did you see that?' he called. 'Wasn't he incredible? Just the one fence and an easy one too, I really think he's going to come good.' He gave High Time a friendly pat on the neck and pulled away quickly as the horse bent, snake-like, to bite.

'He doesn't change,' said Mary ruefully and called Anna and Ben away. She put Daniel in his carrycot and settled in the shade to read to them, for they were hot and tired and in need of a little calm. The familiar adventures of the *Three Billygoats Gruff* and some flat lemonade soothed frayed tempers. Patrick sat next to them, chewing a piece of grass.

'What about Swallow?' asked Mary when the troll had been despatched to a watery grave.

He shrugged. 'Ground's too hard, his leg started coming up as soon as he popped over the practice fence. I'm thinking about having him fired.' It would mean a lay-off but it might well be the making of the horse.

'Fred won't like that, he'll take it personally,' said Mary and he grinned.

'Had enough? We can go home now if you like, beat the rush.'

She nodded and they began to pack up.

No one said much on the long drive home, and the children dozed peacefully. Edna's thoughts were with Sam, wondering how he had spent his day. They had told no one of their plans but they intended to marry after harvest. She felt a twinge of fear as she thought of how her life would change, for unsatisfactory as things had been for some years now, at least she knew what each day would bring and this was a venture into uncharted waters. In the main she feared that she would not prove to be the woman Sam imagined she was, that one day he would wake to find her plain, clumsy and dull. She cast an envious glance at Mary, sprawled in the seat next to her but somehow still graceful. Her hair, though windswept, shone and her skin was touched with a glow from her day in the sun. Edna sighed and tugged at a hangnail.

They turned down the long lane which led to the

house, the verges high and uncut, old man's oatmeal mixed with wild roses. Rabbits scuttered across almost under their wheels and from far away came the whooping call of a snipe. Mary remembered how upset she had been when Patrick had shot one, refusing to pluck it until eventually he went and buried it, calling her a misplaced townee. Grouse and pheasant she did not mind, but the snipe, with his whooping call and outrageous beak, was a magical bird.

A police car stood in the yard. Everyone sat up, each with a different premonition of disaster.

'Something's happened,' quavered Mary, anticipating death as usual.

'I should think it's an unpaid parking ticket,' said Pat, his tone deliberately bored. It steadied her, as he knew it would. 'Can I help you, Officer? I'm Patrick Brogan.'

A policeman stepped forward, young, with a moustache, his cap pulled low. When he peered from beneath the peak Patrick was instantly reminded of a lama.

'If we could talk inside, sir.'

'Yes. Yes, of course.'

The kitchen smelled of cats. Mary bustled about, laden with bags and grubby children. When no one tried to arrest anyone she relaxed a little, and began to go upstairs to run the children's bath.

'If we could talk to the lady as well, sir.'

There, she knew it. The bull had at last killed someone and she was responsible. Or that woman had complained about the dog. She led the way into the sitting room, lovely in the evening shadows and waited for what fate had to offer. The policeman removed his hat. 'It's about Mr

Parsons, sir. I believe he used to work for you?'

'Yes. Yes he did. We parted on very bad terms.'

'So I gather. Perhaps you know he's been working for Mr Felton?'

'I did hear something. Why, has he put his hand in the till?' Patrick's voice was grim and Mary willed him to keep his temper.

'It looks like that sir.' Without his cap the man looked very earnest.

'Good God,' said Mary.

'Does it have anything to do with us?' asked Pat quickly, too quickly.

'Mr Felton thought it might. That possibly something of the sort happened while he was with you but no one said anything. We have reason to believe that he's done this sort of thing before.'

'Not with us he didn't. He never got near the money, thank God.'

'I see. Then why did he leave, Mr Brogan?'

Patrick turned to gaze out of the window. A slight flush touched his neck and Mary thought, it still upsets him. It was all her fault.

'He – he made advances to my wife. I threw him out.' Suddenly he swung back to face them, his eyes blazing. 'And if you catch the bastard make sure you give him something to remember me by. He deserves it.'

The policeman picked up his hat. 'We have Mr Parsons in custody now, sir. But we don't do that sort of thing in England. Thank you for your time.'

He left them gaping at each other, their faces blank with surprise.

Later, with the children in bed, they sat in the half dark and talked.

'I wonder if he did steal anything?' mused Mary.

'It can't have been much or we'd have noticed. Mind you, I haven't seen the stapler in weeks.'

'It's in the kitchen drawer.'

'Oh.'

Mary trailed a finger in her gin and tonic, making the ice cubes nudge each other like flustered cows. 'Imagine. Any of the children could end up like that. It's always somebody's child.'

'Not our kids. We love them too much.'

'I don't think that guarantees their honesty. Oh dear.' She sipped her drink and felt miserable. The day was spoiled. 'By the way,' she said suddenly, 'I spoke to your mother on the phone a while ago.'

'I wondered when you were going to tell me.'

'I suppose she . . .? Well you probably know she wants to visit us in October. If you want me to go and stay with my mother or anything–?'

'It's you she's coming to see. And Daniel.'

'I'd much rather go and visit my mother.'

'You invited her.'

'No I did not, at least I don't know how it came about, it just sort of happened.'

'She's better than your mother at any rate.'

'Not from where I'm standing she isn't. Oh God, I'm so tired.' She slumped in her chair, dropping her glass on to the table from a weary hand.

'Mary, about what you were saying to Tom today,' began Patrick, gazing out of the window.

'What? I'm sorry, I was half asleep.'

'I was saying–' he looked at her closed eyes and sighed. 'It doesn't matter. Wake up, you've got to go to bed.'

Chapter 19

Mary's filly had proved a dud. No one ever said as much and she was not offered for sale but her few outings had been dismal in the extreme. She had no enthusiasm for a fence over three foot high and her gentle nature made her a quiet and placid hunter, despised by Brogan who liked his mounts to have fire. They called her Spindrift, in Brogan's view a waste of a pretty name but he was careful of hurting Mary's feelings. When Mary asked if she could take her out one day no one raised any objections, it was tacitly acknowledged that this was one horse she could not spoil.

They trotted down the lane one close, dull day, each relishing the freedom. Mary glanced behind, half expecting to see Jet and was appalled to recognise the galumphing form of Murphy who was taking his role as faithful companion seriously these days. He had no road sense and her carefree feelings evaporated with the need to bellow furiously at him every time a tractor passed. Spindrift merely pricked her ears delicately. They took the bridlepath that had proved disastrous so many months before with Merlin, but this time rider and mount were in perfect accord, neither wishing to set the world alight. Confidence abounding, they jumped a small hedge at a thin place and trotted along the headland of a cornfield, taking a short cut home. To her surprise Mary saw a man on a heavy grey riding towards her and she arranged her face in a noncommittal smile.

'Good morning,' she murmured as they passed, noting that the man was riding extremely badly despite his handmade boots and new-looking riding mac. She had gone no more than a few yards past when there was an eruption of barks and curses and she turned to see the rider sitting in the corn with Murphy gnawing one of his boots while the horse was a little further on, catching up on breakfast.

'I do so apologise,' she said worriedly as she jumped from her horse and helped him up. He wiped a hand over his face and looked at her, registering first surprise and then dazzlement in a way that made her blush.

'Oh really — it's nothing,' he stammered, trying to hide the toothmarks on his boot. He was in his middle thirties, slightly plump with an open, cheerful face.

'Murphy isn't very bright I'm afraid and he had a nasty experience a little while ago. He doesn't like men very much, thinks they're all going to attack me.'

'I can see why!' he said ingenuously and Mary recoiled and went to catch the grey. 'I mean — oh I say, that sounded awfully rude — perhaps I'd better introduce myself, my name's Jonathan Mayhew, I've taken a cottage in the village.'

'Are you the solicitor? My cleaning lady told me about you. You intend to hunt, I hear.'

'Good heavens, word does travel. Yes, I'm trying to get this chap fit. He's at livery, I've only had him a couple of weeks.'

Mary ran a practised eye over the big animal,
roman nosed and over at the knee but with a kind
eye. 'Looks a good sort,' she commented.

'I say, do you think so? His name's Jason.'

Mary warmed to Mr Mayhew, he was refreshingly naive, a rarity in the horse world. 'I'm sure
he'll look after you. I'm hoping to do some hunting
myself this season, if I can persuade someone to
look after the children.'

Her companion glanced at her left hand and his
face fell. Mary giggled to herself as she went to
mount Spindrift, standing quietly, the perfect
lady. Apologising again, she called Murphy and
rode off, leaving Mr Mayhew holding the grey. A
surreptitious glance behind when she reached the
end of the field revealed the poor man going round
and round in circles as he tried to mount and
eventually, hot and bothered, leading the horse
to a convenient tree stump.

Her spirits soared as she rode home, she felt
young, desirable and vigorous. Things might work
out in the end and nothing revives one so much as
admiration, she thought happily. She had been a
household drudge for too long, it was time she
began to broaden her horizons and she would begin
in the hunting field, watching Mr Mayhew fall off.

That evening she gave Brogan a cheque.

'What's this?' he asked blankly.

'For Spindrift. I'm buying her back, you never
really wanted her anyway and she suits me
beautifully.'

'Damn it, you don't –' he could not continue and
ran a hand over his face. 'I've had enough Mary,'
he said, his voice sounding thick 'We can't go on
like this.'

She sat rigid with fright waiting for him to tell her that baby or no baby, they were finished. The cheque had been intended to please him, to show that her escape fund was no longer so precious to her. There was a knock on the kitchen door. It was Fred.

'Sorry to break in on your evening,' he said cheerfully, 'but I've a few things I'd like to discuss Paddy. Shall we sit down?'

'It's not convenient,' snarled Patrick.

'Well, you know me, business always comes first and I like the people working for me to look at things that way too. Needs must.' He was in a bulldozing mood.

'But I don't work for you, do I Fred? Or has the arrangement changed?'

'Don't let's split hairs, my boy, there's work to be done. Now, I've some figures here I'd like you to look at.' He charged on, and reluctantly Pat bent his head to the papers in front of him.

After a time Fred looked up. 'Mary, my dear, how about a drink?'

Patrick drew a short, annoyed breath.

'Of course, Fred.' Mary was in no mood to argue, she had plummeted from the heights to the depths in less than a minute and wanted only to go to bed and avoid further conversation with Patrick.

'Now, I've been hearing rumours,' said Fred as she placed bottle and glasses on the table, for Fred was not one for subtlety in his drinking. 'About you, Paddy. And me.' He sipped his drink and leaned back in his chair, crossing his legs with the air of one who is about to utter words of greatness. 'As you know I'm not one to keep things hidden, I put my cards on the table and I expect everyone else to do the same. I can't help it, it's the way I am, Yorkshire through and through.'

'Get on with it Fred,' groaned Patrick, who listened to Fred's bluff Yorkshireman act about twice a week, lately with increasing impatience.

'I hear that you've approached other sponsors.'

'Who told you that?'

'Sylvia Priestley.'

Mary stiffened and felt the colour drain from her face. Sylvia! No wonder Patrick wanted to talk about not 'going on like this'. He said nothing to her and then went and confided in that woman. It was too much. She sat and shivered inside, only half listening to the conversation.

'I don't see why you should believe anything she tells you. Anyway Fred, you had only to ask me.'

'As I am doing. What's going on, Pat? Are you going to leave me in the lurch?'

'You know me better than that. The contract comes up for renewal every year and you've as much right to terminate it as I have. I admit, now that this business with Tim has been settled and the papers have booked me as Mr Clean, things are starting to look a bit different. I don't know what I shall do in the long term. But so far I'm happy. Will that suit you?'

'I suppose it'll have to.' Fred's meek acceptance owed something to the fact that Pat's horses were flying and Fred did want to be on television at the Christmas show. Someone might interview him.

'Well then, that's settled. Have another drink,' said Patrick and poured a large glass for both of them. 'Did you hear about the row over the new type of competition?' He launched into a long tale of intrigue and dispute and Mary slid from the room. When Patrick finally came to bed he was drunk and fell asleep half dressed and snoring.

On the day Edna received her engagement ring it was raining and everyone was gathered in the kitchen drinking coffee and feeling bored. When she sidled in, blushing, they all knew what had happened.

'Oh Edna! Can I see?' demanded Mary, and Edna ducked her head, holding out her left hand. Sam's choice was an excellent one for the large solitaire was magnificent on the strong, brown finger where anything smaller would have looked apologetic. Nonetheless Mary suspected that she was looking at the best part of a combine harvester.

'Let's have a look,' said Brogan as Susan, Mary, and the new girl, Jane, oohed and aahed. 'Good grief girl, I should think it's what the Titanic hit.'

'It's lovely,' said Mary and stared meaningfully at Patrick, who rose to the occasion and fetched a bottle of champagne. He teased Edna in a heavy-handed way that she found easy to cope with. 'When's the big day then? When does he get his ball and chain?'

'October I think,' she replied shyly. 'You're all invited, the church in the village.'

'Ooh, a white wedding,' said Susan. 'Can I help you choose your dress?'

'I thought – not white, just a suit or something.'

'I'll help you choose,' said Mary firmly, determined that on this one day Edna should look her best.

York Minster dominates the city, huge and

impressive, almost too magnificent to be real. The summer plague of tourists was abating when Edna and Mary stopped opposite the main entrance to plan their route round the shops and they, like most of the locals, hardly spared it a glance. Only occasionally would Mary stop and marvel at the creamy, unblemished stonework alive with carving and wonder at its age. Today she had other, weightier matters on her mind; Edna's wardrobe.

'I hate buying clothes,' Edna was grumbling. 'I always feel so stupid, there's never anything in my size and the shop girls sneer.'

'We all hate buying clothes and shop girls always sneer, it's the nature of the beast,' replied Mary firmly. 'Come along, we haven't got all day.' She frogmarched her briskly down Stonegate and into an elegant boutique.

'I can't go in here,' hissed Edna, 'it's far too expensive.'

'That's where you've been going wrong,' said Mary. 'Cheap shops always skimp, here the things should fit.'

But it was several hours and many shops later before Edna was outfitted to Mary's satisfaction. She had to be firmly steered away from a spotted suit with a peplum that made her look like a maypole and bodily dragged from a tweed ensemble more suited to a day at a horse trial, but in the end both she and Mary were pleased. They had chosen a blouse in brown silk, loose fitting, long in the sleeve with a tie neck, to be worn underneath a cream wool suit, the skirt flared to mid-calf, the jacket boxy. Mary had ignored Edna's plea for low heels and had bought Italian leather court shoes that made even Edna's muscly legs look slender, and as a last frivolous touch there was a wide-brimmed hat, its trailing ribbons matching the blouse.

'You can choose the flowers yourself,' said Mary, sinking exhausted into the van's dilapidated front seat. 'And your honeymoon nightie, get something sexy.'

'Oh, but I couldn't,' said Edna, blushing.

Mary gave her a searching glance and climbed out of the car. 'I deserve a medal,' she muttered as they marched into the lingerie department of York's most exclusive store. They emerged with a length of pale blue lace, the only respectable parts of which were the shoulder straps.

Her only reward was the happy smile on Edna's face and the exuberance with which she flung herself into the arrangements for the wedding. Mary nobly offered to accommodate Edna's parents, much to Pat's horror.

'My parents, her parents, the kids, this place is like the Dorchester! Are you sure there's no one else you'd like to put up?'

'Well I had to offer,' she remonstrated.

'Why?'

'Oh don't be difficult. I must go and feed the calves.'

In reality she was protecting herself against too much contact with Patrick and her policy was working so well that her only intimate moments with him were in bed. If he showed any inclination to talk personally she pleaded exhaustion and feigned sleep or undressed with studied languor. If that failed to silence him she would twine her arms around his neck, touch his lips with her tongue and undulate her pelvis against him. So far this had been entirely successful, although waking one morning with teethmarks on her breasts and in a tangled knot of bedclothes she wondered who was winning. She rolled towards the naked form beside her, lightly kissing the brown muscled shoulder and running a hand down the hollow of his spine.

'It's time to get up.'

Patrick groaned. 'I can't, I'm shagged out. I hope the hell you enjoyed it, it's killing me.'

'You're getting old. And yes, thank you, I did enjoy it. Lots.' She rumpled his hair and slipped out of bed, but he caught her arm.

'Mary, there's something I want to talk to you about because I'm not happy with the way things are.'

She pulled roughly away from him and almost ran to the bathroom. 'Later, Pat please, I've got to rush, it's Anna's playgroup morning. Over breakfast perhaps.'

'But Mary . . .' the sound of the shower drowned his voice. He aimed a violent punch at the pillow and bruised his knuckles on the bedhead beneath.

Cub-hunting began in the dying days of summer, the leaves still on the trees and the occasional field of corn yet uncut. But the dawns were crisp and the mists hung low on the stubble as Mary hacked along the lanes, hinting at the lean times to come. The year had yielded richly, barns and haystores were full, but these were feeble bulwarks against what winter might bring. It was not to be thought of, today at least. Mary turned Spindrift into a field, taking her at a slow canter towards the small group of riders gathered round the wood. Before the season proper began one came cub-hunting for the pleasure of a dawn ride and the prospect of watching hounds learn their trade, not for the jumping and galloping of November. Jonathan Mayhew turned his big grey towards Mary as she rode up, his face a beam of delight.

'Hello! I thought you might be out today. Bit colder than last week, don't you think?'

She agreed and they talked pleasantly of nothing, hounds, horses, the weather. He was always there when she went out and she knew that if she did not appear he considered his day wasted, but she tried very hard not to encourage him.

After a slow hack from one covert to another she made for home, and Mayhew rode with her. As they turned into the lane, a car drew up and Mary saw that it was Brogan.

'Patrick! Are you off to see Fred? This is Mr Mayhew, the solicitor I told you about. Jonathan, this is Patrick Brogan.'

'How do you do,' said Mayhew, drumming his heels ineffectually against Jason's sides in an attempt to persuade him to walk up. 'I often watch you on television.'

Patrick's face was bleak. 'I dare say. Mary, you're wanted at home, the baby's yelling, Murphy's been sick and Edna's screaming at Susan. If Mr Mayhew – Jonathan – can spare you, that is. He's obviously such a particular friend.'

'Don't be ridiculous, we were only riding back together,' said Mary in a low voice, but Patrick had flung himself into the car, driving off at breakneck speed.

'Damn him to hell,' said Mary softly. She turned to Mayhew who was looking bewildered. 'I must go,' she said curtly. 'Be seeing you.' She set off down the grass verge at a brisk canter.

The familiar grey walls of the farmstead were visible from some distance away and to Mary's jaundiced eye they had all the bleakness of a prison. Waves of noise rose to meet her as she approached the back door, voices raised in argument and the wailing of a baby without hope of comfort.

'I'm not the junior any longer and I don't have to clean the tack,' Susan was saying, shrill with the threat of tears.

'You do what I tell you to do, and no argument,' retorted Edna. 'You've been getting slack, my girl, swanning around in the house wasting time –'

'I can tell you –' shrieked Susan.

'And I can tell you that I want you out of my house,' broke in Mary, striding into the room like an avenging fury. 'While you two are arguing my baby is breaking his heart, and much you care about it. Get out, get out, why don't you all clean the tack since you're all so obviously idle.'

She flung the door wide and both girls slunk into the yard. They had never before seen Mary so cross and it was alarming.

'Murphy's been sick,' said Susan apologetically.

'I can see that for myself since no one's bothered to clear it up,' said Mary with withering point.

Her mood cast a pall over the house for the rest of the morning. She worked furiously, running through an endless mental argument with Patrick in which she made her points with stunning clarity. He was in the midst of a long and abject apology, courteously received by her, when the door opened and he was there. She could think of nothing to say.

'Everything calmed down then?'

'Of course. The girls have been feeding the dog chicken bones.' She was cool, it was for him to apologise for embarrassing her like that. He nodded and strolled round the room, looking at old postcards on the dresser and turning over bills. Stupidly she wanted to cry, and blinked furiously, to do so would be weak.

'I'm going away for a few days,' he said suddenly and for a moment her mind was blank.

'But your parents arrive at the end of the week!'

'I'll be back by then. There's someone I want to see.' Their eyes met and she knew he meant Sylvia. All thought of tears left her, anger was hot in her throat and she reached for her half-empty coffee mug and hurled it at him. It bounced off the wall gouging a lump from the plaster and she reached for another missile. The door closed as her fingers curled round the coffee grinder and she was left staring at it in her hand. She sat weakly at the table and thought about crying but now the tears would not come.

It was plain that he intended to break with her sooner or later and if she pushed him it would be sooner. He even had her replacement in mind, although he would probably head back to Ireland at the first opportunity. He might even argue about the custody of Daniel Patrick, and really was she a fit mother? An impoverished loose woman, hopelessly given to violence and without

visible means of support. If a court failed to give
the baby to Pat they would probably take him into
care, and Anna and Ben as well!

The whole miserable picture rose before her and
it was a white and frightened face, the eyes huge,
that met Patrick as he stormed in with his suitcase.

'I – er – I'll be back on Friday. It's only two
days, Mary.' His anger was evaporating but she
did not speak. 'You will be all right?'

Mary gathered the shreds of her pride into a
polite smile. 'Thank you, Patrick, as always I will
be fine. After all, I can always call on Jonathan,
day or night.'

His fists clenched and he took a step towards
her. 'You'd better be joking, Mary, or so help me
I'll . . .'

'What Pat? Knock me about? Then I can have
a lovely black eye to show your parents. Why not,
you've done it before. Just a minute, I'll call the
children in to watch.' She knew she was pushing
him too far but she felt no fear as he dragged her
from the chair.

'Paddy, don't!' Edna stood in the doorway,
concern on her beaky face and Mary almost
laughed. Now she really would think Patrick beat
her. After a moment he let her go and rushed out.
When she heard the car scream out of the yard
Mary turned her face away and sobbed.

The sports car raced along the narrow lanes,
forcing the few vehicles it encountered to take
refuge in hedges or on the grass verge. Patrick
hardly noticed, he drove automatically, all his
thoughts centred on the row with Mary. The car
rounded a corner at seventy to find a tractor

completely blocking the road and he slewed past in a tearing skid, two wheels in the ditch. He drove more slowly after that, his anger a spent force.

Why was Mary so difficult? From the first she had fascinated him, so cool and contained, yet so desirable. Her face came to life when she laughed and when she made love it was different again, she flamed with passion. But this fierce rejection of him – she hurt him and she did not care. To begin with he had accepted that she was mourning Stephen but as time passed the silent, brooding look had faded. She had seemed happy, and with her pregnancy had even sacrificed some of the independence that had driven him mad. He loved her to need him, he lived for the times when he came home and knew that she was glad to see him, even if it was only to hammer in a nail. But the chances were that she would only ask him if she had tried first herself, and that was Mary for you.

Now she was always on edge, avoiding him or chattering brightly until she could escape. Where were the quiet, companionable evenings they had spent together, when she was soft and open, charming the heart out of him with only a smile? The house had been a warm haven, a place for retreat from the world. Why now would she not talk to him? One word and she clamped her shell shut like a threatened oyster, and threw things at him, God knows why.

It could only be that man Mayhew, but he found it hard to believe that she saw anything in that tubby, ingenuous sort of chap, not when he thought seriously about it. But then, you never knew with Mary, she did such odd things, take that cow for instance, how many women would

have bought themselves a cow? Perhaps Mayhew
had promised her a herd of the things. He grinned
ruefully and turned on to the motorway.

He wondered if she would leave. Before the
baby came he had been surprised every time he
came home and found her still there but since then
he had felt more secure. The thought of the old
house, silent, empty, no toys on the stairs, filled
him with dread. After Barbara he had known
loneliness but it had been nothing to the aching
void that lay ahead of him now. Mary was self-
willed and opinionated, he never understood her,
but she brought his home to life and he loved her.
To lose her would be a taste of dying. He was
damned if he would let her go. With sudden
decision he stamped on the accelerator and
speeded into the fast lane. If he wanted to get to
London in time to catch the agent he would have
to hurry.

Chapter 20

'How do you do,' murmured Mary formally, eyeing the neat figure before her.

Mrs Brogan was small, thin and grey haired, her face weatherbeaten, her eyes a faded blue. She did not look formidable but neither did she look impoverished, thought Mary, her gaze taking in the new station wagon and expensive, if ill-fitting, sheepskin coat. Not so poor these days, it seemed.

'Well, my dear, and it's a fine place you have,' said Patrick's father, showing none of the nervousness evident in his wife. He was already casting interested eyes at the line of boxes, his wiry figure never still for a moment, even his hair, only streaked with grey, springing energetically from his head.

Mary relaxed slightly and smiled. 'Do look round. I'm afraid Patrick's not here at the moment.'

'When will he be back?' asked his mother.

'Before tea I should think,' said Mary vaguely. 'Won't you come in?'

She ushered Mrs Brogan into the kitchen while her husband wandered round outside. She had no idea when Patrick would be back, if at all, and she mentally cursed him for daring to abandon her like this. What was she to say to this woman?

'Did you have a good trip?'

Mrs Brogan shook her head. 'The sea was very rough, it was like a fairground ride, and then we could not manage the English roads. Not so much as a cup of tea did we have all the way from Holyhead.'

Mary took the hint and put the kettle on, noticing for the first time how tired the older woman looked. 'Have you had any lunch?' she asked.

'We're quite all right, thank you. Please don't trouble.'

Mary correctly interpreted this as near starvation and got out the frying pan. The visitors were forced to eat under the enthralled gaze of Ben and Anna who edged nearer and nearer until they could pinch chips. By the end of the meal all four were satisfied and the atmosphere was almost relaxed.

Mary brought the baby into the room and sat with him on her knee. She could feel their eyes on her and was seized with the desire to take her child and run far, far away where they could not even look at him. She felt so hostile she was sure they must sense it.

'Is that . . .?' asked Mrs Brogan after a time.

'This is Daniel Patrick,' said Mary as coldly as she could. She looked up to see the worried, hopeful face of the woman and she relented, she could not be that unkind. 'Would you like to hold him?'

She began the washing up with all her attention on the woman cooing to her child. Charlie was performing complicated tricks with his handkerchief, turning it into rabbits and foxes for Anna and Ben. Oh God, where was Patrick?

Tea-time passed and still he had not appeared and she had run out of excuses. The children were in bed and with them had gone her main defence against probing questions. They sat, very upright, before the sitting room fire.

'I think I'll just take a stroll round,' said Charlie, cravenly deserting his wife. Mary and Mrs Brogan sat on.

'Paddy said he would be late?' asked his mother.

Mary looked at her. 'I really don't know where he is,' she admitted. 'We had a blazing row on Tuesday and I haven't seen him since. He might not be coming back at all!' Her voice broke and she fumbled for a handkerchief.

'And isn't that the whole of it,' said his mother crossly, 'he's changed not a jot. No thought for others, dashing off just as the mood takes him, and his temper's no better, that's plain. I shall have a word for his ear when he turns up.'

Mary blinked at her. Somehow this was not the doting parent she had imagined.

'I well remember,' continued Mrs Brogan, 'he was fifteen when his father last took the strap to him, drunk he was, and fighting. Always a worry, that boy.'

There was the sound of a car turning into the yard. 'He's here,' said Mary, and she felt weak with relief.

Charlie came in with him, father and son talking non-stop. Mary went out to the kitchen as he greeted his mother for he had not, after all, come back to see her. After a few moments he followed her.

'Have you eaten?' she asked stiffly. He nodded and she could have spat to think of him calmly settled in a restaurant while she struggled with his mother.

'Fish and chips at York,' he explained and she grinned at her mistake. He misinterpreted her expression and put his arms round her, holding her close. She sighed and returned the embrace. Even if he had been with that woman she was just so glad, so very very glad, to have him home.

The days gradually assumed a pattern. At breakfast Patrick would ask what they wanted to do and they would make a show of considering the matter, although Charlie inevitably accompanied Pat and his wife remained with Mary and the children. Mary found it an appalling strain. She was never alone and to have her smallest actions observed and commented upon oppressed her. In desperation she searched for tasks for Mrs Brogan to do, and although this eased the situation no one could clean windows or peel potatoes forever, and in the intervals she asked questions.

'She won't leave me alone,' she whispered to Patrick in bed one evening.

'Why the whisper? She can't hear you.'

'I bet she can,' replied Mary fiercely. 'She's always there, whenever I turn round, especially if I swear or yell at the children. And the questions! Today she got a complete run-down of Stephen's financial affairs, through sheer persistence. I didn't want to tell her.'

'She's only curious,' said Brogan defensively. 'At home everyone knows everyone else's business, you can't expect her to change.'

'Oh God,' said Mary dismally and turned her back to him. Two more weeks to go, but at least next weekend would be occupied by Edna's wedding.

'Best bib and tucker,' declared Charlie, appearing just as raffish in his best suit as in his usual rubbed cord trousers. 'Where's the bride?'

'In tears,' said Patrick casually. 'Her mother's been getting at her.'

They had holed up in Pat's study, away from the turmoil.

'Calling it off, is she?' asked Charlie, brightening visibly. 'That's a relief, we can go and look at those youngsters you were telling me about.'

'Oh Mary'll sort it out,' was the airy reply. 'But there's no reason why we can't have a drink to pass the time.' He produced a bottle and two glasses with a triumphant flourish, secure in the knowledge that the rest of the household was far too busy to notice.

Upstairs Mary presided over a scene far less tranquil.

'I'm sure he's too old for you,' Edna's mother was saying gloomily for the eleventh time. 'If only you'd let us meet him before. I said to your father, "Reg," I said, "she should have wed Georgie Bowles what works in the abattoir, when she had the chance." Good steady lad he is.'

'Oh, Mam!' Edna was roused from tears to anger, 'I only went out with him once and anyway he smells.'

'Sam is really very nice, Mrs Mears,' intervened Mary, 'I'm sure you'll agree when you get to know him a little better.'

'I still say he's too old,' insisted the woman, emphasising the point with jerks of her head. The large chiffon hat, perched on a solidly new perm, wobbled dangerously.

'I think a cup of tea would be very nice,' broke in Mrs Brogan in her soft Irish voice. 'Why don't you and I go down and make it?' She took the woman firmly by the arm and steered her to the door.

'But he's too old,' wailed Mrs Mears despairingly before the door shut behind her. The room was suddenly very quiet and Edna and Mary both took deep, restoring breaths.

'Oh dear,' said Mary at last. 'Not the best start to the day.'

'Do you think she's right?' sniffed Edna, begging for reassurance. Her nose, she knew, was red, her eyes swollen and her new hair-do limp from the tensions of the morning.

Mary snorted. 'Like hell she is. Sam's a man in a million and you know it. Look, we're going to be late, go and have a shower while I put the heated rollers on. Grandma Brogan will keep her down there forever, she had a glint in her eye.'

The wedding was at twelve but it was five to before Edna was dressed to Mary's satisfaction, and Mary herself was still in jeans and jumper.

'You look fantastic,' she said firmly.

'Do you really think so?' Edna was pinkly pleased. Her face was framed by soft waves of hair and Mary ignored her plea that she 'never wore eye make-up' hiding all traces of redness under a subtle blend of browns, echoing the colour of her blouse. From the trailing ribbon of her hat to the spots on her tights, Edna looked dashing and elegant.

Mr Mears was sitting in the dining room, alone

and forlorn, his large stomach drooping over his fat thighs. He looked up hopefully as they entered.

'Has everyone else gone?' asked Mary and he nodded.

'Very happy they were,' he said obscurely.

'So they should be. Come on, you'll be late.'

'What about you?' said Edna.

'Oh, I'll be there. Off you go. Best of luck, lovey.' She popped a swift kiss on Edna's scented cheek, almost causing the bride to dissolve.

'Edna! Don't! Think of the eye make-up,' cried Mary, bustling the drooping flower and her flabby father towards the car.

When they had gone she poured herself a fortifying glass of sherry, feeling strangely forlorn. She drank it while dressing, for once refusing to rush. Murphy scratched at the door as she put on her hat, and she let him in with a smile.

'You haven't forgotten me, have you sweetheart?' she said hugging him, careless of the hairs. He snuffled and took a thoughtful chew at her gloves. 'No you don't. Come on, old thing, you can ride in the car.'

They arrived at the church when the service was almost over and Mary slid into the pew next to Patrick during the last hymn. Mrs Brogan was holding a sleeping Daniel with Anna and Ben next to her, clean and very grown-up. Anna had insisted on wearing her long party dress, blue velvet with lace collar and cuffs beneath which white socks and buckled shoes flashed endearingly. She was very conscious of her skirt and kept peering at it to make sure it was hanging perfectly straight. In contrast Ben was miserable, tugging at his shirt and first real tie, his grey shorts gradually losing their grip on his firm round tummy.

'Pull his trousers up,' hissed Mary to Patrick but there was no response. She was about to repeat the instructions when the figure next to her swayed slightly and emitted a belch that would have done credit to a bullfrog. Patrick met her eye with an apologetic smile that slid into a hiccup, looking hurt when she turned stiffly to the front and pointedly raised her hymn book.

Above the roar of the organ swelling for the final verse she became conscious of restless movement in the row behind. One swift glance revealed Charlie trying to extract a silver flask from his pocket with one hand and unbutton the waistband of his trousers with the other. Mary whisked the flask from him and stuffed it into her handbag with such speed that Charlie was left staring at his fingers in horror. After a moment he raised his eyes to the roof and crossed himself, muttering fearfully.

Edna and Sam were coming down the aisle. Sam's beam of pride and happiness illuminated his face, beads of sweat glistening on his forehead in evidence of his anxiety when twelve o'clock had come and gone without a bride. He clutched Edna's arm tightly and she returned the pressure, relief and a new, tentative confidence widening her smile.

The reception was at the White Hart, a short distance from the church. The bride and groom swept grandly away in a Rolls-Royce but the guests walked.

'How you ever got here I will never know,' muttered Mary, discouraging Pat from watering the gravestones in full view of the High Street. 'No Pat, not here for God's sake, wait until we get to the reception. It's all right, Anna, Daddy's feeling ill. I hope.'

She shepherded her brood like an anxious hen, clutching at first one and then the other as Ben tried to dive into a sweet shop, Charlie into the Red Lion. Pushing them before her she arrived breathlessly at the receiving line, her hat askew. The vicar stood next to the bride and groom, a practised smile of welcome on his lips.

'Mrs Squires,' he gushed, holding out his hand.

'Vicar,' she murmured, and noticed he was staring at her handbag, from which a silver flask protruded. 'Such a cold day,' she added hopefully, reflecting that she must find someone else to be a character witness when they tried to take the children from her. With reputation gone for ever she grabbed the first glass of sherry she saw and downed it in one.

'I don't think I know you, do I?' A tall, blond boy of about twenty-five was smiling down at her. 'I'm Edna's cousin Peter.'

'And I'm Mary Squires. Have you come far?' They chatted happily and took adjoining seats for the meal, as far as possible from the drunkards. Afterwards there was dancing and Peter was very good, putting all the fancy bits into the quickstep and insisting they try a foxtrot, one of only two couples to dare. Mary was quite sad when the band retired hurt and the disco began. Still an hour to go before the happy couple left for their honeymoon in Devon and she was exhausted, and rather drunk.

'And now for something romantic,' breathed the

bearded DJ, rooting out Elvis Presley's 'Love Me Tender' and Peter seized Mary's hand enthusiastically. His embrace was ardent and she sagged wearily against him, content just to be steered slowly round the floor. She was almost asleep when a familiar hand seized her shoulder and flung her against a table and she hardly dared look to see what was happening to her partner.

'You seducing bastard,' Patrick was roaring, banging Peter's head on the floor and thumping him at one and the same time. Sam and another man were pulling him off.

'I think I'll go home,' said Mary thoughtfully, gathering up the children. She drifted to the door unseen and strolled towards the van. The dog was asleep, taking up all the back seat, so she pushed him into the front to make room for the children. He perched hugely next to her, wobbling slightly, his bottom obscuring the gear stick. As they passed the hotel she saw Patrick leaning on the wall surrounded by a group of men. She stopped and opened the door.

'Shove him in,' she said, gathering Murphy ever closer to her. The little van puttered slowly through the hills towards home, with everyone apart from an uncomfortable Irish wolfhound, half asleep.

Chapter 21

'Well, Patrick, that was a fine exhibition you made of yourself,' began Mrs Brogan the moment her son made a wan appearance at breakfast.

'Not now, Mother, my head's killing me.'

'And well it might, the Lord knows what you and your father put away yesterday. No more sense than a cartload of monkeys the pair of you.'

'Oh God,' muttered Pat, turning in nausea from the sight of Anna disembowelling a boiled egg.

'And then spoiling that girl's day! I never thought a son of mine would behave so, I was fit to fall through the floor.'

'What a pity you didn't.'

'That's enough from you, my lad. As if Mary was doing more than being civil, as anyone could see whose brains weren't pickled in whisky.'

'Mother, the only person Mary is not civil to is me. You might have noticed.'

'And who have you to thank for that? I tell you —'

'Mrs Brogan,' interrupted Mary, handing Patrick two aspirins in a glass of water. 'Perhaps you could continue this later, as it is I need some help with the calves. Would you mind?'

As she expected, after one searing glance at her son, the older woman obediently followed her outside, but her rage still burned.

'You've been too soft with him, in years to come you'll regret it. I know I've not done too well with Charlie but the Lord knows where he'd be now if I hadn't made the effort.'

Mary took a deep breath. 'Mrs Brogan, I think you should know that Patrick and I are not likely to be together much longer. He wants to return to Ireland and I won't be going with him.'

'But what about the baby? Patrick thinks the world of him.' She stared blankly, her face losing the vigour and determination of moments before.

'I didn't plan things this way, I'm afraid it's just how it's worked out.'

They had reached the calf pens. 'If you could give a scoop of feed to each one, I'll do the milk buckets.'

Later that day Mary left the bustle of the house and wandered into the walled garden. One night in early summer there had been a frost, and in the morning she had found leaves turning black and new growth withered. Now it was as if it had never been, the plants tumbled in a glorious abundance of colour, the urge to live and to grow stronger by far than that brief blight. Each plant had spread its leaves anew to the sun's warmth and had begun again. So it had been with her. When Stephen died the sun had gone in, leaving her cold and miserable, curling inward for survival. She had been so afraid. But no night lasts for ever and the morning, dark and chill though it had been, had blossomed into a sunny afternoon.

But now it was almost autumn, the garden was turning to sleep and it was here that Mary came to escape the people that complicated her life.

Only here could she allow herself honesty and admit that she loved Brogan, and needed him. It had not always been so, in the beginning there had been nothing inside her but despair. She could not say when warmth began again, when she looked and saw someone she could not bear to be without. There was no hope for it, of course, they could not go on like this, fighting a perpetual war, other women lurking in the shadows. If she was ever to make a new life for herself and the children she must go now, while there was still something of herself left, before she was sucked dry. Blinking back the tears that pricked her eyes she opened the rusty gate and walked to the house. She would tell him tomorrow, when she came back from hunting and then she would drive to Leeds.

They were meeting at eight o'clock at Hanging Wood. When the alarm shrilled it was still dark and she had to force herself to venture into the cold. Only the thought of Susan's patient work on the horse prevented her from going back to sleep instead of hunting that day. Brogan was sitting on the edge of the bed.

'Go back to sleep, it's only six o'clock.'

'I'm coming with you. Pass my dressing gown, will you?'

'But you hate cubbing.' Brogan found it far too slow and although he would sometimes let the girls go he never went himself.

'I'm coming this morning.' There was an edge to his voice that precluded argument and she went quickly to turn on the shower. Surely today they need not squabble.

Susan was in the yard, muffled in jumpers, her

hair unbrushed and her face puffy with sleep. She held Spindrift for Mary to mount and then went to High Time's box.

'You're not bringing that brute, surely!' cried Mary before she could stop herself. Patrick did not reply and swung himself into the saddle with a fine disregard for the horse's fidgetings, leading the way out of the yard with set face and back ramrod straight.

The roads were deserted and after a while Patrick hung back to allow Mary to ride next to him.

'Since when have I been going back to Ireland?' he asked suddenly.

Mary swallowed hard, staring straight between her horse's ears. 'You know you are, you can't wait to get rid of Fred. I don't know why you didn't tell your mother yourself.'

'But you won't come with me.' It was a statement, not a question.

'No. You can take Sylvia instead.' She had not meant to say that, in fact she thought she had pushed it right out of her mind until the words sprang to her lips.

'I haven't seen her in months,' said Patrick in an amazed tone.

'Liar! More like three weeks. And how surprising that Fred should hear about your plans from her. Nice of you to tell her, wasn't it? Such a pity you couldn't bring yourself to say a word to me.' She urged Spindrift to a trot but Patrick kept pace with her.

'What she said was only to get back at me. I ditched her for you and she's had it in for me ever since, what she said to Fred was sheer invention

But yes, I have been discussing Irish sponsorship, three weeks ago to be precise, and I'd have told you if you'd damned well asked. Not you though, you'd rather throw things.'

'I don't care what you say, I know you slept with her.'

'So what? I knew her long before I met you and I dropped her because the sex was better at home. All gasp and writhe that woman.'

'God, but you are a rat!' snarled Mary, appalled by this further evidence of the callousness of men.

'Why? I don't deceive you, and that's the truth. On the other hand you have half the men in Yorkshire trailing along.' There was a moment's silence and then he went on in a softer tone, 'So why don't you come? I can offer as much as any of them. Surely you don't want to go to your mother, I must be an improvement on that.'

Mary lifted her head to stare at him. 'Worried about losing your tame housekeeper, are you? All you care about is sex on tap, meals on time and, oh yes, Daniel Patrick, we mustn't forget him, must we?'

'I love all the children, Mary, you must know that.'

'Love? You don't know the meaning of the word. Damn it, I hate you Patrick Brogan, you make me so miserable!' She jabbed her heels into Spindrift's sides, sending her down a grassy track at a fast canter.

She arrived breathless at the wood and reined in with a slither next to the solid shape of Jonathan Mayhew's grey. Brogan drew up beside her, calm and collected.

'Hello, Mary, I am glad you're out today,'

Mayhew was saying. Mary gave a slight smile and he looked warily at the couple, the tension between them hummed in the air.

As the season proper approaches hunts sometimes let hounds run a fox. Today the huntsman was bored, he had a fresh horse and the master wanted some exercise. Within minutes of hounds entering the wood a slim red shape slipped from the trees and they were away. The followers waited in varying degrees of impatience, Brogan, his face impassive, holding High Time with an iron hand while Mayhew heaved and spluttered, his grey plunging about bumping into people.

'Stop it Jason,' he said at intervals in very unhorsemanlike tones but fortunately they were soon on the move, for the hounds were flying along.

The first hedge was small and thin. High Time flew it, Spindrift negotiated it with care and Jason crashed through the thorn with more enthusiasm than skill, his passenger hanging on grimly. All would have been well had he not been determined to follow Mary, who was following Brogan. On a good horse and in a foul temper, Patrick was finding his own line and taking ditches, drop fences and banks in his stride. It was a ditch on the far side of a hedge that brought Mayhew to grief, his horse took off far too early and could not make the spread. Jason scrambled desperately, and made dry land but his rider was left in the water. Mary heard the crash and reined in, thinking that it was time she opted out anyway, for the ditch had given her a horrible fright. She caught the horse as he raced past intent on catching the fox on his own, and went

298

to fish Mayhew out. He was very wet and rather smelly.

'I think I'd better go home,' he said disconsolately.

'Yes. You're not hurt are you?'

'Oh no. And what a fantastic run, I can't wait for the season proper. And what a horse, have a go at anything, won't you, old boy?' He was pink with enthusiasm despite his ducking.

'Next time don't follow Pat,' said Mary sagely.

'I was following you,' he said with a rueful smile.

'Well, I shouldn't have followed him either, we nearly ended up in the same ditch. But I must go.' She swung into the saddle and rode off to find the hunt.

She caught up with them as they hacked across a ploughed field, the fox lost long ago. Patrick's blue eyes blazed at her.

'Where the hell were you?'

'Jonathan fell off. I stopped to help him.'

'I bet you did, why is it you can always spare time for anyone but me? And don't you dare ride off, I want a straight answer.'

'Because you don't need me, I suppose.'

'What about all that exercise between the sheets then? That's not needing you?' He was shouting and heads turned in fascination but neither he nor Mary cared.

'You've got plenty of others for that,' she shrieked. 'They probably form queues!'

'How often do I have to tell you there is only you? I love you, Mary, you stupid bitch, God knows why, you even named our baby after another man.'

'No I didn't, he's Daniel Patrick Brogan if you'd ever cared to look.'

There was a moment's stunned silence.

'Why didn't you say so?' he asked, taking off his hat and rubbing his forehead.

'I left the certificate lying around for weeks, I felt sure you'd have seen it.'

'You always were bloody devious.'

Mary turned her horse and picked her way along a furrow, tears trickling unheeded down her cheeks. Patrick caught her rein and pulled her to a halt.

'Have a handkerchief. Please don't leave me, Mary, please. I couldn't bear not to have you, I love you so much. I know you don't feel the same but if there's no one you'd rather have –' he trailed into silence.

Mary took a shuddering breath. 'Let's get one thing straight, Brogan. There's no one I'd rather have than you and that includes Stephen. I just thought – you didn't care and I couldn't go on, thinking I was just a convenience. When you asked me to marry you it was only for the children, you said so!'

His voice was very tender. 'What about in the snow? And when Daniel was born, and over Tim, and a thousand times when we made love, I couldn't have said it any louder. Couldn't you see?'

Mary looked at him through a mist of tears, for once unable to barricade herself behind a wall of activity and other people. With a sigh she surrendered.

'Oh Pat. I think I've been rather stupid. Darling, darling Pat.'

He wrapped a strong arm around her, kissing her hard. When they parted his face was wet, with her tears or his own, she did not know. Spindrift plunged suddenly, almost unseating her.

'That horrible horse has bitten my mare!' shrieked Mary in outrage.

'Oh God! Why is nothing ever simple with you?'

'I had nothing to do with it, you can't blame me, it's your horse. Come on, we'd better hurry up and plug the wound or something.'

They trotted off, locked in familiar argument.

'Mummy!' cried Anna as they rode into the yard. 'Ben hit me hard on the head, very very hard, Mummy, you will smack him, won't you?'

'Paddy, Swallow's leg's up again, will you come and look?' said Susan.

'There's a man on the phone, says his name's Fred,' broke in Mrs Brogan.

Patrick looked calmly at them all. 'You can all wait,' he said simply, lifting Mary from her horse and leading her to the house.

'Where are you going?' asked Anna.

'To bed,' said Patrick over his shoulder.

'But it's not night-time,' complained the little girl.

'Come along, Anna, let's fetch Ben and go for a walk,' said Mrs Brogan hastily.

The room was very quiet as they undressed, echoing to the small sounds of clothes falling to the floor. She stood naked before him, arms across her breasts. She moistened her lips with her tongue.

'It feels like the first time,' she whispered.

'I'm glad it isn't.' He drew her on to the bed.

'I know every inch of your body, that you like to be kissed here – ' her lips – 'and here – ' her breast – 'and especially – ' his lips travelled down her stomach and over the soft dark mat of hair, ' – here!' She gave a gasp and lay for a moment, her eyes closed, making small, wanting noises. He was above her, his body muscled and proud.

'Say you love me,' he pleaded and she opened her eyes and reached out for him.

'I love you, I love you, I – oh! – I love you!' Her voice broke as he entered her and for a few, precious moments their bodies and their spirits were one.

When it was over they lay together, warm, sticky and tranquil and laughed.

'Why afterwards does it always seem so funny,' chuckled Mary, 'when you don't need it any more?'

'All I know is it makes me damned sleepy.' His eyes were closing and his breath was warm on her cheek.

'You can't go to sleep, there's masses to do!' squawked Mary but his breathing was deep and measured. She began to untangle herself but he was lying on her arm. They would stay here in heaven for just a little time. With a small sigh, she subsided and relaxed into slumber.

Bare wood floors, huge empty rooms and packing cases in the hall. The home which had taken so long to make had been ripped apart in a matter of hours, leaving Mary as desolate and forlorn as the naked house. This time everything was organised with labels and lists proliferating, for the furniture was to go into store while they

302

rented a cottage near Pat's parents and searched for somewhere new, but she could not dispel the notion that her security was locked in these boxes with the saucepans and the pictures.

The children were bubbling with excitement, for they were to go on a ship and they were taking Murphy too. Mary secretly wished it could have been Violet, a far more tractable animal and very much more useful, but she had been sold. Tears pricked her eyes as the little cow stepped daintily into the trailer and she had been unable to speak to the farmer. She had rushed cravenly into the kitchen to spend the rest of the day sorting through drawers with a ruthless zeal. No one had said anything but a few days later a catalogue appeared in the post addressed to her. It was from a firm of Irish livestock agents.

'I think we should have a really good cow this time,' she said thoughtfully. 'We might even show her, that would be fun, wouldn't it, children?'

'Christ All Bloody Mighty,' muttered Patrick, but he didn't say no.

But now that the day had arrived all her enthusiasm had evaporated, leaving only the worries and fears. As she glanced down at her shiny new wedding ring she felt guilt, too, that she was still so insecure. The ceremony had been brief and unpleasantly official but not even the workworn registry office with its brave display of limp flowers could depress her. Afterwards they had gone straight home to a merry, boozy lunch with Anna and Ben singing a party piece they had learned especially for the occasion. No one minded that it was 'Happy Birthday to You' because, as Susan explained, it was the only thing they could learn in the time. She had thought she would be happy forever and only two weeks later she was sitting on a packing case feeling miserable.

The door opened and she arranged her face in more cheerful lines and tried to smile. Patrick sat down next to her.

'Careful, this one's got china in it,' she warned, and her voice wobbled.

He took her hand. 'Hell of a mess, isn't it?'

She nodded. 'Did you see Edna? She came to say goodbye.'

'See her? I couldn't miss her, new Volvo, fur jacket and all. Incredible. And he's even bought her a horse, the man's besotted.'

'She'll be winning shows soon, you know how good she is.'

He shrugged. 'Good enough, but too soft. Anyway, the next thing we know she'll be up to her ears in nappies.'

'Yes. I suppose you're right.' That was always the way, girls held the secret of their own defeat. But in the end they got what they wanted.

'You will like it, love,' said Patrick suddenly. 'I'll make sure you do.'

'I'm not Barbara,' commented Mary with a wry grin. 'Anyway, I'm a creature of habit and I don't change my husbands very often.'

He turned the gold band on her finger. 'You and me. It may not be peaceful but it's what I want. All that I want.'

'We don't deserve this, you know. Sometimes I think we're too lucky and it makes me afraid.' She stood up and went to the window. The paintwork was dirty, the new people would think she was a slut. 'I hate to leave,' she said jerkily.

He came and stood behind her, his hands on her shoulders and she relaxed against him, letting the closeness comfort. 'I think the new people will ruin it. They'll install sunken baths and musical lavatory seats.'

'And turn the stables into garages,' said Patrick gloomily and then grinned at her. 'Much more of this and we'll give ourselves nightmares. Look, the vans are here.'

In a moment the lull had become the storm. There was no time for melancholy as Mary struggled to stop the men taking all the suitcases containing clothes and essentials and putting them into store. When, finally, the ramps had been lifted and the bolts slammed into place she walked through the house for the last time. Nothing had been left, even the rubbish was stacked in a neat pile outside the back door. She went quickly into the yard, there was nothing for her here, the spirit of the house was gone.

It took some time to pile the children into the car with an assortment of toys, books and sweets and when they were ready to set off Murphy had gone.

'He could be away for hours,' wailed Mary.

'If he's not back in ten minutes we go without him,' said Pat. 'We've a boat to catch.'

'You heartless brute, you couldn't leave a subnormal dog to roam the wilds. He's not even bright enough to worry sheep, he's frightened to death of them.'

'You should be happy to lose him, you're always saying what a nuisance he is,' complained Patrick, puffing on a cigarette in an effort to control his impatience.

'Yes, but you're worse and I'm not deserting you, am I?' snarled Mary, gazing wildly up and down the lane. 'There's a car coming. It looks like Fred.'

She cowered against the gate as the limousine hurtled into the yard. It contained not only Fred but a frozen-faced Mrs Swallow trying to ignore the huge and muddy form of Murphy bouncing around on the fawn back seat.

'Found him wandering about two miles away,' boomed Fred, unwisely opening his door and staggering under the impact as Murphy made his exit. Mary hastily caught him.

'It was kind of you to bring him,' said Pat stiffly. 'We were just leaving.'

Relations with Fred had been tense of late. Pat had gone to the opulent, overdone house a week before the wedding and told Fred that he was leaving. It could not have been a surprise but he received the news with a very bad grace.

'Well, Paddy,' he said coldly, 'the parting of the ways it seems. You could have given me some notice, of course, but that's always the way, bite the hand that feeds you.'

'Come off it, Fred,' remonstrated Pat, but the little man took no notice, blowing his nose hard on a capacious white handkerchief.

'I should have expected it, of course, but it's always a shock to have friends turn against you. I'm too trusting, that's always been my trouble.'

'I've noticed. Anyway I don't think you'll have much difficulty finding a replacement, just wave your cheque book about.'

'Friendship means more to me than money,' declared Fred with conscious dignity. 'Give my love to Mary. I only hope you do the right thing by her, at any rate.'

Pat had left before he lost his temper, leaving Fred's wedding invitation on the table. Fortunately he did not come but sent an ornate silver punch bowl and cups inscribed 'To Mary and Patrick, from Fred and Jean Swallow, with fondest love'.

It was hideous, but neither of them could look at it without irrational feelings of guilt.

Today, all was sweetness and light.

'I wanted to have a word with you before you left,' smiled Fred. 'It's about my namesake, Swallow, I've been thinking.'

'Oh yes,' said Pat warily.

'I'd like you to keep the name. Now, we've had some good times together, Pat, and Mary and I have always been the best of friends.' He moved to put an arm around her, then remembered his wife and took a step backwards. 'And I don't think we should lose touch altogether. How about an arrangement for that one horse?'

He bounced up and down on his little legs and Pat smiled in genuine amusement.

'Sounds like a good idea Fred,' he said soothingly. 'But we're in a hurry right now. How about coming to stay when we're settled, then we can talk about it?'

'The wife and I would be delighted,' said Fred, 'wouldn't we, dear?' She sat stony and silent.

'We must be going,' said Patrick hastily and after goodbyes all round they were on their way.

'How could you invite them?' accused Mary. 'One of the few good things about moving was getting away from her.'

'Oh, I like Fred when I'm not actually under his thumb. Anyway, what with Sam and Edna, your parents, Susan, and all the other people you've invited to stay they'll be lost in the crowd.'

'Yes,' said Mary thoughtfully. 'We might need four bathrooms this time.'

'You have the makings of an extravagant woman. You realise we shall never be alone?'

Mary traced the line of his hand on the steering wheel with a languid finger. 'We'll manage somehow,' she murmured and he reached over to put a hand on her knee.

'Mummy, Ben's hitting me,' screeched Anna and a war erupted on the back seat.

Brogan withdrew his hand. 'Damned kids. When the next one comes we'll get a nanny.'

'But I'm not pregnant.'

'Give me time you hussy, we've only been married a fortnight.' He grinned. 'We've got all our lives before us, enough for a football team.'

'Make it five-a-side and I might agree.'

She leaned back in her seat, stretching luxuriously, deaf to the squawks and yells around her. Winter was upon them once again, and the trees were bare, but for her it was summer. She would spread her petals to a summer sun and glory in its warmth. Please God this time there would be no frost.